DEAD MARCH FOR
PENELOPE BLOW

DEAD MARCH FOR PENELOPE BLOW

AN INSPECTOR LITTLEJOHN MYSTERY

GEORGE BELLAIRS

OPEN ROAD
INTEGRATED MEDIA
NEW YORK

Copyright © 1951 by George Bellairs

ISBN: 978-1-5040-9265-4

This edition published in 2024 by Open Road Integrated Media, Inc.
180 Maiden Lane
New York, NY 10038
www.openroadmedia.com

DEAD MARCH FOR
PENELOPE BLOW

A plague upon you, murderers, traitors all!
I might have saved her; now she's gone for ever!

— *King Lear, Act V, Sc III.*

1

THE PERSISTENT SPINSTER

A lovely spring afternoon in London, with the trees by the
Thames bursting their green buds and the Embankment
Gardens looking fresh and attractive after the long winter. The
first holiday makers of the season strolled along the pavements
feeling it was good to be there in the sunshine and cast glances
of mild awe at the great gateway and bright plate which indicated Scotland Yard. Inside, the attendant policeman was not
quite so happy. The same lady had called for the third day in
succession and asked for Inspector Littlejohn and showed
increasing distress every time he told her the Inspector was
away. Now, here she was again...

'Is Inspector Littlejohn in, please?'

Just the same as before. The same gentle voice, timid and full
of alarm, the same sideways cocking of the head, the same
kindly, watery eyes, the same little beaky nose. As she
approached him the policeman shook his head sadly at her to
indicate the answer was unchanged.

'No, madam. He's still away...'

Her eyes filled with tears this time. The constable wished
she'd only been ten minutes later. He'd have been off for his tea

then and someone else could have broken the news. He was a kindly man, father of a family, and his mother had slightly resembled the troubled little woman now hugging her handbag and struggling with her umbrella before him.

'Anythin' I could do, madam? I'm sorry he's not in. He's on business out of town...'

'Where could I find him, please? It's so desperately urgent.'

Littlejohn was at Lewes at a murder trial, but, of course, the bobby couldn't disclose that.

'Sorry, madam. Won't anybody else do?'

By the set of her mouth and her general bearing, he knew what the answer would be. This type were so innocent looking, but so fixed and determined in their ways. No good...

'I'm afraid not, officer. I must see *him*. Mr Claplady said he'd understand and help me best. *And* be discreet. I can't tell it to anybody else. You are so kind, but I can't really...'

The officer managed to get in his question.

'Mister 'oo?'

'Claplady. The Rev Ethelred Claplady, a friend of Inspector Littlejohn, who recommended him to me.'

'Would you spell it, please, madam?'

'C-L-A-P-L-A-D-Y ... Claplady.'

The constable took a pencil from his top pocket, did not lubricate it on his tongue as such officers are supposed to do, and wrote it down on an old envelope in a good, steady hand.

'There! I'll tell him when he comes in...'

'Will he be long?'

Oh dear! Patiently the constable explained that Littlejohn was nearly always out. He did it in the tone of voice he used to his children, slowly, paternally, with just a note of pride, because he, for one, was proud of his acquaintance with the Inspector. Just like one of the Old Guard, who used to boast intimate friendship with Napoleon even if he'd only cantered past him on his horse.

'I can't call again. I've overstayed my arrangements by a day already to see the Inspector. I must get back home. But would you please ask him to telephone as soon as he returns? Here is my card...'

She fished in her large reticule and produced a thin strip of pasteboard. The constable took it between an enormous thumb and forefinger and perused it as though it were a curiosity.

Miss Penelope Blow,
The Old Bank,
Nesbury.

'Very good, madam...'

'The number is Nesbury 0564...'

'Nesbury, Oh, five, six, fower...'

He wrote it on the card.

'And tell the Inspector he must please not ask for me, but for Minshull... Mrs Minshull, the housekeeper. You see, there are others who might answer the telephone, and it would never do for them to know I've been to Scotland Yard. I can trust Minshull and she will let me know that Inspector Littlejohn has returned, and I will then ring him back from a callbox...'

The bobby's eyes goggled at the complicated instructions and he wondered how one so guileless looking could concoct such a cunning scheme.

'You're sure you've got that, officer? It's most important. I'm sorry I can't say more. I will tell the Inspector when he gets in touch with me, however...'

She looked up at the constable and fear crept in her eyes.

'I must go now. Thank you so much, and *please do* let the Inspector know... I cannot call again... I must go back to Nesbury by the five train. Thank you again, and goodbye...'

She turned and then halted in her steps as though faced by some new problem or other. Slowly she unclasped her bag, took from it a small purse, extracted two pennies from it and pressed them in the bobby's palm.

'Thank you, again,' she said, and gathering herself together with her umbrella at the slope, she walked down the corridor and through the door into the fading afternoon.

The officer watched her with a flush of pity in his heart. She seemed helpless and alone, like his own mother after they'd told her of his father's death at sea... He suddenly became aware of his palm. He opened it and gazed at the two pennies.

'Well... I'll be blowed... Tuppence!'

Miss Blow hurried away along the Embankment. She had a one-track mind and could only think of one thing at a time.

'Number eleven...' she said to herself over and over again.

In Parliament Square, she boarded a No 11 bus to Sloane Street. 'Egton Mews,' she kept muttering all the way. The bus put her down at length and, hurrying anxiously still, she threaded her way through two squares and, turning down an alley and under a porte cochère, pulled up before a black-painted door with a large semi-circle of fanlight over it. This was where she stayed whenever she came to London, the home of a former cook at her home. In the window stood a fly-blown card: Mrs Buckley, Select Apartments. Mrs Buckley was as much a spinster as Miss Blow, but, having served as cook in a good family, was entitled to an honorary matrimonial degree.

The door was loose, and Miss Blow quietly let herself in. The long, dark corridor was cool and quiet. The house itself seemed expectant, watching and waiting for something. Two doors, leading from the passage to ground floor bed-sitting rooms, were closed. Their occupants might have been out, or what seemed more likely today, sitting behind them listening for what was going to happen next. At the far end, the kitchen door stood ajar. Still, not a sound. Miss Blow slid her umbrella in the hall stand and the ferrule, encountering the drip-tin at the bottom, created a rattle, which, in the silence, seemed fit to wake the dead. Half-timidly she made her way to the rectangle of light at the far end of the lobby. A large baize-covered screen stood between the door and the room. Behind this Mrs Buckley was in the habit of lurking, and it kept off the draughts whilst enabling every sound in the building to reach her.

Yes, she was there, sitting in a wicker armchair, her hawk's face and insolent eyes set like a bird of prey waiting for the victim. Miss Blow looked at her and then recoiled with a little squeak of panic. Lolling on the old leather couch under the window was a second occupant. A tall, heavy man in his mid-forties. He had a large head with a globular forehead and his eyes were set still and deep in it. His nose was snub and his mouth wide and thin-lipped. You immediately thought of a hydrocephalic child. He was lying there, his legs crossed on the end of the sofa, above the level of his head, which he supported on one hand held at the back of it as though it were too heavy for his neck to bear. The other hand trailed on the floor beside the couch. The only movement seemed to come from the wisp of smoke rising from the cigarette between his fingers. He raised it and took a puff, ejected the smoke slowly and turned his eyes on Miss Penelope.

'Well...?'

'Harold!' she gasped.

Mrs Buckley snapped her lips and looked about to enjoy the scene.

'Where do you think you've been?'

'I... I...'

The hesitant timidity of the frail creature before him seemed to enrage Harold. In one bound he was off the couch and towering over her.

'You WHAT? What do you mean by running out on us like this? We've been hunting all over the place for you.'

'I only wanted a change, Harold. I couldn't bear it any longer. I'm tired out...'

'Tired out! What about us? Why didn't you tell us where you were going, or that you were tired out? Then we could have done something. As it is, we've been scared to death and Honoria's nearly died...'

'Oh... How is Honoria...?'

The name seemed to sting Miss Blow to the quick. She looked wanly round as though seeking a friend and found none. It was obvious on whose side Buckley was playing. As ever, she backed the winner.

'It was only this morning that we got Buckley's letter... I came down by the next train. If this is the way you carry on, we'll have to...have to...'

He paused sadistically.

'Have to what...?'

The little woman whispered it, terrified.

'Never mind. Where's your bag? We're going back to Nesbury by the five train, so we'll have to be quick.'

He paused and then slowly drawing nearer to her thrust down his large face and spoke with terrible precision.

'And what were you doing at Scotland Yard, may I ask?'

'I... I... Oh, please don't be angry with me, Harold. I didn't mean any harm.'

'Buckley tells me you've been inquiring the way there from her. What have you been doing there?'

'Mr Claplady asked me to call and give his best wishes to an Inspector there, Harold. But he wasn't in. So, I did nothing...'

'You're a poor liar, Auntie. Well... I'll talk to you later. Get your things together; we're going. I've ordered a cab and I don't like waiting.'

They said little more. Mrs Buckley rose to see them off. She was very self-satisfied with what she had done, but as was her habit, she kept a foot in both camps, just in case...

'I had to send word, Miss Penelope,' she whined. 'It's not safe for you in London on your own. I only let the family know for your own good.'

Miss Blow ignored her, not from anger or pride, but from sheer fear and bewilderment. The taxi arrived and they bundled her in with her luggage. Harold Blow slipped some notes in Mrs Buckley's talon and spoke to the driver.

'Paddington...'

They drove off without another word. All the way to the station her nephew didn't speak to Miss Blow. First, she lowered her eyes and then turned them up to his own, which looked dead, filmed by his own thoughts. He relished torturing her by his silence, lighting one cigarette from another, throwing the stubs from the window and puffing the smoke about her head until she felt faint from the sickening heaviness of it.

At Paddington, he hustled her in a first-class compartment, bought two cups of tea from a trolley and gave her one.

'Thank you, Harold... So kind...'

She was trying to please him, like stroking an angry dog. He did not respond but got an evening paper and read it for an hour of the journey. Miss Blow looked sadly through the window at the Berkshire scene flying past. Then she hunted in her large bag, found some letters in battered envelopes, read them over and over again until she grew tired, and finally sat back, gazing in a dream at the picture in the panel opposite. She passed to the framed advertisement for railway hotels, reciting the names softly to herself and trying to remember whether or not she'd ever been there...

'Why did you go to Scotland Yard? Is that what you came to London for?'

'I told you, Harold. It was to see Mr Claplady's friend, Inspector Littlejohn. He was away...'

'Don't be silly, Aunt Penelope. You don't expect me to believe a tale like that! Mr Claplady knows a Scotland Yard man, so Aunt Penelope runs away without telling anybody and stays in

London three days just to say howdy-do to him. *What did you want with him?'*

He cast up the last sentence viciously, as though, if they'd been secure from interference, he'd have forced the answer by violence. Miss Blow gathered up as much dignity as she could.

'Harold! I won't have you speak to me like that. I'm much older than you. If your grandfather had been alive, you wouldn't have dared.'

'But he isn't, and I *am* daring. You've been queer for a long time now and you know what they do with people who get queer and do queer things… Come on now, what did you go to Scotland Yard for?'

'Dinner is ready… First sitting…'

The dining car attendant had opened the door and repeated the cry he'd passed all along the train.

'Oh yes, yes… Dinner, Harold. I'm hungry…'

'Meals on the train are foul. I don't want any. Better wait till we get in. I told Minshull to have something ready…'

'But I had such a nice meal coming down. It wasn't foul at all. There was lovely tomato soup…'

'Oh, shut up…!'

They didn't speak again till the train drew up at Nesbury. Blow gathered the bags, left his aunt to scramble out herself, and hurried out to find a solitary taxi in the station yard. The stationmaster, seeing Miss Blow in difficulties, gave her a helping hand.

'Evenin', Miss Blow. Been havin' a little outin'?'

'Thank you, Mr East… Yes… I've been to London…'

'Fam'ly don't seem so pleased about it, by the looks of 'em, miss. You been gallivantin' off without a by-your-leave?'

He was a stocky little man with a large black beard, through which his lips showed scarlet, and little twinkling shifty eyes.

'Come on! The taxi's here. Can't wait all day.' They reached the town hall square at Nesbury in ten minutes. They lived there, the whole family of them, in the large house adjoining the bank. In the old days it had been a private institution, well-known for miles around, Blows' Bank. When the Home Counties Bank took over the business, in the twenties, the residence was far too large for a mere manager, so the retired banker and his family stayed on as tenants. It was an imposing stone building, three storeys tall, fronting on the street, but with a large walled garden along one side and behind. Harold Blow ran up the three steps, beat on the brass knocker and waited without turning to see how his aunt was getting along. She, in turn, struggled out of the cab and the driver followed with the bags.

The door opened and there stood Minshull, the housekeeper, clad in her stiff black dress, her wrinkled healthy face aglow with anxiety. She almost ignored Harold.

'Oh, Miss Penelope... Whatever did you...?'

'Let's get in and close the door, Minshull. We don't want the whole town around quizzing.'

Harold shepherded them all in the gloomy, panelled hall. On the walls were framed pictures of dead and gone Blows, generations of Nesbury bankers, all prosperous-looking, portly and severe.

'How's Honoria? You did look after her?'

'Yes, yes...'

Minshull had grown cautious, almost crafty, watching the vanishing form of Harold to make sure he was out of earshot.

'I saw to her food myself and she's so much better. The doctor's here and he's brought a specialist. They're in with her now.'

'I must go to her...'

With only time to remove her black felt hat and heavy old-fashioned coat, Miss Penelope made for the stairs.

'I wouldn't, miss...'

'I shall... I shall... I must see them...'

She sped upstairs and hurrying to a heavy door, opened it.

The room was stuffy and smelled of used air and medicines. It was large and solidly furnished. In a heavy four-poster, a small-featured, pale, spoiled looking woman was sitting up, clad in a bed jacket and wearing a pout on her lips as though claiming more attention than she was already getting. The last daylight from the big sash window fell full on the bed and its occupant and a lamp overhead exaggerated the shadows on her thin face. She wore a net over her grey hair and her features were similar to those of her sister, Penelope, only more embittered by self-pity and sulking. Minshull hurried to her to straighten the bedclothes and reassure her. In contrast to the dumpy, buxom little housekeeper, the invalid looked almost transparent. The bedside table was a combination of altar and medicine chest. A bible, a prayer book, a little silver vase of primroses, a bookmark embroidered with a sacred text, all mixed up among bottles of yellow liquid, pillboxes, phials, glasses and bed-cups. Miss Honoria pointed to the table.

'Give me my powder. No, not that one... The one in the chubby bottle... Is that Penelope... Where have you been, Penelope?'

'To London, dear...'

'London? I've been so ill. I nearly died. Dr Cross has been coming twice a day. He's got me a specialist. Such a nice man. Dr Tankerstone...'

'Tankerville, Miss Honoria...'

'I said that, Minshull, and don't be impertinent. Go and see what they're doing. They've been a long time. They ought to tell me.'

Minshull crossed to another door leading from the larger room into a small one, which, in the day when this had been the parental bedroom, had served as the dressing room for generation after generation of bankers. She entered and was away a little while. Then, a voice was heard, booming and ill-tempered.

'Well, Minshull, and how long have you been standing there? Get along, my good woman, about your business...'

It was Dr Cross, the family physician, a forthright, tetchy practitioner of the old school, holding a whispered conversation with the consultant he had called in from a nearby large town. He was irritable that day, because he hadn't wanted to take a second opinion, he thought he knew all about the case and took umbrage when asked by the family to obtain further advice. This slur on his technical ability had started with the patient herself and spread through the rest of the Blows. The result was, Dr Cross was being catechised and patronised by a colleague much younger than himself about the condition, history and ailments of a body which had received his clinical care for over thirty years. It wasn't good enough! He took it out of Minshull by bawling at her and she fled before his wrath, out of the sick room, along the corridor and to her own bedroom, where she shut the door, sank in an armchair and had a good cry.

'I must go now to my room and tidy up,' ventured Penelope when the storm had subsided.

'Who's going to look after me? Minshull seems to have run off somewhere. I can't be left alone like this with two men in the room...'

The patient was getting plaintive again. Penelope patted her hand and soothed her.

'I'll find somebody...'

'Where's Ralph and Lenore? They've been out all afternoon and they knew the specialist was coming. They ought to have been here.'

'I don't know, dear. I've only just got home, you know.'

At this, the two doctors returned from their confab in the dressing room. They were both formidable men. Cross was heavy, tall and dressed in grey broadcloth. His lumbering gait and short clipped grey beard made him look like a colonial settler dressed up for a party. A man who inspired confidence in the sick room, however, because of his bulk and bustling self-confidence. He was an excellent diagnostician, but there he finished. Once he'd placed a label on the complaint, he was stumped if it proved obstinate, and if good nursing and the patient's natural resistance to illness did not do the trick, Dr Cross, as likely as not, ended by signing the death certificate. On this occasion he was more aggressive than ever to show he wasn't in the least put out of countenance by the man who walked in beside him.

Dr Tankerville was a consultant on most medical matters, whose claim to eminence was that he was once removed from most patients. They had to approach him through their own doctors instead of directly. He was tall, thin and sallow, with long hands and feet. His bloodless condition and aloofness made you wonder if he were human at all. Impossible to imagine him as a boy or youth; he seemed to have been created just as he was with the sole function of contemptuously pointing out with great precision the ills of the mortals beneath him. He specialised in treatments by hypodermic injection which seemed to result in the patients either leaping from their beds, vigorous and fully cured, or falling down dead at once. In the former event, the feat of magic was trumpeted as another victory for Dr Tankerville; in the latter, the illness was blandly described as the murderer on the death certificate and the doctor passed on to pump medicaments into other bloodstreams...

The medical men entered the sick room in solemn procession, their faces set like those of priests in ritual observance. Dr Tankerville wore a tall white collar, black jacket and striped trousers, and the addition of a black tie suggested that by the mere substitution of black pants for the grey ones, he would be quickly turned into a mourner at the funeral. Dr Cross with gravity told Miss Penelope they would like to see her nephews, Mr Ralph and Mr Harold, who, presumably, as the members of the stronger sex, were best fitted to hear the verdict. She hurried out and left them with the patient.

Below, in the hall, Ralph and his wife were just arriving in. Ralph Blow was the elder brother, another heavy specimen, but better proportioned than Harold, who was a small-town lawyer with a family practice, whilst Ralph, carrying on the family tradition, was a local director of the Home Counties Bank which had absorbed the old firm of Blow. He removed a black felt hat and a large overcoat, examined himself before the mirror, straightened his tie, passed his fingers over his small grey moustache and smoothed down his thin grey hair, plastered to his skull with great care and revealing more of his scalp, as time passed, in a growing tonsure. He looked up and saw his aunt.

'Hullo! You back? Where...?'

Penelope Blow leaned over the balusters and called softly down.

'The doctors have finished and want to see you and Harold...'

'Tell 'em to come down. There's a fire in the drawing room. It's stuffy in Aunt Honoria's room...'

'Will Lenore come up and stay with Honoria a little while then? I must tidy myself...'

Ralph's wife was standing beside him, taking off her heavy fur gauntlets. She wore a black sealskin coat and a little fur Cossack hat. She was much younger than Ralph, in the middle thirties in fact, and it was generally believed that she'd married him for his money. During her pregnancy, her mother had read Poe's 'The Raven' and no other name would do for her offspring than Lenore. It suited her. Her hair was raven black, her face delicately chiselled with high cheekbones and large eloquent eyes. These with the shapely mouth and straight nose, the tall sinuosity of her figure and the soft huskiness of her voice, made men naturally ask what she saw in Ralph and say what a lucky chap he was…

Lenore slid out of her coat, removed the hat, flung them both across the hall chest and slowly and with an air of complete resignation climbed the stairs and made for the door of the sick room. As a bank official, the house really belonged to Ralph and when he had married Lenore seven years ago, he had promised to find other quarters for the rest of the family: his brother, his two aunts and their retinues. Yet, here they still were! Not only that, a further aunt, on becoming a widow, had arrived for a holiday and ended up a resident. She had since died, thank heaven! Lenore wished they'd all die…including Ralph. She was tired of it all. The crazy, eccentric family, their whims, their traditions, their fussiness. They seemed to chase her everywhere. Ralph like a protective, exacting family head; Harold bewitched by her beauty and eating her with his half-dead eyes; the aunts trying to educate her in the ways of a prominent family and the wife of a local bigwig. At first, she had resisted. Now, by some mental trick, she managed to half-anaesthetise her feelings and showed neither pleasure nor disgust. She carried on in silent disdain.

At the door of Honoria's room she met the physicians coming out. Dr Cross greeted her and eyed her with admiration; Tankerville, clinically immersed, hardly saw her but muttered a good day in keeping with his colleague's salute. The procession moved solemnly downstairs, one step at a time, to join Ralph, who, having sought and found Harold, ushered the party into a room on his left. Penelope entered her own bedroom, was there a moment and then hurried out, twittering to herself and muttering for Minshull. During her absence, nobody had bothered about her window boxes. The sills of the two upper stories of the bank house were ornamented by flowers in boxes of soil. When she left, her daffodils were nicely up and budding; now, from lack of water, they were wilting. She hastened to the bathroom and emerged with a large jug of water. Minshull's room was next door. Penelope knocked but it was locked.

'Minshull... Minshull...'

'I'm coming. What is it?'

The voice was harsh.

'You've not watered my bulbs. They're dying...'

No reply. Miss Penelope hurried to render first-aid to the outraged daffodils... It was dark outside, but that did not deter her.

Below, the consultation was in progress. Dr Tankerville spoke to Dr Cross and Dr Cross passed it on.

'Miss Honoria had better go into Dr Tankerville's nursing home for observation. There are points we don't like about the case.'

Ralph hemmed and hawed, stroking his moustache nervously.

'Operation, eh?'

'No. Not exactly.'

'What will it cost?'

That was like Ralph. Rolling in money, people said, but as cheeseparing as they made them.

Dr Tankerville looked pained, as though money were quite a minor affair, in fact, beneath contempt until his underlings sent the final bill.

'Ahem... Twelve guineas weekly...'

He said it with a twist of the lips as though he'd tasted something unsavoury.

'That's a lot...'

'All the same, if it's necessary...' Harold was butting in.

'All right, all right... But what is it? Surely, we've a right to know.'

Dr Cross looked at the door to see that it was closed and then at Tankerville for approval. The specialist slowly nodded assent, like a Roman emperor concurring in the death of a downfallen gladiator.

'Well... To tell you the truth, we both suspect she's being poisoned. The symptoms are those of arsenic poisoning...'

'What!!! Nonsense... Who would want...?'

'Just a moment, Ralph,' said Cross huffily. 'Who, why, or when doesn't concern us at the moment. Our immediate duty is to get your aunt away from here and the source of the poisoning. If our opinion is right, it will be confirmed by observation and tests; if not, suitable treatment will be to hand. But it is imperative that we get her away...at once.'

The Blow brothers looked like pillars of salt. They just couldn't believe it. You could almost see their brains turning it over. Poison! Ralph; Harold; Lenore; Penelope; Minshull; Frazer, the cook; Jelley, their man; Mrs Peevey, the charwoman? Hunting for a suspect...

'She'd better go then...' said Ralph at length. 'All the same, it's nonsense. Who'd want...? How could they...? Nobody here... And what if you're right? What then?'

'The police...' said Cross, and Tankerville nodded with wintry approval.

'The police? My God...! What a scandal!! Oh, it'll turn out all right. You'll see. Nobody would...'

Ralph was being an ostrich already. Things like that didn't happen to the Blows. No fear! When troubles came, they paid somebody to clear them away or deal with them, or else denied their very existence. Ralph had done that with Lenore. When she got troublesome, he just walked out of the room and pretended it hadn't happened. It always worked. Already, Ralph was beginning to smile again. Everything would be all right. With the Blows, things like that didn't exist. Harold didn't look so sure. His pale eyes filmed over, and you couldn't guess what his thoughts were.

'Very well, let her go for a bit. Do all you can. You'll find you're mistaken. When do you want her?'

'Right away. She's better at the moment and can dress and you can drive her to Dr Tankerville's place in Derton. Bring enough for a fortnight's stay, for the time being. I think that's all...'

It wasn't quite all. There was the matter of Dr Tankerville and his consultation fee. Like a few proud and austere members of the learned professions, he pretended, formally, of course, that it was of no account. But you mustn't forget it... Oh dear, no! He cleared his throat for the benefit of Cross, his interpreter.

'Ahem...' Cross tried to look very aloof, too. 'Dr Tankerville's fee...ahem...mine'll do later... Ten guineas...grumha...ahem...'

Ralph counted out ten one pound and one ten-shilling notes from his wallet. Then he carefully counted them again, shuffling each one between finger and thumb to be sure that two hadn't stuck together. He placed them in an envelope from the desk and tried to pass it to Dr Tankerville, who didn't appear interested or to see the gesture. Ralph laid them on the table, from which in the next few moments they mysteriously vanished by a strange feat of prestidigitation, and the two doctors left the room with great dignity after some handshaking.

Ralph, finding nobody else to do it, heavily assisted the medical men into their winter coats and handed them their hats. The latter he got mixed up, giving the best of the two to Tankerville, which caused Cross to angrily snatch at the pair and sort them out with swift gestures like a juggler about to fling them and many more upwards in a perpetually moving circle. Then...

There was from the back of the house a scream, a thud, a crashing and splintering, and another dull impact of something with the cobblestones of the courtyard.

'Whatever's that?'

Downstairs, the house seemed deserted. The two brothers, followed by Cross, hurried to the back door, leaving the consultant standing in the hall and looking extremely irritated.

In the courtyard, illuminated by the hard light of an electric wall-lamp, was lying the body of Miss Penelope Blow, still and face downwards, half-buried by a shattered window box and soil and broken daffodils.

2

DEAD MARCH

I t was obviously an accident. She was watering her plants. A bit excited and shaky, and she leaned on the window box, which was rotten. Over she toppled with the box on top of her...'

Inspector Paston, of the Soke of Nesbury Police, had it all pat. It was as easy as that! Just an accident and the Coroner's verdict of misadventure to make it nice and orderly. Littlejohn wasn't so happy about it, however.

Two days after Miss Penelope Blow's last visit to Scotland Yard, Littlejohn returned from Lewes. He was met by a rather excited constable, who showed him the visiting card she had left and a newspaper cutting.

WATERING FLOWERS.
FALLS TO HER DEATH.

Whilst watering the bulbs in her window box at Nesbury yesterday, Miss Penelope Blow overbalanced and fell to her death.

Miss Blow was a daughter of the late William Blow, banker, of Nesbury, who some years ago caused a local sensation by leaving his fortune to charities. She was sixty-four...

'She was very upset when she found you weren't in, sir. Said it was most important. Wanted to keep her visit secret.'

'Did she indeed? I wonder if her death's all straight and above board. Did she leave any message, Cobb?'

'Yes, sir. You were to ring up a Mrs Minshull, her house-keeper, and tell her to tell Miss Blow to ring you up. You hadn't to say outright who you were or talk to Miss Blow at home. When you gave the word, she'd ring you from a callbox. Sounds a bit fishy, if you'll pardon the word, sir. But then, she looked a bit queer to me...'

'Did she? In what way?'

'Dressed old-fashioned, nervy, almost afraid, I'd say. Said a Mr...'

Here, PC Cobb consulted his notebook.

'...A Mr Claplady'd recommended her to see you.'

'Claplady, eh? I'd better ring him up. Meanwhile, did she come by taxi?'

'I couldn't say, sir. I'll inquire...'

'Right. Let me know, won't you? I'll take the card.'

From his room, Littlejohn telephoned the Rev Ethelred Claplady, his old friend, the lovable and wool-gathering vicar of Hilary Magna. It was somewhat of an ordeal, for the instrument at the vicarage was old and decayed and Mr Claplady's thoughts were not easily assembled.

'Littlejohn here, Mr Claplady...'

'Who?'

'Littlejohn... Scotland Yard... LITTLEJOHN!!'

'Ah, Inspector... How are you...? And Mrs Littlejohn, and... let me see, the dog...is he — or she — all right...? So good to hear from you...'

It took half an hour and after Littlejohn had sorted it out, it didn't amount to very much. Mr Claplady had, almost fifty years ago, been curate at Nesbury and had made a lifelong friend of Miss Penelope, who regularly wrote to him at Easter, Christmas and on his birthday, which she strangely remembered. Then had arrived a hasty confused note, saying he was the only friend in whom she could confide, and could he recommend a discreet detective or lawyer who would investigate a matter for her. It was terribly urgent and secret, and she would tell him about it later. That was all...

When Littlejohn told the Rev Ethelred of Miss Blow's death, the good man became so incoherent and the call so confused that Littlejohn had to ring off and promise to go to see him at a later date.

'Go to Nesbury if you like, but it's on your own head, you know,' said Chief Inspector Shelldrake, to whom Littlejohn went for advice. 'If you get treading on the corns of the local police, there'll be hell to pay. The Chief Constable of the Soke is a tartar. Keep out of his way...'

And he went on to remind Littlejohn of the case of the Three Red Men, who planned to blow up, simultaneously, all the Cabinet and all His Majesty's Opposition and establish a Communist dictatorship, and who almost got away in an aeroplane whilst Colonel Cardew was arguing the niceties of police jurisdiction...

'Why was the box on top of her?' asked Littlejohn of Paston. 'You'd expect her to be on top of the box if it was as you say.'

'We thought she might have caught it with her body as she fell and dislodged it. Besides, who'd want to push a nice old girl like Miss Blow through the window? Harmless, and everybody liked her. Look... That's her funeral starting now.'

The police station was on the opposite side of the main square from the Home Counties Bank, formerly Blows'. The square was a large, cobblestoned space on which were held a general weekly market and periodic cattle fairs and auctions. On two sides, rows of shops, modern chromium-fronted monstrosities, cheek-by-jowl with a few remaining old-fashioned ones. A block of prosperous-looking, handsome Georgian houses, now the offices of lawyers, auctioneers and accountants and a number of opulent heavy buildings, including the town hall and its appendages, respectively made up the two remaining sides of the rectangle.

The Home Counties Bank stood at the end of the Georgian row and before the door of the bank house a hearse and two official mourning cars were assembling.

Even as they did it, a number of other vehicles, full of top hats, black crepe, and male and female faces bearing fixed expressions of spurious grief, tacked themselves on the end of the cortege and vanished from sight in a long queue up a side street.

The two Inspectors stood at the window watching the scene.

'A very influential and historic family in Nesbury were the Blows. Everybody liked Penelope...'

'So it seems...'

The Market Square seemed dead everywhere except in front of the house, now the centre of activity. Two policemen were keeping the large, silent crowd within bounds, with restrained, almost reverent gestures. You felt that at any moment they would begin to parade about on tiptoes. From the hearse descended a frock-coated figure, majestic and top-hatted, bearing a scroll of mourners and their precedence in his huge red hand. He was followed by a small, prancing man who acted as his master of ceremonies and official door-opener and closer. The undertaker mounted the broad steps up to the house and indicated to the underling that he might ring the bell. Instead, the small man beat softly, like death itself, on the panel of the door with his crooked index, and they were admitted.

The coffin emerged, then two carloads of wreaths; the MC

opened doors, bowed in the mourners, and then closed them. The voice of the undertaker could be heard, like a herald's, intoning the order of the procession. One after another the cabs filled and moved on to make room for the next. Then, just as all was ready for off, a diversion occurred. The band of the local Salvation Army, marshalled in a side street, emerged and posted itself at the head, before the hearse. Paston thought some explanation was due.

'Miss Penelope was a great friend of the Salvationists. You see, her father, by his will, left them money to build a local citadel and she took a great interest in it. They thought the world of her...'

'Good! Old Blow left money where it would do good...'

Littlejohn liked the Salvation Army folk. He'd made a lot of friends among them years ago when he pounded the beat.

The procession to the cemetery began and the band started to play the Dead March in Saul. The solemn heavy drumbeats and the wailing air on the cornets struck a chill down your spine! Slowly the file of cars in bottom gear wound its way through the square and vanished down the main street. The Dead March repeated over and over again, got more and more diluted until it mingled with the rising noises of the town, and then died away. The shops grew busy again, the blinds of tile bank and the adjoining house were raised by invisible hands and Nesbury became itself. Now and then, the spring breeze blew an odd bar or two of the Dead March back over the square. The overture of a ghastly drama soon to be played out with the little town as its stage...

'I don't know why she should have called at Scotland Yard. She was a bit eccentric you know. Perhaps imagined things...'

'Maybe...'

Littlejohn and Paston withdrew from the window and sat at the local Inspector's desk. Littlejohn looked bothered. Miss

Blow had wanted his help and he hadn't been there to give it. What was it all about?

'Look here, Paston, this is a bit awkward. I don't want to meddle if the case is closed...'

'Case? Closed? What do you mean?'

'I want to satisfy myself about Miss Blow. She called three times at Scotland Yard, made a great mystery of what she had to tell me, arranged for me to ring her up, and then fell out of the window before I could get to her. It might have been an accident, or it might not. I want to make sure.'

Paston rubbed his chin irritably with the back of his fingers.

'As you said, Inspector, it's a bit awkward. Our Chief's a terribly jealous man about the force. He thinks it's a reflection on his capacity if anyone suggests outside help...'

Littlejohn looked Paston in the face. A slim, tall, ruddy officer in his middle forties, with his rather bushy hair already turning grey, he looked a decent sort...

'Are you jealous, too?'

'Who? Me?'

Paston laughed and pulled a pipe and tobacco from the drawer of his desk.

'Have a smoke, Littlejohn,' he said, passing over the tin. They filled up their pipes and lit them without another word.

'Chief or no Chief, nobody's going to murder Penelope Blow in cold blood and get away with it. I'm not saying she *was* murdered. But I'm as anxious as you are to get to the bottom of what she was wanting at Scotland Yard. Tomorrow, the Chief's going with his wife and daughters to London for a few days. It's Tuesday; he'll be back at weekend. As he goes, I suggest you move in, but not officially, mind you. I can't do that. But you can come and go without interference or the usual unholy row. That do?'

'Thanks a lot. That'll suit me fine. Maybe it will turn out to be a mare's nest, but I'd like to satisfy my conscience.'

'Right. We've most of the afternoon to talk things over and lay our plans. The Chief won't be calling in till late. We'd better not be seen too much together, if you don't mind, but we'll meet regularly to swap notes and ideas. Sorry, therefore, I can't take you to lunch, but they'll do you tolerably well at the Duke of York, over there across the square. Come back after and we'll get started. I'm glad you're here. To tell you the truth, there are one or two things going on at the old bank house I don't quite understand. We'll go into 'em...'

The Duke of York, which had at one time been a coaching-house, had not long been acquired by a London company who had already started to make it abhorrent and to deprive it of character by extensive alterations. Littlejohn entered by the revolving door and stood for a while in the entrance hall. Nobody took any notice of him, so after a few abortive attempts he found the dining room and seated himself at an empty table. This was a signal for the head waiter to materialise from somewhere and tell him the table was booked, although there was no indication to that effect. It is a way such potentates have and is a disciplinary measure to let guests know the place doesn't belong to them. Having done this, the head waiter left Littlejohn and did not reappear for some time.

A few diners were assembling as it was half after noon. The room looked large enough to accommodate all the population; it was used for balls and public meetings as well as feeding. The floor was thickly carpeted, the furniture modern, there was a bar in one corner and the walls were decorated with panels in which were set mural paintings of shepherds, shepherdesses, lords and ladies disporting themselves in groves and on swings, in decidedly poor imitations of Watteau and Boucher. The directors of the hotel were very proud of these monstrosities, called them their artistic 'decor', (a word left behind by the artist who had worked best whilst drunk and had eventually run off with the head barmaid), and brought parties of friends from far distances to see them.

A plantigrade old waiter, a dear and polite relic of days long gone and only retained because replacements were hard to get, at length arrived and took Littlejohn's order. As such survivals are, he was paternal and talkative.

'Sorry to keep you waiting, sir, but we're busy today. There's a funeral party coming in...'

He indicated a long table, set apart by the windows, with places laid for a score or more. The head waiter was now telling another customer that the table he had chosen was engaged. He moved him to the one Littlejohn had been told to vacate...

'The Blow family, sir. Miss Penelope's been buried today, and many people have come from long distances. In normal times, I guess they'd have entertained them at home before seeing them off, but as it is, what with rations...'

The head waiter, who resembled one of those dusky French colonials who hawk carpets in Paris, signalled angrily to the old-stager to get a move on. No time to be polite to clients; get 'em fed and out...

'Sorry, sir. Would you like a drink? Very good...'

Plantigrade made off as fast as his poor feet would take him and returned with a plate of tomato soup bearing in itself a curdy precipitate...

Then the funeral party arrived, ushered in by the manager. The Blow family had shares in the hotel, word had gone round the staff, and most of them were on their toes. The head waiter ran here and there, trying to manipulate the chairs of all at once.

A tall, heavy, middle-aged man was apparently the fugleman of the party and received most of the managerial homage. He had with him a lovely woman, apparently his wife. She wore a dark fur coat and Cossack hat and held herself proudly. By her side, a queer-looking fellow whom the guests addressed as Harold, tried to give her his undivided attention. The rest, a mixed assembly, looked like relatives and friends. Some were prosperous-looking, one answered by the name of Sir Nigel, another was addressed as Mister Mayor, whilst two or three rather nervous hangers-on, the poorer branch of the Blows from the looks of them, sat down in their shabby black and were left to fend for themselves.

Littlejohn was not far from the funeral party, yet, but for a stroke of good fortune, would not have gathered much from them, for they said little and said it in undertones. The local Blows were simply here to see their remote-dwelling relations fed and off. It was a bore to them but had to be tolerated. The manager had been instructed to get it all over expeditiously; the head waiter, therefore, concentrated all except the veteran waiter on the Blow table and left the other diners to hunger.

Littlejohn's stroke of luck was in Sir Nigel Clapp, a second cousin of Penelope Blow and fabulously wealthy from brewing. He was turned seventy and told everyone that the last time his doctor had overhauled him he'd said he was as good as a chap of forty. He attended in triumph all the funerals of his contemporaries. His only physical failing seemed to be in his ears. He was deaf, stone deaf. He was also very curious about everything. Deaf or not, he insisted on receiving a bawled account of all that went on. His soup finished, he set about his neighbour, the family lawyer, Mr Copplestones, a man of his own age and huge bulk, but sound of hearing if not of liver.

'Sad business about Penelope... Used to play with her when we were nippers. Always was a plain Jane... In love with a parson in her twenties, a curate in the town. Her father put his foot down, and right, too. She never looked at another man after, though many a one would a been glad to take her on with all that money...'

The family looked uncomfortable and tried to appear not to care; the proud ones assumed fixed expressions which indicated that Sir Nigel really wasn't with them...

The brewer continued to talk through the next course. He was determined to get to the bottom of everything before he went home to Clapp Towers, where his wife was awaiting a full account. She led the baronet a dog's life and having quarrelled with the Blow branch of the family was more than normally interested in them. If he didn't return with a full story, she'd blister him...

'What was Penelope doin' fallin' out of the window? She wasn't a child...'

Mr Copplestones muttered something through a mouthful of meat and potatoes.

'Eh? I can't hear.'

The lawyer swallowed hastily, raised his eyes to heaven to indicate to the rest assembled that he couldn't help himself and spoke louder in his reedy tenor.

'It was an accident. She was watering her bulbs in the window box.'

'Did nobody see it happen?'

'No. Honoria was in bed ill and Lenore was with her. Mrs Minshull was in her room and the rest were downstairs.'

Mr Copplestones thereupon turned to his other neighbour and started an eager whispering, but Sir Nigel wasn't being cheated. He prodded the lawyer in the ribs until he winced.

'Where is Honoria?'

'In a nursing home. She is not well.'

'What's the matter with her?'

'Under observation... Dr Tankerville...'

'Tankerville? Bah! Quack...'

Sir Nigel forked his meal pensively. He was thinking what to ask next.

'Where's Minshull? Thought she'd have been here.'

'She's a servant, Nigel. What would she be wanting with the family?'

'Can't hear. Damn, Alfred, speak up. Whisperin's rude.'

'She's gone to her sister's for the afternoon. She's been upset by all this...'

'Didn't know she had a sister...'

'Yes... Married to the Mayor's steward, Parker...'

'No need for her to be upset. All got to die sometime...'

Mr Copplestones was getting fed up.

'I thought you had one of those ear-aid things, Nigel. Where is it...?'

'In my overcoat pocket. Don't use it at mealtimes. Awkward...'

'I'll get it...'

'Eh?'

'I'LL GET IT...'

Copplestones didn't stay to argue; he rose and made for the cloakrooms, where, presumably, he rifled all the pockets, for it was a long time and the strawberry roll had gone cold before he returned, bearing in his hand Sir Nigel's hearing contraption. This he hastily handed to the baronet, helped him to switch it on and then, in low tones, which Littlejohn couldn't catch, began to satisfy his friend's curiosity.

Littlejohn finished his meal and sat for a minute or two unobtrusively eyeing the rest of the company. Ralph, as someone had called him, was at the head of the table, a pompous, unbending sort of fellow, without sense of humour and full of his own importance. His wife, sitting beside him, looked like a lovely model out of *Vogue*. The light, catching the fur of her hat, seemed to cast a nimbus high above her beautiful well-chiselled face, with its high cheekbones and dark, clever eyes. A slight curl of disdain about the lips expressed her thoughts on the company and maybe on her husband and his family as well. The man they called Harold, apparently the brother of Ralph, kept trying to catch the woman's eye and failing. The trio seemed to take the emotional limelight of the scene. The atmosphere around them was somehow charged with strange feeling; the rest of the party were like a lot of supers in a play, with Sir Nigel and Copplestones as a couple of traditional comic parts.

'Damn, Copplestones, you're the family lawyer. You ought to know,' bellowed the brewer out of temper with the cautious solicitor. They reared up at one another bellicosely, like a couple of contentious seals, their moustaches bristling and their poached eyes popping.

Ralph Blow rose without waiting for coffee. He'd had enough. The rest got to their feet a little surprised, and one of the poorer relations hastily filled his mouth with the remnants of his trifle and asked his neighbour if coffee was being served elsewhere. The party formed a ragged procession and slowly filed out. The head waiter presented Littlejohn with a bill and stood waiting for payment.

'Leave it, please,' said Littlejohn and dismissed him. He waited until little plantigrade came in sight, beckoned him, paid the bill and tipped him. They exchanged a friendly word or two and then Littlejohn, too, went his way.

The mourning party were sorting themselves out and making for their cars, parked in the centre of the square round the large statue of some local worthy, a rugged Victorian gentleman, with one hand raised, finger pointing to heaven and the other holding a scroll. The pigeons had anointed him liberally with white splashes like large exclamation marks. The poor relations were asking about trains and buses, with a peculiar, pleading intonation, which suggested that a lift in a car would be better for their health. Nobody took the hint and they made off, after obsequious farewells, in the direction of the inquiry office. Parting seemed to bring back the recollection of the purpose for which they had all assembled and their faces grew mournful. Sir Nigel had switched off his talking-box and departed, amid loud goodbyes, to a distant town where he was due to open a political bazaar...

Littlejohn strolled over to the Town Hall, a large stone edifice with Olympian pillars in front. The Mayor, having also detached himself from the funeral party, hurried across the square and vanished inside the building before Littlejohn could get there. At the inquiry office, the Inspector asked for Parker, the Mayor's steward. He arrived and proved to be a tall, stooping, elderly man with military moustache, black trousers and a brown morning coat, a uniform he wore when attending on His Worship, who was about to take him and the municipal chain on an official trip to greet a delegation from the Board of Trade. Parker looked in a hurry.

'Good h'afternoon, sir. I'm just goin' out. What was you wantin'?'

Parker was, with the exception of startling items of news gathered from the morning paper or from the gossip of the Town Hall, quite illiterate, but he looked very impressive on occasions of state, at which, of course, he never needed to open his mouth. Mayors came and went, but Parker remained a politically neutral symbol in his bearing of the mace and chain of office for Mayor after Mayor, of the continuity of authority.

'I won't keep you, Parker...'

Parker stood to attention, for he sensed from long experience, the official tone, the poise of authority.

'Yes, sir?'

'You're brother-in-law of Mrs Minshull, I hear, and she's at present at your home with your wife?'

'Yes, sir.'

'I wanted to see Mrs Minshull. Might I go round to your place?'

'Of course, sir. Twenty-four Albion Street, just round the corner there. She's in, but very upset, sir. Bin to the funeral... Sad business. Was you from the press or...?'

'No. Just a friend of Miss Blow. I couldn't leave without

seeing Mrs Minshull of whom she's spoken quite a lot in the past...'

A bell rang in the room nearby. It was the Mayor summoning his acolyte.

"That's for me, sir. Perhaps I'll be seein' you again...'

'Very likely, Parker. Thanks...'

With that, Parker put on a top hat and hurried across to Blows' Bank to pick up the golden chain of the Mayoralty, and Littlejohn turned down Albion Street for his first interview.

3

POST MORTEM

No 24 Albion Street was a new council house, built on standard lines with a small square of garden at the front and a hundred or more similar buildings on every side of it. Mr and Mrs Parker had acquired it with great difficulty after a marriage contracted late in life. Previously Parker had been a sworn bachelor living in a large old house with his mother. On the death of the latter he had married mainly from a utilitarian point of view, Maria Light, in service at the Blows along with her sister, Anna Minshull. They had tried to squeeze all Arthur Parker's heavy Victorian furniture in the new house, for he couldn't bring himself to part with any of it. The place looked like a repository.

Littlejohn beat upon the knocker and Mrs Parker answered the door. You could guess she'd been a cook: a homely, buxom, yet masterful type of woman who'd taken Littlejohn's measure and come to an opinion about him before a word had been said.

'Is Mrs Minshull here, Mrs Parker? Your husband said...'

'Yes, she's here. What do you want?'

'I'm wanting a word with her about Miss Penelope Blow. I believe she left a message for me...'

Mrs Parker's lips tightened.

'They've just buried her, and my sister's a bit upset after the funeral. Won't another day do?'

Mrs Minshull had evidently been listening to what was going on, for she appeared behind her sister in the doorway. She, too, was buxom and homely to a less degree than her sister, however, and her face was harder and more masculine. Harder features and thick, dark eyebrows which were exaggerated by the greyness of her thin hair.

'What did you want?'

She'd been weeping, not from great grief for her lost mistress, but from a multitude of other little things. She'd been invited to the funeral and then treated like a stranger; they hadn't buried Miss Penelope properly because there hadn't been a proper funeral feast after it and such as there was, she'd been ignored when the invitations went round. A whole host of petulant complaints...

'May I come in for a minute or two?'

'Of course, if you must see her now...'

'It's all right, Maria. I feel better after a cup o' tea. Come in, sir...'

There was a small vestibule and then Littlejohn found himself in the sitting room. The walls looked ready to crumble from the pressure of a huge sideboard, with a sofa, armchairs, small chairs, corner cupboards, whatnots and tables to match. The place was like a menagerie, too. A dog with two puppies and a friendly cat on the hearth, a canary hanging in a cage in the window, and a budgerigar performing feats of gymnastics on a small ladder and ring in another cage suspended from a stand in one corner. The arrival of an intruder caused a commotion. The dog began to growl, the puppies to whine, the cat to spit, the budgerigar to talk and the canary to chirp.

'God Bless Winston Churchill!' shouted the talking bird.

'He did that all through the war. Cheered us up no end in the bombing, he did,' explained Mrs Parker. 'Don't mind the dog; she won't bite and the cat's that jealous of the pups, she can't bear anybody near them.'

The canary emitted a few bubbling notes and then burst into lovely unrestrained song.

'Pretty Dick,' shouted Mrs Parker.

'What was you wantin'?' asked Mrs Minshull, bringing them all back to earth.

'I believe Miss Blow was in London just before her death, Mrs Minshull.'

'Yes... She went off without telling anybody and Mr Harold 'ad to go and bring her 'ome. He was mad about it, too.'

'Didn't you know she was going? Didn't she tell even you?'

Mrs Minshull looked upset. Her lips trembled and she gripped the solid arms of the oversized armchair tightly.

'I'll just get a bit done upstairs,' said her sister, with great tact, and taking a duster from one of the large receptacles in the furniture, vanished aloft.

'I... I... Well, she did sort of tell me, sir. You see, she wanted to get somebody's advice and couldn't trust anyone else to go for her. Yes, she told me, but I wasn't to tell anybody. There's no harm in tellin' you what you seem to know, is there?'

'Did she leave any message with you? Anything you'd to tell anyone?'

'I oughtn't to be talkin' like this to a stranger. Did you say you was a friend of hers?'

'In a way. I'm a friend of Mr Claplady, who, I understand, was also a friend of Miss Blow.'

'That's right, sir, he was. I did hear that one time, many a long year ago, before I came to the family, and I've been with them forty years, Miss Blow and the Reverend wanted to get married. Her father wouldn't hear of it. Made an awful bother and even got them to move the Reverend a long way off to keep them apart. They always wrote to one another and never married... It was a pity...'

'I see. Well, my name's Littlejohn. Inspector Littlejohn, of Scotland Yard. I'm not here officially, really, but I've come to find out, if I can, why Miss Blow wanted to see me or, at least, talk to me.'

'Oh, sir...'

Mrs Minshull was in great distress. She didn't know what to say.

'Do you know?'

'Well... Yes and no, sir. You see, the family said she was going a bit queer and I don't know whether I ought to tell things.'

'Come, come, Mrs Minshull. Whatever you tell me will be used with discretion.'

'Very well, sir. Miss Penelope'd got it into her head that somebody was poisoning her sister, Miss Honoria.'

'Is that the one who's gone to a nursing home?'

'Yes, sir. The doctors were fast in her case. They didn't say so, but that's what it was.'

'And how did Miss Penelope know her sister was being poisoned?'

'She said Miss Honoria told her.'

'And how did Honoria know?'

'She said she felt it. It certainly was mysterious, sir. She started to be ill with her stomach. Couldn't keep anything down. Sick and such like. In the end, she said only Miss Penelope was to give her her food. That was after she had to go to bed.'

'And did Miss Penelope do that?'

'Yes. Prepared it all, too. She got a bit better after that.'

'What happened whilst Miss Penelope was in London, then?'

'I got it ready. She didn't get any worse, but not much better, either. She asked Dr Cross to bring in another doctor. He was mad, but he did it. So they took her off.'

'Did you think she was being poisoned, Mrs Minshull?'

'I don't know. She said so, but who and how could it have been done to her? I'm sure they'll find she's wrong. It's Miss Honoria, not Miss Penelope, who's queer, if you ask me.'

'Were they both wealthy?'

'I don't know, I'm sure, sir. They seemed short of nothing. It wasn't my business to inquire what they'd got.'

'I heard their father left his fortune to charity.'

'He left a lot. All sorts of charities. Nobody knew what was happenin' till the will was read. It was like a joke. The only sensible thing was leavin' money to the Salvation Army to build a sort of church for them. They needed one. Miss Penelope seemed to think he'd like her to see that they got a proper Citadel, as they called it, and she used to go regular to their meetings. Left a wish behind that the band should play her to the cemetery, she did. That's why they was there today. The family was terribly mad at it, but Mr Copplestones said it was only right to respect the wishes of the dead.'

'Why did William Blow leave his money that way?'

'Spite!'

Upstairs Mrs Parker sounded to be moving more heavy furniture, the canary began to sing again, and the budgerigar shouted, 'God Bless Winston Churchill'.

Mrs Minshull was warming up to her tale now. Properly in her stride she needed no persuasion. Outside a cart drew up and a hawker began to cry fresh fish.

'Spite?'

'Yes. There was him and his nephew, Mr Theodore, the only son of Mr William's dead brother, Rufus. Mr Theodore had three sons, and Mr William only got three daughters. That made him mad. Then, when his wife ran away from him with one of the men in the bank, he never got over it. He hated women and couldn't bear his daughters about the place. It was awful for nearly thirty years in that house.'

'So Mr Ralph and Mr Harold are Mr Theodore's sons?'

'Yes, sir. You see, there was some arrangement about the head of the Blow family livin' in the old bank house and being on the board of the new bank. When Mr William died, Mr Theodore having passed on before 'im, Mr Ralph came in.'

'I see. What about the third son?'

'Killed in the first war. That killed his father, too. Mr Henry was the nicest of them all.'

'So, Miss Blow wanted to see me about the poisoning, Mrs Minshull?'

'Yes. She was nearly out of her mind with worry.'

'Were you there when the accident happened?'

'I was in my room. Dr Cross had been very rude to me, because he said I'd been listening to him and Dr Tankerville. I hadn't. I was hurt and went and shut myself in my room.'

'Did you go to the bedroom after it happened?'

'Yes, sir. She screamed as she fell, and I rushed along. The window was open and there she was, poor dear, lyin' dead on the stones below with all the bulbs and soil and wood all over her.'

Mrs Minshull began to cry. Her whole frame grew convulsed, for she was tightly corseted, and her sobs threatened to explode the tight envelope of black silk in which she was laced.

Littlejohn waited until it had all subsided and until the dogs and the cats had ceased the noise her outburst had stimulated.

'What happened? Do you know?'

'Well, the place was full of police. They all said she must have been leanin' hard on the box and it gave way under her.'

'Was it an old box?'

'Rotten, you mean, sir? No. It hadn't long been mended and painted. It was on the sill and fixed to the wall with iron things. I can't understand how it happened, unless the irons was rusty.'

'I suppose the police looked into it?'

'Oh yes, sir. The box wasn't rotten. I saw it. It had broken with falling or else a weak spot had given way. They said it was accidental and that was right, too, sir. Nobody would have done that to Miss Penelope. Besides, there was nobody there to do it.'

'How do you know?'

'Well, sir. I wasn't long going to see what it was all about, and I saw nobody.'

'How long?'

'I'd bin cryin', I must say, about what the doctor said to me and I... I... well, I had to unfasten me corsets, I felt that bad. When I heard the scream, I fastened myself up quick...it didn't take a minute...and then I went.'

'And you saw nobody?'

'No, sir. Except the gentlemen in the hall in a bunch and then they ran out to the yard.'

'Where was Miss Honoria?'

'In bed, sir. Waitin' for the doctors, again.'

'Was anyone with her?'

'Yes, sir. Mrs Ralph. She was looking after her till the men had finished. They was in the drawing room havin' a talk.'

'I'm not here officially, Mrs Minshull, but with Miss Penelope having called to see me, I'd like to make sure that right was done to her. In other words, that I didn't, by my absence when she called to see me, cause injury to be done to her.'

'I see, sir. You wasn't to blame. Anybody might be out.'

'Yes, but I don't want to return with it on my conscience. Will you help me?'

'If I can, sir.'

'I'd like to look quietly round the house and where the accident happened. But I want to do it privately. The family or anyone else mustn't know. Can you arrange it?'

'I think so. I generally know when they're all bein' out. They tell me on account of meals. I could telephone or let you have word some way.'

'Very well, thanks. And not a word to a soul, not even your sister, Mrs Minshull.'

'I won't, sir.'

'And now, can you tell me a bit about the family. Who they are and what they're like, going back to William Blow's time?'

'Yes, sir, although I shouldn't really, you know. It's bad for servants talking about their masters outside...'

This seemed to voice the well-known below-stairs ethics of bygone days. You mustn't, if you were in service, talk to your 'betters' about your employers, although, to your equals in similar jobs, you could say as much as you liked.

'This is exceptional, Mrs Minshull. It isn't just gossip, it might save another life, you see.'

Mrs Minshull threw up her hands in horror, uttering a wild, startled cry which made the animals growl with anger, the canary chirp and the budgerigar shout 'Down with Hitler'.

'Surely not, sir. I'll tell you what you want to know rather than that.'

'What sort of a man was William Blow?'

'Domineerin', sir. Always wanted his own way. Even wanted to dictate to the Almighty whether he had boys or girls and then sulked because they was girls. He led Mrs Blow an awful life with his tantrums and bullyin', till in the end she ran away.'

'What made him that way?'

'He thought because he was town's banker, everybody must do just as he said. Now, Mr Theodore was a gentleman, sir. Quiet and kind, but his uncle bullied him too, and though they was nearly of an age, Mr Rufus bein' much older than his brother, Mr William, Mr William was the master.'

'Did Mr Theodore leave his money to his sons?'

'Yes, sir.'

'Were they wealthy?'

'At one time, sir, they was the wealthiest people round here, but things didn't go well for them. So much so, that they do say the old bank was in difficulties when the Home Counties bought them over. The Blows was said to do pretty well out of the turnover, though things were never the same with them. They do say that Mr Ralph and Mr Harold have to work for their livings and if they didn't, they wouldn't make ends meet.'

'Are Ralph and Harold married?'

'Mr Ralph is; Mr Harold's a bachelor. Mr Ralph married Lenore Broome, daughter of the one-time cashier of the bank. She's a beauty, but a proud one. All the town said how well she'd done marryin' a Blow, but I don't know. Mr Ralph's twenty years or so older than her. They've never had any children though they've been married ten years or more and she seems bored with it all. I don't blame her really, with all that lot: two aunts, Mr Harold and all living in that big house, as well as her and her husband...'

'I think I saw them over lunch...'

Mrs Minshull's face assumed a pinched, pained expression.

'They never asked me... That ud be them.'

'Middle-aged man, a lovely dark girl in a black fur coat and a tall, loosely-built man with a large head?'

'That's it, sir. With Mr Harold — that's the one with the head — hangin' on every word Mrs Ralph says? Disgraceful! He never ought to live with them. Both brothers wanted her, and she chose the one with the most money and influence. Now she's unhappy.'

'You like her?'

'She's all right. They're all all right to me. I've been in the family since the boys were little. It's a good, comfortable job if you look after yourself, sir.'

'You said three daughters of William Blow. Where's the other?'

'Dead, sir. About three or four years since. That was Miss Katherine, the youngest. She married the Town Clerk here. They'd no children and was very fond of one another. When he died, Miss Katherine was like somebody lost. They took her in at the bank house for a bit and there she stayed till she died, not very long after. Her heart was broke with her husband dying. She took bad and never got up again.'

'What was the matter?'

'Enteritis, I think. She just pined away.'

'Did the sisters get on well together?'

'Oh, yes, sir. Miss Katherine and Miss Penelope was the quiet ones. Both of them had fallen in love, though Miss Penelope was unlucky, but it never made her bitter, I must say. Miss Honoria was the haughty one and liked fine livin'. Balls, receptions, parties, driving around in carriage and pair and bein' a Blow suited her. The men of the town was scared of her. I never heard of any of them fallin' in love with her, though there was rumours of her fancyin' one of the doctors of the town, but he packed up and went away...'

'So after the official mistress of the house, Mrs Ralph, Miss Honoria was head?'

'Yes. She ran the place for 'er father when he was alive, though he didn't take much notice of her. And then when Mr Ralph moved in, Mrs Ralph seemed quite content to let her keep on. It suited Mrs Ralph to shed the responsibility.'

'Now about this problem of Miss Penelope's; Miss Honoria told her she thought somebody was poisoning her. How long is this ago?'

'Nearly twelve months since Miss Honoria started with her do's. Sickness and such like. Then she'd grow better and then begin again.'

'Was Miss Penelope upset? How did she take it?'

'Well, sir... Miss Penelope used to talk a lot to me. The best and kindest of them all, she was. She'd come into my kitchen and tell me her troubles. "Minshull," she'd say, "my sister tells me she thinks someone is giving her poison. What do you think?" "I think it's all nonsense and another of her silly fancies,

miss," I said. "Who'd want to be poisoning her?" And that
seemed to comfort Miss Penelope for the time being. But Miss
Honoria kept on at it, till, in the end, Miss Penelope started to
be afraid. She must 'ave told Mr Claplady and he told her to see
you, sir.'

'Silly fancies, you said, Mrs Minshull; was Miss Honoria full
of fancies?'

'Very self-centred, sir. The most selfish of the lot. And the
things she'd do to get her own way. Pretend to have headaches,
go sick, take to her bed, if things just didn't suit her or if people
wouldn't give her what she wanted. That was due, to my
thinkin', to her mother spoilin' her when she was little. She took
her about with her a lot and the child talked and acted just like a
grown-up. It doesn't do to let children get that way...'

'Miss Honoria kept it up all her life, did she?'

'Yes...'

There were noises from above after a long spell of quiet. Mrs
Parker was on the move and preparing to descend upon them.
Footsteps sounded on the stairs and there she was, pretending
to be astonished and evidently determined that she was going to
partake in any more talk that was going.

'Are you two at it yet? Must 'ave a lot to say to one another.
It'll be tea time soon...'

The small menagerie made loud noises of joy at the return of
their mistress. The dog whined, the cat rose, arched her back
and started rubbing round the table legs and purring volup-
tuously. The canary gurgled a note or two and then burst into
song and the budgerigar began to call down repeated benedic-
tions on Mr Churchill. They apparently agreed that it was tea
time.

Littlejohn rose and bade them both goodbye and thanks. It
was nice to get in the open air and smoke. He puffed his pipe
with pleasure and made his way back to the police station.

Paston was busy writing at his desk but seemed pleased to

see Littlejohn. The detective told him where he had been and what had happened.

'Not letting the grass grow under your feet, are you, sir?'

'Might as well get it over as soon as possible...'

'Yes. Good job you didn't call earlier. There might have been some awkward questions. You see, the Chief called in sooner than I thought. He's decided to go to London by road, so has made an earlier start. He's dominated by his womenfolk and I guess they've made up their minds they'll take the car. He's gone...'

They smiled at each other like schoolboys in mischief.

'Good...!'

'All right for you, sir,' said Paston with a wry smile, 'but I'm in a bit of a cleft stick. Superintendent Hempseed, my superior, and acting Chief when Colonel Cardew's away, is laid-up with lumbago. He's in bed. Now, if anything turns up in this case... I mean, if matters grow worse, I'll have to act in the absence of the Chief. If Hempseed were here, it would rest with him whether or not to call in you chaps from Scotland Yard. But he's away, so if we re-open the case, I'll have to get in touch with Colonel Cardew in London and that would finish it. He'd never call you in...'

'Why can't you, as acting Chief, do it and present the Colonel with a *fait accompli* when he returns?'

'That's the awkward part about it. You see, I don't want to blot my copybook with the Colonel. Hempseed retires next month and I'm on the shortlist for Superintendent of the Soke. If Cardew gets mad with me, he'll veto that and one of the outside applicants will get it.'

'Ah! Bit awkward... All the same, if you could solve the case...if case there is...before Cardew comes along, your name would be made. They'd elect you on the strength of it.'

'You don't know Colonel Cardew. He'd never forgive me. Unless... Yes... I'll go up to see Hempseed. He's a sport. He'll advise me. He wants me to follow him. If *he'll* call in Scotland Yard, Bob's your uncle!'

The telephone bell interrupted their plotting.

'Yes... Paston here...'

It was Dr Cross. He wanted to see Paston urgently and at once. Most important and too grave to discuss over the wire.

Littlejohn removed his pipe and smiled gravely.

'What's the betting they've found arsenic and he's coming to inform you officially?'

'Arsenic? What do you mean?'

'I was going to tell you after we'd planned our campaign. Miss Penelope came to Scotland Yard to ask me what she'd better do; somebody was feeding arsenic to her sister Honoria. Or, at least, that's what Honoria said.'

'Well, I'll be damned. Let's hear Cross and then, if you're right, I'm off to talk to Hempseed right away.'

At the Blow house opposite, the door suddenly opened. Lenore Blow hastily descended the three stone steps which led to it, and walking quickly, crossed the square and disappeared down a side street. As Littlejohn watched, the door opened again, and Harold Blow emerged. He looked to the right and to the left and then, almost running, took the same route as his sister-in-law and vanished as well. Then, the pair of them were followed by Ralph, who repeated their performances and, after some hesitation, took the wrong side street and hurried down it.

'Foiled again!' said Littlejohn.

'Eh?'

'They seem to be having a general turn-out at the bank house. Like the cinema closing... Lenore Blow hunted by husband and brother-in-law...'

'A mad lot, the Blows!'

'You're telling me!'

4

ARSENIC

Dr Cross was a very superior type of person. Cold and objective in his bearing, you would have thought the Lord had placed in his power the ultimate decisions of life and death, instead of very limited means of keeping people alive without curing them. The only times on which he showed the least signs of passion were when he was crossed, or his opinions challenged; he then burst into indignant eruption. He had indulged in such volcanic manifestations when asked for a second opinion on the case of Miss Honoria Blow. Now, it seemed that the request was fully justified. He'd diagnosed ulcers, possibly malignant growths; it turned out to be arsenic. He entered the police station on the side of law and order in hunting down the criminal who'd thus made a fool of him.

Dr Cross wore the black gloves, frock coat and top hat in which he'd earlier that day attended the funeral of poor Penelope, who had managed to die without his assistance. He looked a bit out of date, a throwback to the times of mustard plasters, castor oil and wooden stethoscopes.

'Good morning, doctor,' said Paston cheerfully.

'I want to see you,' replied Cross, without returning the

greeting.

'This is a colleague of mine, Inspector Littlejohn...'

'Littlejohn, Littlejohn... Where have I heard that name before? Were you mixed up in the case of the death of the Bishop of Greyle?'

'Yes, sir.'

'I read about it in a book. Took you rather a long time, I thought. Criminal was obvious...'

'You think so, sir?'

'Yes. All the same, glad to meet you in the flesh. You down here on a case?'

'Not exactly, sir...'

The doctor shook hands. To Littlejohn it felt like clasping a dead fish.

'Can't waste much time. I called to say that we've now had time to examine the case of Miss Honoria Blow. We think she's been given arsenic. The tests prove that.'

He spoke collectively, although he'd only read a report. He sat down irritably in a chair, removed his gloves and placed his tall hat on the table as though about to perform a lot of conjuring tricks.

'Yes... And now it's up to you, Paston. And, if I may say so, it's as well you've got a man from Scotland Yard here with you. From what I gather the local force wants a bit of waking up.'

Dr Cross and the Chief Constable were at daggers drawn.

'I beg pardon, sir.'

'I don't mean you, Paston. The higher-ups want clearing out. This place is a disgrace.'

He spoke as if the Soke of Nesbury were a hotbed of crime and corruption.

'Can you tell us the full story, doctor?'

Cross rubbed his fingers across his stubbly beard. It was evident that talking shop with laymen went against the grain with him.

'It's rather delicate… You see, it concerns a well-known and highly respected family in the town. It wouldn't do…'

Littlejohn intervened.

'Excuse me, doctor. Highly respected or not, if one member of the Blow family has been giving another lethal dose of arsenic, the matter becomes a criminal one, and, therefore, public. I may as well tell you that the reason for my being here is that Miss Penelope, before her death, called at Scotland Yard to tell me that she suspected that her sister was being poisoned…'

'What! Then, why didn't she tell me? How did she know?'

'Miss Honoria said she suspected it herself…'

Dr Cross ran his hand across his bald head.

'They're mad! Mad as hatters. Here's a woman, ill in bed, with her doctor attending her daily, more sometimes, and she thinks she's being poisoned, and she doesn't mention a word to him. I give it up.'

'I can't explain it, either, doctor,' said Littlejohn. 'We've got to get at the bottom of it, though, now that it's been definitely established. What are the details?'

'Miss Honoria is suffering from slight potassium arsenate poisoning. The whole thing's a mystery. About twelve months ago, she started being unwell. Burning in the stomach, nausea, vomiting, purging, thirst…and other symptoms which I needn't enumerate. I put it down to something she'd eaten. There's a lot of rubbish in food nowadays. She recovered in the course of a few days. Then, soon afterwards, the symptoms were repeated. Thus it went on. Relief, recurrence, relief, recurrence… Until a few days ago, the family suggested a second opinion. Had there been any deterioration in Miss Blow's condition, I intended taking additional advice myself, but she was never seriously ill. I was beginning to suspect either ulceration or malignant obstruction of some kind…but…I confess arsenic never entered my head. A family like that! Who would think…?'

'It may not be the family, doctor.'

'You suggest servants? Old retainers, with them all their lives, more or less? Hardly.'

'Did Miss Honoria go out much?'

'Fairly often until she began ailing. But for six months she's hardly been out of doors, and if she did go out, it was just for an airing in the car or a little walk in the park. She does rather tend to coddle herself and dwell on her ailments. How she suspected poison, I can't think.'

The whole of the doctor's discourse was delivered in indignant tones. He was obviously affronted at his patient and with things in general. Somebody had stolen a march on him!

'The poison you mentioned, sir...potassium arsenate...is it a common drug, a familiar form of the drug?'

'No... It belongs to the past the analyst tells me. I've never come across it before... In fact, I've never encountered any cases of criminal poisoning in all my long career. It used to be used in what was called fly-water, I believe, compounded with sugar, and you soaked paper or blotting paper in it and dried the paper. Then, the flies came for the sweet paper and the arsenic killed them. Who and where the stuff came from, I don't know.'

'We must find out, sir.'

'Yes, Paston, you must. Because Miss Blow is not returning home until it's safe for her to do so. Oh, yes, and by the way, the analyst did say potassium arsenate known as Fowler's Solution is used for sheep-fly, too... The whole thing is confusion.'

'Do you think, doctor, that a lethal dose had been given?' asked Littlejohn.

'Don't know. Certainly, our tests showed arsenic in the system, but not in large quantities and yielding only to careful analysis. None of the other traces of chronic poisoning, such as presence in the nails and hair, eruptions, and so on...'

'Perhaps we might have a copy of the report, sir?'

Dr Cross looked amazed, and then resigned.

'Maybe, although such things are strictly confidential. In

fact, this whole business is confidential. I feel it is my duty to inform you of it, but it must not be made public until all has been most carefully checked.'

'Of course. The police surgeon had better consult with you, doctor.'

'The police surgeon! Oh, yes, I understand. Very well. Arrange it then. And now I must go. Very busy. Remember, strictest confidence...'

'And on your part, too, sir,' added Littlejohn.

'What do you mean? Think, I'm going to shout it from the housetops that Honoria Blow's being poisoned by her family?'

'No, doctor. But as little must become public as possible. We don't want to scare away whoever's trying to poison Miss Blow.'

'I see. Very well. Don't need telling to keep it dark. Good afternoon...'

And with that he swept up his hat and gloves, placed the former solemnly on his head and made off.

'Pompous ass!' said Paston. 'What do you make of it, sir?'

'I don't know. Funny affair. Small doses of arsenic in antiquated form. Victim first off-colour, then better. Then she finds out herself that she's being given arsenic. How did she guess that? It beats me.'

'If you ask me, sir, it beats me more. I think we'd better call in Scotland Yard officially. I'll go and see Superintendent Hempseed. Care to come and meet him? He's a very nice fellow.'

'I don't mind. Can't do much now until I'm authorised to act. By the way, you said there were one or two funny points about Miss Penelope's death. What were they, Paston?'

'Just that I didn't quite follow how that window box managed to fall so easily. If she'd fallen out by over-balancing, yes. But to crash down because she put her weight on something which gave way, well... I just don't understand it. The box wasn't old or rotten and was fastened to the wall by iron brackets. How it came adrift is a mystery to me.'

'Another point for reconsideration?'

'Yes. Now let's go and see the Super.'

Superintendent Hempseed lived in a nice little semi-detached villa on the outskirts of the town. His wife, a buxom, homely woman, opened the door to the officers and her face lit up at the sight of Paston.

'Hello, Inspector. I'm so glad to see you. Mr Hempseed's still in bed and as bad-tempered as can be. Come in, both of you.'

During a lull, Paston introduced Littlejohn. Mrs Hempseed said she was pleased to meet him. The name of Scotland Yard seemed to strike no admiration, awe or terror in her heart. Her main concern was the Superintendent, to whom she was utterly devoted, and the similar little villa they had just bought at the seaside and to which they were shortly to retire.

'... It's a bit awkward lumbago striking him like it did at a time like this. He was wantin' to get to Bexhill in his spare time and get the place ready for us.' She turned a happy smile on Littlejohn. 'We're retirin' in six weeks and then I'll have him all to myself. No more police and courts and cases. Just me and his hens and his tomatoes in the greenhouse and the like. It's made him wild, this lumbago. Struck him just like that...'

She snapped her fingers.

'He was takin' down the corner cupboard and had got it on his back. Lumbago struck him stiff and he had to shout for me. I was bothered, though I could have laughed the way he looked...'

'Could we have a word with him?' asked Paston, as the good woman came up for air.

'Of course. It'll cheer him up. He's all of a sweat at present. I've just ironed his back with my electric iron and brown paper. Then, I put him on an electric blanket. Before that I gave his back a good rubbing with liniment. He ought to get better after that. He's so hot now he's steaming...'

Outside the bedroom door they could hear the victim groaning and talking to himself.

'That you, Minnie? Come and turn off this blasted blanket, girl. It's like a furnace.'

The 'girl' giggled and led in the visitors.

'Hullo, Paston. Oh, dear. Never get lumbago. You can't move and they do all sorts of things to you in your helplessness. I wouldn't mind if I could read or something. But all I do, is lie and sweat...'

If the face was a symptom of what was going on inside the bed, it was something hot and cheerful. Hempseed had a long, humorous, clean-shaven face, furrowed with what might have been the results of a perpetually pleasant smile. On his bald head and wide brow, beads of sweat stood like peas and his complexion was red and radiant as though the sun had been at him. The sheets were tucked right up to his chin. He looked like a mummy beneath them, trussed and still.

'This is Inspector Littlejohn, of Scotland Yard, sir.'

Hempseed's lower parts began to move, and he looked to be making preparations for rising from his bed. Then, his lumbago struck a blow and he subsided.

'Oh, blast this lumbago... Sorry, Littlejohn... Glad to see you. Courtesy call?'

'No, Superintendent. That's why we've called. We want some help.' Before Hempseed could answer, his 'girl' gave him a large dose of medicine from a large spoon. The Superintendent made a wry face.

'What, again! I've only just had some. And it doesn't do me any good, Minnie. Can't you turn off this heat? It's like the tropics.'

'No,' said his wife firmly. 'You stay and sweat. It'll do you good and the gentlemen won't mind. And you were grumbling about my rubbing you. You'd better ask Inspector Paston to give you a turn. He'll not be as gentle as I was...'

'I'm not complaining, girl. You did your best...'

'I should just think so. I'm glad your temper's better...'

With that she left them and sharply shut the door.

'I'm fed up with being in bed. It's a week now and the doctor's done me no good. In fact, his assistant called this morning; my own doctor's down with lumbago himself... What were you wanting, Paston?'

'We've run into trouble, sir. As you know, Miss Penelope Blow fell through the window at the bank house and killed herself the other day.'

'Yes; they buried her this morning, didn't they? Something go wrong?'

'No, sir. But just after the funeral, Dr Cross called at the station and reported Miss Honoria's been poisoned with arsenic.'

'What! And me in bed with lumbago... It would have to be now...'

Hempseed struggled feebly beneath the bedclothes and then, goaded by his complaint, gave it up with another cry of pain and annoyance.

Between them, Paston and Littlejohn told Hempseed all that had happened hitherto. Miss Penelope's visit to Scotland Yard, her fears for her sister, her own nervousness and distress when she found Littlejohn absent, her death, and, finally, her sister's removal to a nursing home where they'd found she was being given arsenic in a form once used for fly catching.

Hempseed forgot his lumbago. Littlejohn began to wish the Superintendent had been on his feet and able to act, for Hempseed was alert and intelligent, in spite of his present tribulation, which, in the intensity of his interest, he now and then forgot to the extent of raising himself in bed and crying out as his pains smote him. His outstanding endowment, however, was his prodigious memory. He had been, as Constable and then Superintendent, a member of the local force for over thirty years and seemed easily to bring to mind all that had happened over the period.

'What strikes me,' said Hempseed, after deeply pondering what had been told, 'what strikes me is the symptoms you've described as given by Dr Cross about the arsenic. Do you know, Miss Katherine, Mrs Ferrier, the married sister, died of stomach trouble three and a half years since. I remember asking one of the men at the bank what ailed her, and he told me. I wonder...'

'Do you know the set up about the Blow fortune, sir?' asked Littlejohn.

'I guess so. Old William hated his family. He wanted boys and got girls, and then his wife ran off with a cashier in the bank. He left his fortune to charities and just an annuity apiece to his daughters. His brother Rufus was the better man and somehow the two families got mixed up, living together and such like. Very close-knit lot, though among themselves they quarrel like Kilkenny cats. Miss Penelope was the best of the bunch, I reckon. I don't like that window box affair. We'd better go farther into it. You can say you're just clearing up a thing or two. The poison business will have to be handled quietly.'

'Yes, sir. That's where I want your advice. It was Miss Penelope's calling at Scotland Yard brought Inspector Littlejohn here to see us. I think we ought to call them in...'

'Ho, ho! So, that's it. What will the Chief say, eh?'

'With his being away, I thought maybe you, as Acting Chief...'

'Me? You're OC. But I understand. All right. Call 'em in, on my responsibility. I've only a week or two to go and he can't sack me; only take the huff and not speak to me for weeks. I can stand that.'

'I'm very grateful, sir...'

'Now, you can do something for me, Paston.'

'Anything, sir.'

'Switch off this ruddy electric blanket. It's killing me.'

5

THE CROSS-EYED WINDOW CLEANER

D r Tankerville's nursing home was a very exclusive place and charged exorbitant fees. There was only room for eight patients, there was a long waiting list and you were only admitted as a previous inmate went out, alive or dead. Miss Honoria Blow had been fortunate in gaining immediate admission; that afternoon a millionaire who was in the habit of retreating to the home for a rest from his wife had learned that stock markets were falling and had hastened away to do some rigging...

A cheerful sister met Littlejohn at the door. Tankerville had been warned of the Inspector's visit and had granted the necessary permission. Littlejohn was the first visitor Miss Blow had received since her entrance, and she was pleased to see him. She had had herself specially prepared for the occasion and greeted him sitting in bed, clad in a sumptuous bed jacket.

The room was white and clean and overlooked a trim garden. The home had once been a private residence and, purchased by the doctor at the bottom of the property slump, had proved a first-rate investment. There were plenty of flowers about the room and fruit and chocolates on the bed table. These had been provided by the home and would duly appear on the bill. Food, drink, visitors and even flowers from outside sources were, at the time, regarded with suspicion and forbidden.

Honoria Blow was quite unlike her late sister. She had been a spoiled darling and at the time of the family tragedy had hardly given up the idea of getting married. Somewhere, romance was round the corner for her, she thought, and her dress, make-up and bearing blended efforts at attraction and coyness nauseating in one of her age. She pretended to be shy because the Inspector had found her in bed.

'Oh, dear… Forgive me receiving you like this, Inspector,' she twittered as the sister introduced them. 'But the doctor won't let me get up, yet, and we must obey our doctors, mustn't we?'

The nurse smiled and shrugged her shoulders.

'If it's fine tomorrow, Miss Blow, you're to get up a bit, and before the week's out, maybe you can take a turn in the garden…'

With that, the nurse tucked her patient tidily in position and left them.

'I'm almost like a prisoner here, Inspector. I can't understand it.'

'We'll soon have the matter cleared up and then…'

'They haven't told me what the matter is, but I know. Someone has been trying to poison me, Inspector.'

'How do you know, madam?'

'I read a book once about it. It told how an old lady was poisoned by her niece to get her money and described how it felt. When I had been ill once or twice with those awful pains in the night, I remembered and got Minshull to bring up the book. It was just as I felt.'

'Did you tell your late sister about it?'

'Yes; and at first, she wouldn't believe me. But when my attacks kept happening, I made her believe. She said she would come and tell you.'

'But why not your family or the local police?'

'That was Penelope's idea. She said suppose, after all, it merely turned out to be as Dr Cross said, a form of colic? So, she asked the advice of a friend of hers and he said to come to you.'

Littlejohn was sure Honoria Blow didn't act like this at home. She was said to be spoiled and domineering. At present she talked and behaved like a child, in a bewildered, affected tone, as though struggling for sympathy and comfort. Outside visitors were coming and going on tiptoes and with muffled coughs and voices like somebody in church.

'I do wish somebody would visit me.' She whined it, almost with tears. '... But, according to what the doctors say, it wouldn't be safe yet.'

'Why?'

'Well... They make out I'm too ill. But I know what it's all about. They think one of the family gave me the poison and may try to do it again. Whatever shall I do? I can't trust anybody. Even my own family...'

She squeaked it out in an infantile voice. Judging from the half-empty chocolate box, the half-read romance on the eiderdown and the get-up in bed jacket and wavy hair, she was thoroughly enjoying it.

'Do you suspect anyone?'

She'd been waiting for that! Her face assumed an arch and stubborn look.

'Really, Inspector, I oughtn't to say...'

She wanted him to coax her and sat waiting for the next move. Littlejohn rose and stood before the window.

'Nice view from here...'

'But you were asking me, Inspector...'

'Oh, yes. Maybe I oughtn't to have done that. Seeing that it's probably one of your family. One ought to be sure, oughtn't one?'

'But I am sure. It was Penelope... That's why she threw herself out of the window. She knew they were taking me away and her plan would fail. She wanted my money...'

Littlejohn spun round and faced the woman in the bed. Someone had hinted that the Blows were a bit mad. Here was one of them.

'Surely, if your sister wished to kill you, she would have kept it quiet, Miss Blow. Instead, she called to see me at Scotland Yard to enlist my help. She also said you yourself suspected you were being poisoned and had confided your fears to her.'

Honoria Blow got impatient. With a flick of her flabby hand she brushed all arguments aside.

'That was to divert suspicion from herself and put it on someone else. She was very cunning.'

'That's not what I've heard. She was universally loved and respected in Nesbury, they tell me.'

'They didn't have to live with her. She was most trying...'

'But what proof have you that your sister was trying to poison you?'

'She brought me the food that made me ill. She pretended to look after me and all the time...'

'In that case, then, I suppose it will be quite safe for the doctors to allow you to go home as soon as you are fit to move?'

'That's what I say, but they won't let me...'

The sister entered again.

'Don't tire her, sir. She's not very strong yet.'

Honoria Blow suddenly remembered that she wasn't strong yet and wilted.

'I think I'll settle down in bed and try to sleep, nurse. I'm very, very tired...' in a thin, squeaky voice, like that of a five-year-old.

The sister arranged her patient low in the bed with a pillow behind her shoulders and Honoria lay quiet regarding Littlejohn solemnly.

'We were just saying, sister, Miss Blow'll soon be able to return home now.'

'I wouldn't say that, sir. I suppose you know all about the circumstances which have brought her here. It would hardly be wise to let her return yet, would it?'

'But she tells me that the source of the danger has now gone...'

'I didn't, I didn't. I said nothing of the sort, nurse. He's questioned me that much I don't know what I'm saying...'

Honoria Blow began to whine again.

'So you don't feel safe yet, Miss Blow?'

'No. I don't feel safe. I never said I did.'

'I think I'd better leave you if my presence distresses you so. I'll call again when you're feeling more like yourself. Meanwhile, I wish you a quick recovery....'

There was no reply and Littlejohn followed the sister out into the corridor. A patient was being wheeled out of the operating theatre to one of the rooms and Tankerville followed the procession wrapped in a white smock. He ignored Littlejohn with the vacancy of a high priest too immersed in his functions to observe small fry.

'Miss Blow baffles me a bit, nurse. First, she says she's safe: then she says she isn't. She tells me her sister, Penelope, was the one who gave her the poison...'

'But that's nonsense, Inspector. She doesn't know what she's saying. Miss Penelope was the sweetest thing. It's unthinkable.'

She was pretty and dark, and her cheeks flushed a becoming red with indignation.

'I thought she seemed a bit beside herself. She must have been brooding.'

'You see, she's been kept in the ward since she arrived and no visitors. The family will probably be allowed to see her tomorrow. As a precaution, however, one of the staff will be there and nothing eatable will be allowed to be given to her...'

'A bit awkward...'

'Yes. But a precaution for all their sakes.'

'Quite...'

As Littlejohn left the nursing home, he found the grounds alive with the various activities of keeping the place clean and of feeding the inmates. Two vans were discharging milk and fish, fruit, vegetables and fowl. They didn't seem short of food there, and at the rate Tankerville charged, they certainly oughtn't to be.

With his ladder sprouting from a flower bed, a window cleaner was at work on the first-floor windows. He glanced down and caught sight of Littlejohn as he wrung his wash-leather. Littlejohn looked up and met the man's eyes, or rather tried to do, for they carried a terrible squint which made you feel sorry for the fellow. It didn't seem to bother him, however. He brandished his leather at the Inspector and crooking a finger, cried 'Hisst...'

Quickly, almost like a monkey descending for food, the cross-eyed window cleaner hurried to terra firma and again beckoned Littlejohn.

'Hisst... You the London detective 'as come about the Blows? Saw you with Inspector Paston... Good job you come. Somethin' wrong there...'

To add to his infirmities he had just had his teeth extracted at the country's expense and chewed his words as he spoke. His mandibles took on a rotary motion.

'Name o' Slype. John William Slype. That's me. Registered window cleaner...'

With the leather he still held he pointed to a small handcart attached to a bicycle. A sign on the latter repeated the information its owner had already given with the addition of the news that he was fully insured against accidents.

JOHN WM SLYPE

Window Cleaner

(Fully Insured)

Est '21

Mr Slype was small and cat-like. His nose had been badly broken and as badly set, and above it he suffered the most awful squint, an after-effect of whooping-cough in infancy. He wore a cloth cap which was too large for him. To see his cap and face beneath it peering at you from a height through glass as he pursued his trade was a fearful ordeal, although the fact that the eyes never stared straight at their object must have been a comfort to those caught in compromising behaviour by his sudden ascents.

'Wanted a word with you, sir...'

'Speak up, then, Mr Slype. What can I do for you?'

'It's this way, sir. A bit awkward. You see, in my trade they's ethics, like, just as in doctors, lawyers and bankers. Whatever we see as we oughtn't, we keeps mum, see? Of course, they's some window cleaners as is unscruperlous...don't keep to the rules o' the trade and blabs all they see. But one like me, and me father afore me... Well...anybody in town'll tell you, Slype and father before 'im was allus to be trusted. Models o' discreetion, as you might say...'

He chewed away and the words came out amid flecks of foam.

'Well, Mr Slype?'

'Well, sir. As yore the police, I can tell you in confidenks what's bin troublin' me ever since the death of the late lemented Miss Penelope Blow, sir. Sad loss, sir. I'm a Salvationist myself, and well I know 'ow we'll miss 'er.'

'I'm sure you will, Mr Slype.'

'Yes. She's safe in the Everlasting Arms now, sir; but that doesn't mean that right's not right and shouldn't be seen to, sir. There was somethin' queer about that fall Miss Blow had.'

In spite of its terrible shortcomings, the face of Mr Slype was an earnest, kindly one. It was a pity that the eyes could not reflect the kindliness that was hidden behind them. He drew close to Littlejohn and placed a forefinger on the Inspector's chest...

'Somebody'd been fiddlin' with that window box, sir, before Miss Blow fell down with it.'

'Indeed! This is important, Mr Slype. Please tell me more...'

'I'm goin' to, sir. Now I've started, I'm gettin' it off my conscience proper. I cleans the windows at the Blows'. Me and me dad cleaned Blows' windows ever since we started in busi-ness. A nice contract we got there. Well... I was up at the bedroom windows, back and front, the day that Miss Blow died. It's a bit of a tricky job with them window boxes there. Of course, some window cleaners — no names mentioned — would just clean level with the boxes and leave the rest dirty. But not J WM Slype. I got me reputation to keep up. I did the lot. I got a garden of me own and nachurall was a bit interested in the bulbs cumin' up in the boxes. Lovely show round the bank from them boxes when they're all out... Lovely... Well, as I was sayin', sir, I looked at the boxes and found the one on Miss Penelope's windowsill was loose. The screws that 'old the brackets that 'old the box safe'd been tuck out.'

'You knew it was Miss Penelope's room, Mr Slype?'

'Well...'

Mr Slype looked a bit bashful as though he'd been caught peeping where he shouldn't.

'Well... In thirty years, sir, you're bound sooner or later to find out, at least, whose room you're cleanin' the windows of. It's only nacherall... Allis confidential, of course. Good window cleaners never talk... It's ethics, sir...ethics...'

He ground the word out between his gums with great relish.

'You're quite sure that the screws had been recently removed?'

'Yes... I'll tell yer for why... I'm interested in them boxes, bein' as I'm a gardener myself and watch 'em closely. Last autumn they was painted, repaired and new screws put in 'em for the winter. Now, if you was to ask me now, without me spectacles, I wouldn't be so sure. I've broken 'em and it takes weeks to get 'em mended with so many 'avin' new 'uns at the government expense, like. When I'm without me glasses, me eyes turn. Been that way since I was a kid. Whoopin' cough. When I get me glasses on, I see straight. I had me glasses when I noticed them winder boxes.'

'How were they fixed...?'

'The box stands on the sill, like, and then there's a straight iron piece, fixed one end on the side o' the box and the other end screwed into the wall of the window side, like. The screws goes into wooden plugs in the wall. Now them's good screws and put in proper. Somebody must 'ave tuck 'em out and poor Miss Penelope Blow, leanin' on the box to water the bulbs, must 'ave toppled the box over and gone with it.'

The anxious, distorted eyes searched Littlejohn's face. The man was eager to help and avenge Miss Blow. A common-sensed, practical fellow, and hardly likely to make up a cock-and-bull story to bring himself into the limelight.

'Very good, Mr Slype. I'm much obliged to you for troubling to come down and tell me this. As you'll realise, it's most important.'

'Yes. Practically makes it a murder, doesn't it, mister?'

'Looks like it. Where can I find you again in case I need your further help, Mr Slype?'

The window-man fumbled in his pocket, produced a battered wallet and from it a grubby business card.

'That's me, sir, and complete with address. And now, if I'm not needed anymore, I'll be gettin' back up me ladder. Lot to do. Busy these days...'

He gave a brief, respectful nod and was back and up his ladder, plying his leather, before Littlejohn could reply.

Paston was rattled when, back at the police station, Little-john told him about the window box and Mr Slype's revelations.

'Slype's reliable enough. Honest working chap. What annoys

me is we missed the point of the window box. When we examined the frame, we assumed that she irons had been wrenched from their places and the screws torn out. We'd better go back to the bank house and have another look at the things. Bit awkward. We'll have to tell them we're re-opening the inquiry... and after the coroner's verdict, too.'

'Well, it'll have to be done, Inspector. Was Miss Penelope a heavy weight...? I mean, if she put her full weight on the box for support...?'

'No, no. Quite slim and light. Light as a feather, I'd say. We can't accept that as a theory. We'll have to go to the house and begin again. What had Miss Honoria to say, sir?'

'Accused Miss Penelope herself of giving her the arsenic.'

'She's mad! How could that poor old soul...? Besides, why come to Scotland Yard and set the police on herself? It's fantastic.'

'I don't understand it myself. There's something queer behind it and we must find out what it is.'

'Well, if you're ready, we'll get along to the bank house, then. There'll be a lot to do there with that funny lot. We'll have to do some questioning and they'll resent it like blazes.'

'I'm ready then. I'd better phone first for my colleague from the Yard, though. He's priceless in ferreting out these family secrets...'

Littlejohn felt happier after he'd spoken to Cromwell and fixed up for him to join him in Nesbury. He wanted someone to talk with and a familiar companion. Cromwell was just the man in a community like this.

The two officers put on their hats and made off across the square to the Blow residence.

6

THE WINDOW BOX

It might have been the nineties in Nesbury, instead of halfway through the twentieth century. There was hardly a soul about; a horse harnessed in a cart stood quietly munching the contents of his nose bag whilst his driver refreshed himself at a small pub. The animal shook the bag in a frenzy of getting the last bit of crushed oats and pigeons alternately picked the crumbs which fell away and floated aloft to the head and shoulders of the statue which they anointed afresh with white droppings. The monument was in memory of an MP of the pocket borough of Nesbury who had, in his time, been regarded as a philanthropist by a certain section of the community. He had underpaid his work people and fought like a tiger for the repeal of the Corn Laws to make their bread cheaper and justify further wage cuts. He was now only given space because his memorial added local colour and broke up political disturbances which arose in the square from time to time. His name was almost worn away, but with a bit of effort you could just make out the word Blow. He was the founder of Blows' Bank.

A neat pony and trap stood in front of the bank and a coachman in livery and the bank porter were busy removing a basket of plate from it and taking it to the vaults for safe keeping. An elderly man in a top hat, greatcoat with astrakhan collar, and spats over his boots, toddled past swinging a Malacca cane... Paston seized the brass bell-knob which projected from the doorframe of the bank house and vigorously tugged it. Somewhere inside a bell jangled and, as if in answer, the clock over the town hall struck twelve cracked notes.

The door was opened by an old servant who looked as if a breath would bowl him over. He was tall, thin and very frail. His tottering gait gave him the look of being on stilts. This was Jelley, the family butler, who, as pantry-boy, footman and then butler, had been with the family for nearly sixty years. He supported an ailing sister who had died a natural death at the same time Miss Blow was suffering violence and had been absent during the family tragedy and funeral. He was of little use now, except as a symbol of other days, and for answering the door and slowly cleaning the silver. Now and then, he waited at table. The Blows, ruthless as were their menfolk, hadn't the heart to sack poor Jelley. Besides, Miss Penelope, in her day, wouldn't hear of it. Now, it might be different. Jelley wore the impassive look of a retainer to whom nothing comes amiss, but his grief was deep. He could hardly drag one foot after the other.

'Good morning, sir...'

Jelley recognised Paston and knew why he was there. He even looked relieved to see the police.

'Please come in, sir... Gentlemen, I mean.'

Voices were raised in the drawing room. It was Ralph in a thoroughly bad temper, upbraiding his wife. 'I tell you I won't stand for it...'

'Well, you know what to do!'

'What do you mean?'

Jelley coughed and tapped on the door. Silence.

Then Lenore Blow, her cheeks flushed, her eyes blazing,

magnificent in anger, strode out, ignored the group of men standing there and mounting the stairs with rapidly accelerating steps, entered one of the upper rooms and slammed the door with a crash that shook the whole place.

Littlejohn caught a brief glimpse of Ralph Blow, puffed out with fury, standing on the hearthrug, a sheaf of what appeared to be bills in his fat fist. He turned to the door as Jelley entered and closed it. Blow did not trouble to lower his voice.

'What is it?'

The replies were inaudible.

'Who? Police? What do they want?'

'I can't be bothered now... Eh? Urgent?'

'Show them in then, but I've no time to waste.'

Blow was dressed in tweeds, as though ready for a day in the country. The recent tiff with his wife had upset him. His face was livid, the dark veins of his cheeks were inflated and another across his temple had risen until it looked ready to burst. He mopped his forehead with a silk handkerchief which he then stuffed angrily in his breast pocket. He faced the Inspectors.

'Well?'

'Good morning, sir. Sorry to bother you, but I've called to introduce Inspector Littlejohn, from Scotland Yard. There are one or two points concerning the death of Miss Penelope on which we aren't quite satisfied.'

The banker looked ready to explode. Jelley thought it prudent to withdraw and plodded out as fast as his tottering old limbs would bear him. At first, speech forsook Blow; then he managed to articulate thickly.

'You what? You're not what? What do you mean?'

'It has been reported to us that the window box which figured in the death of your late aunt had been tampered with.'

'Who reported that?'

'I'm not in a position to say, sir, but it makes it necessary for us to look into the affair again.'

'But the coroner found a verdict from misadventure. I refuse to be pestered and badgered like this about a matter which is closed. Why Scotland Yard enters into it, I don't know. But as far as I'm concerned, it's finished. I want to hear no more about it and refuse to have you poking and prying around...'

More footsteps on the stairs and across the hall and then the front door slammed violently. Blow jumped at the impact. It must have been Lenore running out again, only this time he wasn't in a position to follow her.

Littlejohn intervened.

'I think I ought to tell you, Mr Blow, that just before her death, your late aunt called at Scotland Yard and asked for me. She wished to enlist my help in a matter which was troubling her. She suspected that someone was trying to poison her sister, Miss Honoria.'

Blow pawed the air and stamped vehemently on the rug with both feet. The sad eyes in a stuffed stag's head over the door looked down reproachfully on the unseemly behaviour of its owner. It bore beneath it a small plaque.

Balgussie, 1887.

'Rubbish! Rubbish! My aunt was an eccentric woman who saw trouble everywhere. Surely, you've not come all this way to bother people about a tale like that.'

'I have, sir. And it would seem there was a measure of truth in your aunt's suspicions. It is reported to us that Miss Honoria is suffering from arsenic poisoning...'

'Who told you that? It's all nonsense. How could she? Why, she never leaves the house and I can assure you that none of us would...'

'That remains to be seen, sir. Meanwhile, we'll be very grateful for your cooperation. We want a free hand, if you please, to make further inquiries on both counts. We'll be as little trouble as possible.'

'You'll be no trouble at all. If you dare to enter this house again, or if I see or hear of you prowling around on this cock-and-bull business, I'll make a complaint in the right quarters. The matter of Aunt Penelope's death has been properly dealt with and a verdict given. As to Aunt Honoria's latest sensation, well...the family will deal with it. There'll be no more talk of arsenic, I can assure you.'

He turned to the bell-knob beside the fireplace, shook it and Jelley appeared, looking more pale and thin than ever.

'Show these gentlemen out. I've business to do and I've no time to listen to their tales.'

Jelley sighed and held open the door. The police took the hint and made their exit. Then, Littlejohn paused, re-entered the room and went quietly up to Blow. He met the banker's furious stare steadily.

'Mr Blow, I just want to say that you mustn't on any account imagine this affair is closed. Your aunt asked for my help. I was away and was too late to give it. I feel I owe it to her to make amends. That I will do, and nobody is going to prevent me. I don't believe Miss Penelope was eccentric or as mad as you would have me believe. I think she met her death by violence and I'm going to find out who did it. Good morning...'

Blow only recovered his speech as Littlejohn reached the threshold.

'Hi, you! Who do you think you are? I warn you...'

Littlejohn gently closed the door.

'As soon as you have a minute to spare, Mr Jelley, I would like a word with you at the police station,' he said as the butler handed him his hat.

'But, sir... I couldn't... It's as much as my place...'

The poor old fellow was knocking at the knees.

'Don't worry. We won't compromise you. But you were fond of Miss Penelope?'

'Yes, sir. She was the sweetest lady... The best of them all... I shall miss her very much...'

Jelley's shrunken jaws worked emotionally.

'Then help us find out who did her violence...'

'Is that true, sir? She didn't fall herself?'

'No, Mr Jelley, she didn't.'

The old man pulled himself together.

'Very well, sir. I'll come as soon as I can. Probably in a quarter of an hour. The family will all be out. Mrs Blow should have been in for lunch, but now she's gone out...'

'Yes, we heard her!'

'Jelley! Damn you, where are you...?'

Mr Blow was bellowing for his man, who hadn't answered the bell.

Littlejohn and Paston crossed back to the police station.

'That's done it. Now for it!' said Paston. 'We're not sure about either Miss Penelope's tumble or Miss Honoria's poison. Yet, you've made it seem that we've proof of both. If we don't...'

'Don't worry, Paston. Nobody's going to treat us like that, banker or no banker. Mr Ralph Blow threw down the challenge; I've taken it up. Now it's up to us. From now on, if you agree, the case is mine...and Cromwell's, for here he comes, if I'm not mistaken.'

A taxi had just drawn up at the police station and there was Sergeant Cromwell, arguing about the fare and taking over his own and Littlejohn's luggage which he'd brought with him. He broke into wintry smiles as he spotted Littlejohn and the taxi withdrew with its furious driver muttering to himself.

'Hullo, sir. That blighter wanted to charge me five bob from the station. About a mile...'

He shook hands with Paston, and they went in the office, Cromwell carrying the bags. His own contained as usual a complete outfit for any sort of case, law books, toxicology books, books on his favourite hobby of bird watching, pairs of handcuffs and his ubiquitous chest-expanders.

'I'll book you rooms at the Duke of York,' said Paston. 'I guess you'll be here for a bit...'

Across the square a garage mechanic was drawing up in front of the Blow residence in a small car. He climbed out and rang the bell. Ralph Blow appeared, muffled up in a greatcoat, squeezed himself in the driving seat and drove away. As soon as he had vanished, Jelley appeared wearing a bowler hat. He stood on the steps for a moment like a pointer scenting game and then, turning his nose in the direction of the police station, he made straight for it, holding on his hat as he went.

'Come and sit by the fire, Mr Jelley,' said Paston charitably. The old man looked as if he needed a good thawing-out.

'I hope nobody has seen me coming here,' trembled the butler. 'If Mr Ralph got to know...'

'We'll look after you, Mr Jelley,' said Littlejohn. 'But first, are all the family out, and could you trust the rest of the servants not to talk if you let us have a brief look round the house and garden?'

The butler shuddered like a man with the palsy. He passed his tongue over his dry lips and tried to speak but couldn't.

'It's simply to find out all we can about Miss Penelope's death. We'll have to rely on you and the rest of the staff. The family are obviously opposed to our investigations.'

'I'll do it, sir. But you'll have to be careful. Somebody will have to keep watch and if any of the family show up, you'll have to go away without being seen...'

He wrung his hands.

'... I shouldn't be doing this, sir. The first thing about a good servant is loyalty. I've been with the family ever since I entered service and I'm nearer eighty than seventy. It goes against the grain with me.'

'You're serving Miss Penelope, you know.'

'Very good, sir. There's none left now worth serving...'

And with that the old man's reserve broke down. His pale cheeks flushed, and he raised his thin hands in denunciation of his present masters.

'All my life I've served 'em faithfully, and what do they do to me in my old age? Treat me like a dog. When I wanted to change to better myself, Mr William swore if I left them, he'd see I didn't get another job in the county. Then, when I'm old and other people's wages go up because it's harder living, what do they do? Because I'm old, they say I'm not worth anymore. I get paid the same now as I got fifteen years ago... It's not good enough... And Miss Penelope was the only friend I had in the family. I'm old, gentlemen, and the little I had went on my invalid sister who's just passed away. Thanks to the Blows, when I'm no further use, it's the workhouse for me...'

Tears ran down his face, his voice was shrill, and he clutched the air with his thin hands. The skin of his skull tightened, revealing the bone formation clearly if you'd peeled him, it seemed that nothing, but a death's head would have remained. He collapsed, panting in his chair.

Paston opened a cupboard, poured a few fingers of whisky in a thick teacup and passed it over.

'There... Take that, Mr Jelley, and pull yourself together. We're your friends here. We'll see you through.'

The butler slowly recovered and stood ready to accompany them. His black suit was a bit threadbare, but well pressed and smart, and his linen spotless. He was doing his best in spite of it all. He put on his bowler.

'I want a long talk with you, too, when you've time, Mr Jelley. You must know a lot about the family,' said Littlejohn.

'Yes, sir. But as I said...a good servant...'

'I understand. But this is for Miss Penelope.'

'I'll come.'

Whilst Cromwell went to the Duke of York to get the pair of them signed up and installed, Paston and Littlejohn followed Jelley back to the house. They entered by the back door, which they reached through a wicket gate let in the high wall along the side of the building. This gave on a walled garden, with neat lawns and paths and a glasshouse and vegetable plot beyond. Between the back of the house and the garden, a paved court-yard, with outbuildings, the stables and coach-houses of past days, now mere garage space for the brothers' two cars.

Paston pointed to a spot in the yard.

'That's where Miss Penelope was found...'

Littlejohn looked up. All the other sills had window boxes in which the green spikes of spring daffodils were showing. One window had none.

'Yes... That's the room.'

The yard had been swept and cleared up and there was little to see there.

'Where did you put the remnants of the box?'

'The contents were thrown on the garden... Nothing much there. But we took the box away. It's still in the yard behind the police station. I'll show it to you when we get back.'

'Was the soil examined?'

'Not particularly. What had you in mind?'

'The screws which held the box to the wall. The window-man, Slype, said it was loose. We could have confirmed that. If the screws had been removed...'

'Yes. Let me see...'

Paston looked around. In the greenhouse a man was moving about among the young plants. Paston beckoned him a time or two before he saw the gesture. Then he emerged. A small, thick-set, bald-headed man, wearing a cloth cap and an old grey suit. He had a small, snub nose and a large moustache, clipped across his upper lip and fanning out droopily round the corners of his mouth, like a rope frayed at each end.

'Want me? Ho-ho-ho…'

'Yes, Betts. Can you come here?'

Betts was quite a character. Imperturbably cheerful, he supported a nagging wife, an unmarried daughter with a child, and a drunken son who now and then came home bellicose, turned the family out of doors and wrecked the furniture. Betts, it seemed, took to laughter as others, in their extremity, took to drink. It was his safety valve and, if mirthless, certainly kept him sane.

'What was you wantin'?'

Betts, his big hands covered in soil and a trowel sticking from his pocket, slowly approached.

'Where is the soil we dumped out of Miss Penelope's window box, Betts?'

'Good job I'm not doin' much out o' doors. Ho, ho, ho. It's where you put it. Lucky, eh?'

'Yes. Let's go see it.'

They followed Betts, who shuffled along to a heap of compost in the far corner of the vegetable plot. The last of the Brussels sprouts and winter greens protruded forlornly from the earth. There was the heap of soil, just as they'd left it.

'Got a riddle, Betts?' said Littlejohn.

The gardener produced a sieve from an outhouse.

'Let me do it, sir. He, he, he. Guess I know what you're after… Them screws, eh? Ho, ho, ho.'

He almost danced about in glee, like a mischievous gnome.

'Yes. Why? What do you know about it?'

'Thought the same maself. "Where's them screws?" I sez. So, I looks. None there. You can try, but you'll find none of 'em. Ho, ho, ho. Somebody tuck 'em afore…'

'You've got brains, Betts.'

'Got it up here,' said Betts, tapping his temple with a large finger without the top joint, which had been removed by a circular saw in the days when Betts worked in a sawmill.

They left him, talking and chuckling to himself. 'One day, come back. I'll tell 'ee some more...'

Littlejohn turned.

'What more, Betts?'

'Oh, things...ho, ho, ho. I got it up 'ere. No doubt o' that.'

The half finger went up to the temple again.

There was no time now. The family might return.

'I'll be back.'

Jelley let them in the back way. They passed through a scullery and on to the kitchen, where at a table, Mrs Minshull and another woman, Mrs Frazer, the cook, were eating a meal. The pair regarded the procession with wide eyes. A buxom kitchen-maid appeared from a small room leading off and stood aghast at the crowd in the room.

'These are Mrs Minshull, the housekeeper; Mrs Frazer, cook; and Dolly, the kitchen girl...'

'I've met Mrs Minshull already, haven't I?' said Littlejohn. 'I may as well tell you that we're here making further inquiries about the death of Miss Penelope...'

Mrs Minshull started, Mrs Frazer's jaw tightened, and her lips formed a very thin line. Dolly stood still and goggled. But not a word was said. They knew something.

'... We're here without the consent of your employers. In fact, they've forbidden us to carry on here. It's only through the good will of Mr Jelley. So, I'll be grateful if you'll keep our comings and goings to yourselves and not mention them to anyone. We don't want to get Mr Jelley in trouble, do we?'

'We do not,' said Mrs Frazer firmly. 'And as far as we go, we've seen nothing, heard nothing, and'll say nothing. Eh, Mrs Minshull?'

Mrs Minshull nodded.

'And you, Dolly, don't stand there gawking. You heard what the gentleman said. Not a word. *Not a word*. You hear? If I hear of you saying anything, you go without references and box your ears in the bargain…'

Dolly squealed dismally and began to sniff.

'I won't, Mrs Frazer… I swear I won't.'

'No need to swear. Just keep quiet. There's things gone on here as won't bear mentioning. I only hope you clear it all up. I can't sleep nights thinking of the awful things…'

'All right, Mrs Frazer. That will do,' interposed Jelley, exerting his below-stairs authority. 'And now, we'll be getting along. I want you, Mrs Minshull, please to keep watch against the family returning. If they do return, ring the handbell in the hall. We will hear it… And stop sniffing, Dolly. Nobody's going to hurt you.'

The three men climbed the stairs. Jelley took them straight to Miss Penelope's room. It was small and neat, but of the second-class variety at the back of the house. The heads of the family, Ralph, his wife, and Harold, had the best on the front. All signs of occupancy had already been removed, leaving the great double four-poster bed, the chest and dressing table, solid Victorian survivals of great weight, bare and cheerless. Littlejohn crossed to the window and thrust up the sash. The sill was black from the soil which had percolated through its former window box, which had filled it entirely, rising on each side to a depth of about nine inches.

'The boxes were held, I believe, by iron stays, Mr Jelley?'

'Yes, sir. I was away with my sick sister when it all happened. I know no details.'

He was trembling and it must have been with emotion, for it was quite warm outside.

About six inches from where the top of the box must have reached, each side of the upright wall of the window frame had been plugged and a wooden peg inserted to take a screw to hold the bracket of the box. Littlejohn examined and fingered the wooden plugs.

'These haven't been split, and in that case, had the screws been there, would have held the box. It looks as though they've been removed. Or else, when the boxes were taken down for repair and painting, somebody forgot to replace the screws. That may have happened, and Miss Penelope might have died through a workman's carelessness.'

'I'm sure Mr Hornblower, the joiner, wouldn't have done that. He's a most careful and conscientious man. He works for himself, not for anyone else.'

This from Jelley, who was watching the procedure with extreme interest.

'We must find out. Could we have Mrs Minshull up a minute? Ask the cook to keep *cave* for a bit.'

Jelley tottered out and returned with the housekeeper.

'You were here when Miss Blow fell, weren't you, Mrs Minshull?'

'Well, yes, sir, in a manner of speakin'. I was in my room but hurried out. By that time, she was gone...'

'Where were the others?'

'Cook and Dolly in the kitchen. Mrs Blow in Miss Honoria's room gettin' her ready to leave for the nursing home. And Mr Ralph and Mr Harold in the dining room below, with the doctors.'

'Did you hear anyone moving about?'

'No, sir.'

'You're sure Mrs Blow and Miss Honoria were in Miss Honoria's bedroom when Miss Penelope fell?'

'Well, sir, I couldn't take my Bible oath. Miss Honoria's room is next door, you see. Miss Penelope had fallen when I got here. They could have... But why should they? Miss Honoria wasn't to be left.'

'Could Miss Honoria walk about? Was she strong enough?'

Mrs Minshull's lips tightened.

'I shouldn't say it, but it's true. She could walk about. But she liked to be waited on and sitting up in bed like a lady. Of course, she could get up, if she'd wanted. Begging your pardon for the liberty, I'm sure.'

This for the benefit of Jelley, who was looking outraged.

'All right, Mrs Minshull. That will be all, thanks.'

They all left the room, but on the threshold, Littlejohn paused. He turned to the next door on the other side from Miss Penelope's room.

'What's in here, Mr Jelley? It's locked.'

Littlejohn turned the handle and shook it. Jelley began to knock at the knees again and lick his dry lips. 'It's quite empty, sir. Just a lumber room.'

Littlejohn beat the panels with his clenched fist. 'The door sounds very solid. Is it reinforced, or something?'

Jelley stood there dumbly, looking in great distress.

'Is this the family secret, Mr Jelley? I think you'd better tell me. I noticed from the yard that the windows were barred.'

'That is true, sir. The door, too, is strengthened by a thin steel sheet inside.'

'Why?'

'It is never mentioned, sir.'

'Look, Mr Jelley. You want to help us get to the bottom of this business, don't you? Don't you think you'd better not hold anything from us?'

'This has nothing to do with… It was long ago…'

'All the same, please tell me. *Who was shut in that room?*'

'It was Mr William, sir. At one time, he got very low. It was towards the end of his life. He imagined things and tried to take his own life. They had to make a bedroom there for him and lock him in.'

7

THE CITADEL

W hat exactly was the trouble with Mr William Blow?'
They were downstairs again, sitting in the butler's private room, with Mrs Minshull still keeping watch for the return of the family.

Jelley tugged at his collar and his prominent Adam's apple rotated nervously.

'I don't quite know, sir. He was never taken away. They had him locked in his private room for a while, and Dr Cross kept coming. Then, one day, he seemed better and came out and was normal again... Or so it seemed...'

'So it seemed? Why?'

'Well, sir, he was different ever after. More kindly and considerate, yet cunning and with little will of his own. He died not long after...but...somehow, if I might put it that way, he seemed sorry for the things he'd done, yet hadn't the will to make amends. I mean, for instance, he was kind to me, but he didn't increase my wages as he ought to have.'

'But what events caused him to be shut up at all, Jelley?'

The butler pulled his long, fragile fingers until the joints cracked. At each explosion, Cromwell winced.

'I never quite got to the bottom of it, but it was said he got religion, if you understand what I mean.'

'Some sort of conversion?'

'That's right. They did say that in the course of some business with the local head of the Salvation Army here, he suddenly saw the error of his ways, sir... I do know, that Simon Jacques, the "Major" as they called him in the Salvations, came to see him quite a lot. And Mr Blow went to a service or two at the meeting room they had over a laundry at the time, not having a citadel, as they call it, in those days.'

'Did it drive him mad?'

'Not exactly, sir. He got to shutting himself up in his room for hours at a time and you could hear him prayin' with the door locked. Then he started talking of his sins and redemption and must have come to the conclusion he was lost. He tried to take poison, sir.'

'Poison? What kind?'

'Well, in those days, they used to use a sort of arsenic water for catching flies... Mr William took a good drink of it. It made him very ill, but they got the doctor in and he pulled him round. There was such a scene. Dr Cross said, either Mr William was watched night and day till he got round, or else he'd certify him insane and have him in the asylum. That door was made then.'

'How long is that since?'

'Getting on a dozen years, sir. I remember, Munich happened at the time he was locked in the room above, and us saying whatever was going to happen if there was war and bombs falling and Mr William mad on our hands.'

'What happened to the poison? Did the police enter into the case?'

'No, sir. It was hushed up to avoid scandal. The Blows, sir, couldn't stand a scandal. You can see for yourself, sir, how they managed to convince the police about Miss Penelope's accident. If you hadn't arrived the matter would never have been fully seen into. As for the poison...well...I don't know what happened. It was missing when Dr Cross ordered it to be handed over to him. Quite a flutter it caused, but these things have a habit of dying down.'

'And Mr Blow left all his money to the Salvation Army?'

'Oh, no, sir. He left them enough to build and keep a citadel, as they call it, going. But other charities benefited, too. He made his will just before he went queer. The lawyers said it was quite legal. The family talked of going to law about it, but they learned it was no use. Now, if he'd made it after his attack, it would have been easy. But before, no, sir.'

'What did his daughters live on, then? By the way, they weren't really aunts of Ralph and Harold's, were they?'

'He left them right, I gather. Bought them annuities. But not very generous, by all accounts. You see, sir, it was done in spite. He never wanted girls and he hated his daughters, 'specially after their mother ran away. Miss Penelope and Miss Honoria were cousins of the present Mister Blows, but being so much older, the custom of calling them aunts sprang up somehow.'

'Was Mrs William ever seen again?'

'No, sir. She died in France later, we heard.'

'His conversion made him remember the Salvation Army but not relent about his daughters, then?'

'That's wrong, sir. He'd made his will before he fell under the influence of Major Jacques, as they called him. He'd evidently picked his charities and started to investigate them. It was his saying how he wanted the money spending on the citadel, as they call it, that brought Major Jacques, as they call him, here. The will was made before the madness took him. Then, of course, he couldn't alter it, because the family would have said he was non-compos-mentis, as they say, and got it set aside...or else, the charities could have done. In any case...'

The handbell in the hall rang furiously and Mrs Minshull, hot with emotion and panting, rushed in.

'Mrs Blow, sir... She's crossin' the square...'

The detectives were let out by the tradesmen's entrance and Littlejohn asked Jelley to call for another chat at the police station as soon as he got an opportunity.

'That I will, sir... But 'urry, 'urry...'

They could hear the front bell ringing furiously in the kitchen...

'Pretty kettle of fish,' said Cromwell. 'Where do we go from here, sir?'

'To the hotel, then dinner, then to the Salvation Army Citadel, my dear Cromwell,' said Littlejohn. 'Are you in good voice?'

'I could be,' answered the sergeant, who had, at one time, been an enthusiastic member of the Metropolitan Police Choir, 'but on this occasion, I beg to be excused...'

THE SCOTLAND YARD men had been told where to find the citadel, but exact directions were not required. They only needed to follow their ears. It was band and choir practice night as well as the occasion of many more activities at the meeting house. The latter was well-lighted and sounded as busy as a beehive as the two visitors stood before the main door. Brass and human voices blended joyfully, and people were running about making the room sound like a factory.

The gust of sound and cheerful zeal of the place struck Littlejohn and Cromwell dumb on the threshold. On a shallow platform at the far end of the large hall a brass band of about a dozen players was gathered, and with them a choir of ten or more. They were practising for next Sunday's open-air service. But that was not all. It was spring cleaning time at the citadel, too, and eight members, five women and three men, were on their knees in a ragged line scrubbing the floor. They moved backwards, crabwise, as they worked in time with the band and, in spite of their vigorous efforts, managed to sing as they scrubbed. This working to music seemed to please them all, for they glowed and grew convulsed with the ardour of their task. They greeted the Scotland Yard men in full song.

I'm h'aitch-A-P-P-Y, because I'm S-A-V- E-D,
I'm H-A-P-P-Y, because I'm F-R- double E.
Once I was B-O-U-N-D in the chains of
But now I'm h'aitch-A-P-P-Y, and glory to the end.

The blast of music hit you like something solid as you opened the door.

One of the men on the floor rose and wiped his hands on the sackcloth apron which covered him from the waist. The rest of the scrubbers smilingly closed the ranks and included his pitch in their own. He approached the detectives with a beaming face.

'Well, sirs? What can we do for you?'

He eyed them up and down. There was a hostel next door for wayfarers and poor folk where you could get a bed for the night for next-to-nothing. These didn't seem like vagrants, however.

Littlejohn paused.

'Is the chief in?'

'The Major, friend? Of course. He's in the hostel. I'll get him. Just wait here...'

He took them to a small room formed off the main hall by movable glass partitions, gave them a couple of chairs, and hurried off on his mission. Outside the playing and singing continued.

I'm H-A-P-P-Y...

Cromwell's lips pursed and he began to whistle.

'Jolly lot,' he said. 'Seem to have just that little extra bit of somethin' the rest haven't got, eh?'

On the wall a marble tablet.

To the Glory of God and in Memory of
WILLIAM BLOW
by whose kind benefactions this Citadel was built
and who entered his Eternal Home
June 24th, 1939.

That was all. Least said, the better!

Outside the band, playing non-stop for the benefit of the scrubbers, struck up again, accompanied by the choir, who shook their tambourines vigorously. The door at the far end opened and the man who had greeted them brought the Major to Littlejohn and Cromwell. He was the only one among them wearing uniform. He was stocky, round-faced, red-cheeked, with shrewd bright eyes and as clean as a new pin.

'Good evening, gentlemen...'

The noise going on in the hall was too great to speak against, and Major Towse took them to his own room, an austere, clean office where the business of the local body was transacted.

'Now?'

It came as no surprise to Towse when they told him who they were and what they wanted. He'd evidently summed them up beforehand and had probably learned from his widespread flock what they were doing in Nesbury.

'We are seeking background about the Blow family, sir. I hear that Mr William and Miss Penelope were actively interested in your cause. Can you help?'

'Certainly, my friend, but what do you want to know?'

'First, the circumstances in which Mr William Blow left you so much money... Oh, I'm not for a moment suggesting there was anything wrong about it. I can't think of any charity he could better have favoured...'

'Thank you, Inspector.'

'But his connections with the Salvation Army seem to have altered his outlook on life...'

'I should hope so, Inspector. For the better, I trust. Otherwise, our task would be a vain one.'

'Yes. But I'm trying to find out just what occurred.'

'I can't help you there. It was before my time. But my predecessor is still alive. He's a grand old man of well past eighty and long retired from the burden and heat of active service. But he comes here when he can. He lives in the town on his pension. He could tell you quite a lot. Major Jacques is his name. He was here when our people gathered in quite a small room and his contacts with Mr Blow resulted in his leaving us enough to build this fine place. He goes to bed early, but tomorrow...'

'I'll call on him then. How long have you been here, sir?'

'Seven years.'

'Have any other of the Blows been actively connected with your organisation...? Other than Miss Penelope, I mean.'

'No, sir. I think they hardly regard us in their class. Furthermore, I gather they resent the very appearance of this place, which, in its very bricks and mortar, represents a part of the family wealth. Miss Penelope was a good friend...'

'So I believe. Why?'

'She was a good woman, Inspector. She wasn't a regular attender. She hadn't been brought up in the evangelical school, you know. But she came to many of our special efforts and services. She said her father had found comfort in our message in the last years of his life and she owed us a lot. She took it as her duty, too, she said, to see that his wishes were fulfilled in that we got a meeting place which did credit to his memory. I think you'll agree that we did.'

'I'm sure you did...'

'We do a lot of charitable work in the town, too. There's a lodging place attached and also a café which serves food to the needy and travellers. Perhaps you'll come and see it later.'

'With pleasure...'

Major Towse beamed and gave Cromwell a friendly nod as though signifying that his boss was a good fellow.

'Miss Blow helped a lot with our charities. I don't think she was a wealthy woman, but she did what she could.'

'How do you know she wasn't wealthy?'

'She told me so. Her money came from annuities. Although she could raise quite a sum on occasions.'

'What do you mean, sir?'

'Well... We used all the money William Blow left to build this place. There then arose the question of building the hostel and canteen during the war. There were a lot of soldiers and WAAFs here with no suitable place to go to. We wanted to put up a place where a bed and some food could be got. I told Miss Blow and she found the money.'

'How much, if I might ask, sir?'

'Five thousand pounds...'

'Five thousand...! And all her money in annuities?'

'Yes. And the family didn't provide any. She said she couldn't ask them. They were so bitter about William Blow leaving us what he did... No, she had some other source...one she wished to be kept secret.'

'I see. So, it looks as though...?'

'Yes. It looks as though she had other funds somewhere. I could make a good guess... But I promised Major Jacques...'

'He knows, then?'

'He has a shrewd idea. Ask him. I'm not in a position... It was in confidence, you understand, and only a chance word which...'

'I understand, sir.'

'And now, Miss Penelope Blow, sir. Do you think she died naturally...or rather by an accident of her own doing?'

'I really ought not to be talking about it, but, if your inquiry will result in some justice being done to her dear memory, I will speak. I don't think...nay, I know, that the way she fell to her death was not entirely her own doing, at least.'

'What do you mean by that?'

The Major took off his shining spectacles and polished them. His bright little eyes grew grave. Outside, the band and singers were raising the roof with their joyful chorus.

> *Shall we gather at the river,*
> *Where bright angel feet have trod...*

'Miss Penelope may have fallen through leaning out too far. I grant that. But if, as was suggested, she fell through leaning hard on the window box, which gave way, then someone assisted her downfall...'

'How do you know that?'

'After the inquest, one of our members came to me. He's a joiner who does the work at the bank and the bank house. A very decent, honest fellow, whose family have served this town faithfully for generations. He was worried. The box, they said, had fallen and let Miss Blow down. But how had it fallen? he asked. He himself had repaired and painted it in the autumn. It was all right then. He said he had fixed it securely with four-inch screws, put in wooden plugs in the wall, firm enough to last a dozen years. The timber itself was good, too. At the inquest, it wasn't suggested that the wood was rotten, but that the box in its entirety had fallen. Our man wanted to know how and why. He was very upset. I'm glad you called about this. It's saved my coming to see you. Hornblower, that's the joiner, is a shy man. I told him to see the police after the funeral, which was

on the day he brought his troubles to me. But he was quite put-
out. Asked if I'd do it for him...'

'This only bears out what we've already heard from the
Blows' butler and gardener. The screws had been removed.'

'This is terrible. To think...Miss Penelope... Why, she hasn't
an enemy in the world.'

'Are you sure, sir?'

'Well... One would think not... But they are a strange family.
All the same...I can't think...'

'Did Miss Penelope ever mention to you about trouble at
home?'

'Not really. She was a simple soul who didn't see much
wrong in the world or with her fellows. Little childish things
she'd talk to me about. She had very few friends outside the
family in whom she confided.'

'Such things as...?'

'Well... The cat got ill, and she told me of that in great
distress; and then Miss Honoria being taken with bouts of sickness from time to time...'

'The cat? When was that?'

The Major and Cromwell looked at Littlejohn in astonishment. The cat! Cats were always picking up something and
being sick about the place...

'About twelve months ago, Miss Penelope talking to me after
a hostel meeting, mentioned she was worried about the cat. It
had been very sick and lay like a dead thing. It recovered,
however, so that needn't concern us.'

'And Miss Honoria... When was she mentioned? Her illness I
mean?'

'Not long after the cat, strange to say. But, of course, the two
aren't connected.'

Cromwell threw an admiring look at Littlejohn. Yes, the
cat...and then Miss Honoria. How did the saying go? Try it on
the cat! And here was Miss Honoria being poisoned...and the

cat had been laid out. He wanted to point it all out in triumph to Major Towse, but that wouldn't have done.

'Is there anything more, gentlemen? It's supper time in the canteen and I reckon to be there to see that all's right?'

'How many hours a day do you work, Major?'

'I don't count 'em. Morning, noon and night, as the saying goes and happy at it. It's my hobby as well as my work.'

Nothing self-righteous or sanctimonious about it all. Just a business-like getting about his work.

'Care to come along and have a bit of supper? We may meet Hornblower there. He comes and helps two nights a week.'

He led them through the main hall. The spring cleaning was going along fine and the tempo the bandmaster was setting was slave-driving, but the scrubbers revelled in it.

Yes, we'll gather at the river,
The beautiful, the beautiful river,
Gather with the saints at the river,
That flows by the throne of God...

Through a door at the far end and then along a passage. The canteen was an old Nissen hut, and beyond it a brick structure in which stood six beds. The whole place was plain and neat. In the canteen were a number of small tile-topped tables at which workmen were sitting. Round the fire a few easy chairs occupied by clean, vagrant-looking men and an old regular or two. One of them had arrived in drunk and was being allowed to sleep it off. 'That which was lost...' as the large placard on the wall announced concerning the flotsam and jetsam which came and went in this place.

The Major bade his guests be seated at one of the tables and joined them. They were approached by a large, flabby man with the face of a wondering child.

'What'll it be, sirs?'

He had taken off his jacket and wore an apron. The empty plates on the other tables announced that the rest of the diners had been served.

'Hullo, John...'

'Evenin', Major Towse.'

The man was bashful. He blushed as he spoke and looked ready to turn and run. With his fingers he pleated his apron and smoothed it out again.

'Everything all right?'

'Yes. Shipsides arrived in drunk again. His wife's turned him out. He's sleeping it off. Then we'll give him a bite and put him to bed. He'll be right by mornin'...'

'This is John Hornblower of whom I spoke. These are Inspector Littlejohn and Sergeant Cromwell of Scotland Yard, John. They're here about the death of Miss Penelope Blow...'

The big hands of John Hornblower grasped large folds of his apron; he looked ready to tear it to shreds.

'Not before its time, too. Wrong's bin done there and oughter be righted...'

And then, as if amazed at his own temerity, Hornblower stepped back a pace, blushed right over his bald head and stared at the three sitting men as though expecting them to strike him down.

'What'll it be, gents?'

'What you've got...'

Three plates of oxtail, a chunk of bread, a mug of cocoa were placed before them.

'Sit down a minute, John,' said Littlejohn.

'I've got to... The kitchen... It's my turn for duty... I...'

He was quite put out of countenance.

'You wouldn't think John here had a family of five, would you? You'd think they'd cure his shyness... Do sit down, John...'

Hornblower eased his great body on one of the chairs and

coiled his long, heavy legs under the table. He looked ready for any torture that might be coming.

'Have a cigarette, John?'

At the sight of Littlejohn's case, envious eyes from all parts began to glint. He passed it round and when it was empty, followed it up with a packet from his pocket.

'Now, John...'

The cigarette looked a bit ridiculous in John's huge face. He smoked a foul pipe of strong tobacco all the time he worked in the daytime and the speed with which the glow sped along the cigarette showed how hard he normally puffed.

He thumped the tiles of the table with his huge fist when they asked him about the window box.

'I fixed it good and proper. It couldn't 'ave fell of its own... Somebody screwed out the screws. And she fell out... She was only a little mite... Harmless... What could anybody...? And her tending her flowers... If I could only lay...'

He stretched out his huge paws in the direction of Cromwell, whose hand flew to his neck in protection.

'Now, now, John...'

'I'm sorry. Better be gettin' on with me work. But it's not right...'

'That's why we're here, John. Thanks for the information and the supper.'

Hornblower passed his hand over his bald pate in embarrassment.

'That'll be all right... I must be off... Be seein' you...'

He backed a few steps from the table, turned and fled.

'A good fellow... Terribly shy... Makes one shy as well to see him so uncomfortable...'

It was ten o'clock. The whole of the floor in the main hall had been cleaned and re-polished, the choir had gone home, and the band were slinging the moisture out of their instruments and packing them away.

Major Towse took his guests to the door and bade them good night. The town was quiet. A blue lamp over the police station and a square of light behind the window of the Blow residence. The town hall clock struck ten-fifteen. A taxi drew up in front of the bank house and Lenore Blow stepped out. There seemed to be another figure inside the cab, but the detectives couldn't make out who it was. She rang the bell and before they reached their hotel, the house door had opened, and Lenore had gone inside.

'Good supper,' said Cromwell. 'Bet the Duke of York couldn't do better.'

He hummed to himself.

'You'll get nothing at all there at this hour, except maybe a drink if they condescend. What's that you're humming?'

'One of those band-pieces. Quite catchy, I thought.'

I'm H-A-P-P-Y, because I'm S-A-V- E-D,
I'm H-A-P-P-Y, because I'm F-R double E...'

8

THE JOVIAL SALVATIONIST

Even if it turns out to be murder, what can the motive be? If, as you say, the daughters of old Blow lived on annuities, which, presumably, die out at their deaths, what sense would there be in killing them?'

They were holding a further council of war in the police station. Littlejohn, Cromwell and Paston.

Paston wasn't comfortable about the investigation. Being turned out of the bank house so churlishly by Ralph Blow had shaken him badly. In a small town, small things mean a lot. Furthermore, he realised how much, on the strength of the Blow family, he'd taken for granted before Littlejohn arrived.

'All the same,' said Littlejohn, 'Towse at the citadel talked of Miss Penelope finding five thousand pounds from somewhere. If she'd only an annuity, she must have borrowed it. But it may have been that she had money in her own right. Bit awkward being in the opposite camp from the surviving Blows, but we've got to find out from somewhere. What about the family lawyer?'

'Copplestones?' asked Paston and laughed mirthlessly.

'I see what you mean. I've already met...or rather encountered...the gentleman. Big, pompous chap?'

'That's him. He'd soon put you in your place. He'll side with Ralph, of course. Pays him to do so...'

'What's his firm?'

'Copplestones, Jervis, Bentley and Brett. Just across the square there.'

'This square is a real solar-plexus in Nesbury, isn't it? All the life and nerve centres here...'

'Yes. With the Blows slap bang in the middle of it. This office is a good observation post, too.'

It was early morning and men were already erecting stalls of tubular steel round the statue of the great Blow. As each stall was ready a member of a waiting crowd of would-be holders took possession and began to set out his wares. A number of market-gardeners' carts piled high with produce for the market stood nearby ready for unloading. There were women, with large baskets of cakes, eggs, cheese and shrimps for sale as well. And a motley flock of carpet, cloth, clothing, pots and small ware merchants eager to be making a start. Cars of all kinds were gradually accumulating. Ramshackle farmers' vehicles, the more trim ones of better-off folk, and then buses bringing in people from outlying places in the country and depositing them in the square...

'Things are getting busy...'

'Yes. It'll be pandemonium till late afternoon. What's your programme, Inspector?'

Littlejohn filled his pipe and lit it.

'Is Copplestones the only member of his firm, Paston? I mean, has he any partners who might be more friendly to us?'

'Yes. Young Brett. You might try him, although not today. The courts are sitting, which means I must be off, too. Try tomorrow. I'll tip you off when Copplestones leaves the office and you might slip over and try to get hold of Brett. He's quite a nice chap and may talk to you about the Blow affairs. You can only try...'

'Till then, there are plenty of other things. How far's Hilary Magna from here?'

'Hilary Magna?'

'Yes. The vicar there was, I think, a close friend and maybe confidant of Penelope Blow. I think I'll call on him if it's possible.'

Paston opened a drawer and took out a bunch of road maps.

'Hilary...Here we are... Looks as if it'll take you a week to get there and back by train. Take one of the police cars. Hilary, by the looks of it, is about seventy miles by road. Two hours there and two back.'

'Right. If it's all the same to you, I'll accept the offer of the car. I'll drive myself. Now, Simon Jacques...the Salvation Army man who was in charge when William Blow was alive and doing the Army some good. Towse said he lived at some alms-houses on the edge of the town...'

'Yes...I know them...'

Paston smiled.

'What are you laughing at?'

'You'll be surprised... Or will you? They are called W Blow's Retreat...'

'No!!'

'Yes. They were part of the original charity. He included them in his will along with the Salvation Army and others. There are six of them. All in a row and very nice, too. Two inmates are nominated by the Salvationists, two by the Mayor and Corporation, and two by...guess whom...?'

'Come again...'

'The committee of the police charities.'

'Good! A very good lot, too. Old Blow must have been a shrewd bird...and not so bad at heart, either.'

'You get him wrong, really. All the charities bear the name Blow in big letters. The Blow Alms-houses, the Blow Citadel, the Blow Ward at the infirmary, and the Blow Dogs' and Cats' Shelter... The last was his best joke...'

'I see. Self-advertisement...'

'Not at all. Just to parade before the family the hated fact that he'd left his money away from them; a way of goading them after he'd been put under the sod.'

'Well... That's not getting you off to court. I must be off to Hilary, too. Cromwell, here's a job for you. Will you go down to the Blow Alms-houses...?'

'Retreat, you mean...'

'I'd forgotten... The Blow Retreat and find out old Simon Jacques. Get to know from him all you can about old Blow's charity, his conversion, as they call it, and anything else the old Major can tell you...'

'Right. Whereabouts is it, Inspector Paston?'

Paston gave him directions... A two-penny ride on the bus out of town. Cromwell kept smiling to himself at some private joke.

'What's tickling you?' asked Littlejohn.

'I was wondering if he endowed an Old Blow's Almanac, as well?'

Then they parted company. Paston gathered up his notes on three drunks, two shoplifters, five parking offences, four food and black-market malefactors and a Communist who'd thrown a brick through the Mayor's window and, after seeing off Little-john in a natty little car, went to prosecute before the magis-trates. Cromwell, still smiling at his almanac joke, caught a handy bus and rode off to find W Blow's Retreat. The bus conductor eyed him up and down when he asked where it was. After setting aside the ideas that Cromwell might himself be putting his name forward for retreat, or trying to sell the inmates something, that official decided that the sergeant was an evangelist and grew very civil. He gave him a brief history of the charity and said he'd drop him at the very door.

'But if it's religion you're calling about, you won't do much good there. They're all old and their minds are made up. There's four ladies and two old men. Three belong to the vicar and the rest are dissenters. But old Jacques looks after 'em all. He's sort of chaplain there. Prays with 'em, sick visits, in fact, he's like a little bishop there. A grand old chap...'

'Is he fit and well?'

'Oh, aye. Unsteady a bit on his legs. You and me'll be a bit shaky when we get eighty if we're still here, which is very unlikely.'

'Speak for yourself...'

'I am doin'. But you'll find with all this rushin' about and rotten food we're havin', we'll be lucky if we see sixty. Chaps like old Jacques belongs to another age. The doctors are better than they used to be, or so I read in the papers. But the times are a jump ahead of 'em. They can't give you a new 'eart for the one that's wore out with runnin' here and runnin' there, now can they?'

The conductor raised his pug face to Cromwell's and looked at him with large, puzzled spaniel's eyes. He seemed to want an assurance that, in spite of it all, he himself would reach eighty.

'Oh, by the time we're old, they'll have new hearts for us. You'd be surprised the things they do now...'

'You really think so...?'

Thus comforted, he punched Cromwell a two-penny ticket, took his money and almost at once told him he'd reached his destination.

''Ere we are. Give my love to old Jacques. He'll know me... Just say Joe... He often 'as a free ride with me and my mate.'

The mate was glaring at Joe from the glass of his cab, wondering what was holding up the bus. Joe gave the bell a double ring...

'S'long... New hearts...! Well...well...'

Retreat described the place well. You approached it through

a large white gate, passed through a coppice of trees and bushes on either side of a well-made path, and there it was, a neat, long, single-storied bungalow affair, with six little doors, built in mock-Tudor style, black and white, with tall, fancy chimneys leaping upwards. It was only half-past ten, but smoke was rising from the fires inside and three of the inmates were already in their gardens; two frail-looking old ladies and a chirpy old man, who was digging among his plants.

The ladies were gossiping over the privet hedges which divided their homes.

'Mr Jacques?' said Cromwell, raising his hat to one of them. They stopped talking and the old gardener raised his head, grunting a bit as his bent back teased him.

'The end house...'

'Thanks. Nice morning...'

'Very nice,' said all three of the inmates, and their eyes followed Cromwell's tall, heavy frame as he made his way to the end of the row. He knocked, but it seemed that the occupant had already seen him from afar off, for it flew open at once and there stood Simon in his shirt sleeves, a potato in one hand and a short, sharp knife in the other.

Jacques was small and thick-set. He looked about sixty until he began to move, when his tottering gait told a different tale. A fine head rose from a sturdy neck and he had a gentle old face, ruddy and serene from good living and his own particular brand of philosophy. His hair, dishevelled from his housework, floated like a snowy nimbus, thin and silky, to finish off a very pleasant appearance.

'Good mornin', friend...'

'Good morning, Mr Jacques.'

'I'm just getting my dinner ready. Come in, sir, come in.'

There was a small living room on one side of the door, a bedroom on the other, and behind, the kitchen and other offices.

'Take off your coat, sir, if you're staying a bit. You'll feel better for it when you go out again. I'll hang 'em up here. The pan's on the stove for tea... Tea's always better when taken in company. There'll be enough for two...'

The old fellow gave Cromwell a chair whilst he made a brew. In the little room were cluttered, neatly, the precious possessions collected in past times. Old comfortable furniture, a sideboard bought for a bigger house, a small table...and on the walls a dozen or more framed photographs, all of Salvationist rallies and other events. Cromwell recognised in one of them General Booth himself. Over the mantelpiece a picture of Mr Jacques, much younger, with a happy-looking woman by his side. They were both in uniform.

'You lookin' at my pictures, sir...?'

The old un had entered quietly.

'Yes. They're interesting.'

'That's my dear wife. In God's keepin' these fifteen years... And there's me...and the old General himself. He spoke a lot to me that day. It was a privilege, I assure you, sir. Blood and Fire, it was then...'

Jacques was not ostentatious in his religion. He said grace over the tea, but his speech was free from evangelical fuss. Funnily enough, he seemed to take Cromwell for granted. He made him at home without the slightest inquisitiveness concerning the visit.

'Do you know why I've called, sir?'

'No. You'll tell me when you're ready. You're welcome, even if you've called for no real purpose. Took to you right away. All the years have given me a way of knowing when a man's all right. I think you're all right...'

Cromwell felt a blush start at the bottom of his back and slowly creep in the direction of his collar-stud. He sipped his tea.

'Smoke if you like. I never smoked myself, but if it gives you pleasure...'

Cromwell took out a pipe like Littlejohn's, filled it with the same mixture as the Inspector smoked, and lit up.

'I called for a talk with you about Mr William Blow, sir.'

The smiling face of the jolly old Salvationist grew even more happy.

'There now. That's strange. I've never talked about him properly for years. Though he's always in my thoughts. God in His mercy granted me the privilege of showing His love to William Blow. He was saved from his own sin and pride just before it was too late. In my humble way I wrestled with the devil for William Blow and by grace he was saved. Hallelujah!'

'Will you tell me about it? But first, I must tell you who I am, sir. I'm a police officer from Scotland Yard. You see, we aren't quite sure that Miss Penelope Blow met with an accident. We suspect she suffered violence.'

'Oh...'

It was almost the roar of an old warrior scenting the devil again.

'But I thought the coroner said accidental death...'

'It seemed so at first, but since, well...we've even discovered that the box was loosened so that when she leaned on it...'

'Oh...'

'Before we can be satisfied, sir, we must find out whether anybody would want to get Miss Penelope out of the way. I mean, if it would pay them to kill her.'

'But how could anyone kill such a good Christian woman? If ever there was a good woman, it was her. I've known her for nearly forty years.'

'So, we're trying to find out from her friends, of which you were one, a sort of picture of the Blow family...'

'I could give you that, young man, but the Lord says vengeance is mine. I'm not a vengeful man.'

Mr Jacques sipped his tea and grew lost in thought.

'It's not that, sir. I have my duty to do and I'm asking you to help me do it. If you don't help me, I'll have to find out the information from elsewhere; it won't be so easy, sir, and will waste a lot of time. Meanwhile, the wrongdoers, if any there be...'

'I'll tell you what I know about the Blow family, though all this suspicion and evil grieves me greatly. I'm an old man. The Lord has seen fit to bless me with length of days. I don't want the end to be in darkness.'

'I'll be as little trouble as I can. Suppose you tell me, sir, all about Mr William Blow and how he came to endow the citadel and how you influenced him for his good.'

'Yes; I can tell you that...'

'Bread!!'

The old man from farther down the row had arrived with a loaf of bread, apparently part of a cargo delivered from the town. He entered, leaning on his stick and glanced keenly from Jacques to Cromwell, noted that they were *tête-à-tête* and looked for a spare chair on which to sit and join in.

'Thank you, Albert. I can't ask you to stop this morning. I've a visitor talking private. I'll come and see you later.'

Albert drew himself upright. He was indignant at receiving such short shrift, especially from Sim, his old-age pal.

'Oh, I don't stop where I ain't wanted, Sim Jacques. I ain't no busybody. Nobody can say I am. Mind yer own business, is Albert Biles's motter. So I'll bid yer good mornin' and take meself off, not bein' wanted...'

Old Sim led his buddy to the door and Cromwell could see him in the garden making his peace with Albert, who was trembling with senile fury at not finding out what was going on indoors. At length, shaking his head in semi-pacification, he toddled off to vent his annoyance on the two old ladies still gossiping at their doors.

'It was when I was in charge of our body here...'

Old Sim got down to his tale right away. His mind was as clear as a young man's and he wasted no time in metaphors or irrelevancies.

'We worshipped in a small room we rented at that time. Far too small it was, because we were growing in numbers. So many answered the Call in those days. Well, one day Mr William Blow sent word from the bank that he wanted to see me. I knew him all right, because in those days I was plumbing in my spare time and I used to do jobs for him. I was surprised, because I never did any banking myself. I wondered what he wanted. He soon told me. He was leaving in his will enough money to build us a grand new citadel in the town...'

The old man was living it all over again. His face grew flushed and his voice shrill. He was getting excited.

'... It was the miracle we'd always prayed for. Every time we held public Knee Drill, we asked God in His goodness to give His flock sufficient accommodation to meet their growing needs. And here it was! I couldn't understand it, sir. Here was a man known for the hardness of his heart suddenly turning from his evil ways and giving £30,000 to the Lord...'

'Did he say so, Mr Jacques?'

'No. He soon took me up when I put it that way. "Don't you think I've got religion," he says. "Nothin' o' that sort. It's simply that I'm leavin' nothing to my family. If I don't will it away from them, they'll get it all the same. So I'm givin' it to charity!"'

The old man got up and poked the fire violently.

'I couldn't accept it, sir. I didn't say so right out, though. I'd my own ideas and I said I'd call and let him know. Meanwhile I'd pray about it...and I thanked him very much. It worried me, sir. There seemed too much of the devil behind it. Pride and spite and malice. I wanted it to be given to the Lord or nothin'...'

'Quite right, too.'

'I knew you'd see it as I did. I prayed and the Lord showed me the way. I sent word to London headquarters and they sent down a man to talk it over with Mr Blow on equal terms. Matter of fact, the man that came...I forget his name, sir...my memory for names is gone...the man that came had been in banking, seen the Light, and joined our body as a financial adviser. He talked a lot to Mr Blow... He told him of the Word... and of Redeeming Grace...and believe me or not, sir, he convinced William Blow of the way to Salvation.'

'Did he, indeed?'

'Yes. One day, Mr Blow sent for me. Saw me in his private room and asked me to pray for him to begin with. I was amazed. And yet in another way, I wasn't. God moves in a mysterious way, sir, His wonders to perform, and the spirit bloweth where it listeth. He looked ill, sir. Said he hadn't been able to sleep thinkin' of his sins. I told him, sir, they'd been washed in the Blood of the Lamb, and with that, he broke down and cried, sir. Very troubled, he was. Well, sir, in short, he said to me, "Here I was, hatin' my daughters and the memory of my dead wife so much that I'd left them almost without money in my will. Not only that, what money I'd left them was left in a way to breed more hatred..." What he meant, sir, I never knew. I told him that rather than that, we would do without the citadel money. But he said no, there would be plenty for all. He'd take it from the dogs and cats, whatever that meant, and give it to his girls and the citadel could be built, too. He was going to alter his will and make it all right so that no wrong and sin should enter into it.'

'And he did?'

'I don't know, sir. What I do know is that we got the citadel after his death, but he hadn't altered his will. You see, before he could do it, he fell ill. Religious mania, they called it and I did hear he was locked in his room and not allowed out. After that, he was always queer. The Lord chastened him...He does that way with some He loves...'

'So what you call his sinful will was never altered?'

'I don't know, sir. I saw him once after that. He was very queer. I was doin' a bit of plumbing at the bank house, and he suddenly appeared on the scene. He was very secretive, like. Put his hand to his lips and whispered. Somethin' to the effect that they said he was mad. His relatives, Ralph and Harold, was lookin' after him. He told them he was goin' to alter his will. They said he couldn't...they wouldn't let him... They'd say he wasn't mentally fit to make his will... You see, sir, he told me they didn't know how he'd left the money in the first will. Thought it was all to the family. And now they thought he was going to do somethin' daft and leave it all to religion. The first will was sealed up and he cheated them properly. When it was read after his death, all went to charity, except some insurance of some kind...not much, I heard, for the girls. So we got our citadel...'

'But I don't understand, Mr Jacques? Why did you accept the money if you thought it was evil?'

'Ah... That was just it. Let me go on. You see, before Mr Harold found him talkin' to me and took him off, Mr William had told me what he'd done. "They won't let me alter my will. So much the worse for them. But I've gone round them. I've dodged them. I've looked after my girls in another way." He swore it on his honour.'

'Did you confirm that?'

'Yes, sir. I got hold of Miss Penelope after the funeral. We took him to the cemetery with the band... It was in the will that we had to...He said it would please the family very much. I can't say I agreed when we turned up to do it. They looked daggers at us... But as I was saying, sir, Miss Penelope told me it was quite right to accept the money. Mr William *had* looked after them, as promised... So that was that... And it's all I know. It was a very sad business... Mr William died of a stroke suddenly and answered to his Maker, and the family, except Miss Penelope, tried to forget all of him but the money and the will...'

'Thank you for telling me all this, Mr Jacques. It's been very useful indeed. Sorry to have taken so much of your time.'

'I've been very glad to see you, sir. Come again. Well...here comes Albert Biles again, so I'll bid you good day and God bless you, sir...'

Albert was toddling up the garden path very purposefully this time. He wasn't going to be gainsaid.

'Goodbye, then, Mr Jacques. Thank you and good luck.'

And utterly confused by the story he'd heard, Cromwell went to catch the next bus back to Nesbury.

9

MR CLAPLADY CONFIDES

It was pouring with rain when Littlejohn arrived at Hilary Magna. The wind swept and tortured the bare trees and he could see nothing ahead save what the two triangles of semi-opaque glass, cleaned by the windscreen wipers, revealed. Suddenly, these too became obscured by a large cape and regulation helmet.

'Well, well, well... I am glad to see you, sir,' said a voice from long ago, as the Inspector lowered the window to greet the apparition. It was Sergeant Harriwinckle, the law in the two Hilaries. 'And what brings you to these parts?'

'Good day to you, Harriwinckle. The pleasure's mutual. I'm just calling on Mr Claplady.'

'And just at the right time, too, sir. Flewker killed a pig yesterday...'

Radiating goodwill and pleasure, in spite of the weather, the worthy bobby closed one eye slowly, opened it again, tapped the side of his nose and leered conspiratorially.

'... Mrs 'Arriwinckle'll be glad to see you, sir. Welcome as the flowers in May, as you might say, sir.'

The place hadn't changed much since Littlejohn left it years ago after solving the case of the dead busybody. A few more council houses, a small deserted camp, and Harriwinckle a little older and rounder... That was all. He wondered how time had treated the saintly, absent-minded vicar.

'How is Mr Claplady, Harriwinckle?'

'About the same, sir. Older, like us all. Still chasin' about after swarms o' bees in their seasons, sir, and forgettin' the time and date, like he always did. Only a fortnight since, there was no parson at mornin' service an' somebody went off to see what was the matter. The reverend was busy among 'is bees, sir. Thought it was Saturday...'

'Otherwise, all right?'

'Yes... Though these last few days 'e's bin worse than ordinary. I seen him wanderin' abroad in the lanes lookin' terrible distressed. Somethin' must have upset 'im. And he's not easy upset by the things o' this world...'

'Well... I must be off. I've a longish journey before evening. I've come from Nesbury...'

'Good 'eavings! So, you won't... Mrs 'Arri-winckle will be disappointed, sir. She'll take it out o' me proper...'

'Don't worry. I'll be with you for lunch. I'll not be long with the vicar.'

'Okay, sir. We'll be ready. Roast pork, sir... Ah!!!...'

The bobby smacked his lips, saluted, and Littlejohn was off.

The vicarage looked more deserted and forlorn than ever. All the leaves had fallen from the creepers which covered the front and sides, leaving twisted stems and dark walls. The gardens, thanks to the attentions of the men of the parish who did a lot of tidying up out of sheer affection, were neat, however. There were more beehives than ever sheltering under the wall of the churchyard. Littlejohn took the shortcut between the graves, picking his way among the slanting old headstones, past the gypsy's grave in unhallowed ground, and round to the front door. He tugged the old-fashioned bell-pull.

The old housekeeper was ageing fast. She peered in the Inspector's face as though it roused some dim recollection.

'Inspector Littlejohn, Mrs Younghusband...'

'Well, upon my word! You look cold and wet, sir. How are you? Come in and let me take them wet things... Mr Claplady's in 'is study. Not so well, poor soul. Some bad news reached him about an old friend who died. He took it hard and on top o' that, he's took a cold... He will go out givin' them old bees their sugar in all sorts o' weather. I told him... But there, go in, sir.'

The Reverend Ethelred Claplady was cowering before a large fire in his large, untidy study. On the table, the battered manuscript of his still unfinished, monumental work on bees. He was wearing an old dressing gown over his clerical clothes and had a large woollen scarf wound several times round his neck.

'Oh, dear...' he said softly to himself as Littlejohn entered, then he raised his dim, tired eyes and fumbled on the little table by his elbow for his glasses.

'Excuse me... I can't see without them... There, that's better. My dear Inspector...!! How glad I am... You find me a very poor soul...full of cold and sorrow...'

'I'm glad to see you again, sir, and sorry about your troubles. What are you taking for the cold?'

Littlejohn cast his eye over the contents of the small table top. Smelling salts, a physic bottle, books, papers, a reading-glass and a large jar of honey.

'I'm taking honey, Inspector. I find it good for so many complaints. I don't know what I'd do without it... Oh, dear...'

The vicar coughed hoarsely. Like a dog barking. And fumbling among his many garments he brought to light a large handkerchief and trumpeted in it.

Littlejohn passed over the pocket flask of brandy which he always carried.

'Try that, sir...'

He sat down opposite his friend before the roaring fire of logs.

'Really, Inspector... With the exception of an odd glass of sherry now and then, I'm teetotal...'

'Medicine, sir,' said Littlejohn and smiled knowingly.

'Very well, then, if you say so...'

Mr Claplady poured rather a copious dose into a medicine glass from the table and drank it calmly in a single gulp.

'Oh... Ah... Dear me... Well, well...I feel better already.'

Littlejohn emptied the rest in a clean tumbler. 'Take some more soon, sir. It'll do you a lot of good.'

'I will, I will...'

Mr Claplady looked better already. He had been low in spirits and the brandy was just what he wanted. He grew quite chirpy, took another absent-minded gulp of the rest of his new remedy, and then began to talk of personal matters and exchange many experiences since their last meeting.

'... But you've not called to bring me brandy and ask about bees, Inspector. I think I know why you're here...'

'Yes, sir. It's about Miss Blow. I'm very sorry to tell you we suspect foul play.'

'Foul play! But that is monstrous. Why, Penelope was the finest woman I ever knew. Nobody would want to...want to... Was she...was she murdered, Inspector?'

His voice fell to a whisper and he rose and thrust his face close to that of his visitor.

'I'm afraid so, sir. I'm very sorry to bring such news...'

The old vicar staggered backwards, fumbled blindly for the arm of his chair and slumped down in it.

'To think it should all end this way... I should have been there to pray with her and hold her hand and close her eyes when she was dead. As it is... Oh, dear... I have been a weak, miserable wretch...'

And he burst into tears and sobbed noisily.

It was very painful. Littlejohn didn't know what to say or do. He just let the old man calm himself and settle and then resumed as though nothing emotional had happened. He told him of the window box and the daffodils and how the screws had been removed. Then of Penelope Blow's visit to Scotland Yard and of her death. The vicar sat quietly, slumped in his chair, his eyes red, his muffler awry, his grey hair in disorder...

'I am not a vengeful man, Inspector, but...but...I curse the one who caused the death of such a good woman...'

He said it standing on his feet, his hand raised, a priest pronouncing the fatal words. Then he told Littlejohn how, in his early days, his first curacy at Nesbury, he had fallen in love with Penelope Blow and how William Blow had hounded him from the town and locked his daughter in her room.

'I ought to have been firm, Inspector. I ought to have remained and, if necessary, released her and eloped. As it was...'

Littlejohn looked at the vicar. Every man, he thought, remembering the Eastern saying, bears his fate on his brow. There was nothing of the violent, decisive man about the Rev Ethelred Claplady. Faced with unreasoning physical strength and power, he would be all at sea. He wouldn't know what to do, except yield to it. On the spiritual side, yes; but faced by William Blow, no.

'As it was...I just went and left her. That is nearly fifty years since, Inspector. She forgave me, I know. We wrote to each other on birthdays and at Christmas. She sent me this scarf, Inspector. Made it herself... When I left her, I thought soon to go back. I would make a success of myself and claim her... I never did, so I never returned. I have been here, on a small stipend in a rambling old house, for more than forty years. I was a nobody to offer myself to such a lovely, gracious lady. She suggested our meeting...but, somehow, I felt inadequate, sir. I was ashamed...'

Perhaps it was all for the best, thought Littlejohn.

The old man was living still in his love for a lovely young girl of fifty years since. He remembered how they'd described her at Scotland Yard and Nesbury... Old, plain and fussy... Well, well...

'But what can I do to help you bring this monster to justice, Inspector?'

'You've kept in touch with Miss Penelope by correspondence, sir. Maybe, she has told you things from time to time which might help us.'

'She has told me such a lot. They were a strange family and I think I was her only confidant... Unworthy as I was...'

'Perhaps it would be better then, sir, if I ask you a few questions about things.'

'By all means do.'

The vicar took another nip of his medicine. It was doing him good. He looked brighter, his eyes sparkled, and a bit of colour came back to his cheeks.

'First of all, then, you recommended Miss Blow to contact me at Scotland Yard. Why was that, sir?'

'She telephoned and wrote... Her sister, she thought, was being poisoned. I almost went myself to see if I could help. But then...well...imagine me in an emergency... I thought of you. I hope I did right, Inspector.'

'Perfectly right, sir. In fact, had you not intervened, Miss Penelope would have been buried as an accident case and forgotten...'

'Not by me, Inspector, not by me...'

'I realise that, sir. Was that all she told you?'

'About the poisoning...yes. She was indeed distressed about it. She said she would go to London right away and stay with an old servant...Buckley, I think, who kept a little boarding house in Egton Mews... I remember Buckley... Well, she said she would go there and call on you.'

'I was away and never saw her, but I got her message. That

was how I became involved in this case. The family are opposed to my presence and investigations...'

Mr Claplady sprang to his feet again.

'Inspector, I beg you... They have done enough to her, and to me, in life. I beg you let them not wrong her in death. Let right be done...'

'I'll see to that, sir. Now another question. When William Blow died, he left a will giving all his money to charity. Is it true he hated his daughters and never forgave their mother for not bearing sons and then leaving him for another man?'

'That is true, Inspector. Penelope told me that in a letter after his death. His will left all his possessions, except the house and all in it, to charity. But something strange happened; he made provision for the daughters in another way.'

'Yes, I heard about the annuities.'

'More than that, Inspector. Cash. He gave them cash before he died. He atoned somewhat. Had he not done so, he would have been truly damned, for even the annuities were fraught with evil.'

'In what way, sir?'

'It was a single annuity, Inspector, on their three lives. It was known as a tontine, I think. Penelope wrote about it at the time. The annual payment was divided in three shares, at first. Then, when one annuitant died, the same sum was divided in two; and when only one remained the original annual sum came to her. Monstrous... It meant that an evil annuitant would want the other two to die... Might even be tempted to violence to get their shares as well as her own.'

'But all the Blow daughters got on well together, didn't they? Surely, he couldn't, wouldn't, hope to set them one against the other.'

'That is what he intended, Inspector. I knew him well and I knew of what he was capable. He was an evil man...but God in His mercy saved him just in time. It was almost like a miracle.

He left a large sum in his Will to the Salvation Army to build a place of worship in Nesbury. Somehow, in the course of his contacts with the Salvationists...he met them often because he wished to arrange with them exactly how the place was to be erected...in the course of his meetings with them, they were able to show him the evil of his ways. He became so obsessed with a sense of sin that it unhinged him. The male members of his family locked him in a special room in the bank house and relieved him of responsibility. Thus, he was unable to alter his will.'

'But what about the cash, sir?'

'Before he died, he sent for Penelope. He said she was the only one he could trust. You see, Katherine was married, and her husband might have become involved, and Honoria...well... she utterly despised her father. She was always on her mother's side and a proud, haughty, selfish girl... No, he dealt with my Penelope and she served him well. He gave her thirty-thousand pounds in bearer bonds... They were in a strong box in the bank; but not his official one. He had built up this reserve in case of need. When the firm was a private bank, they got in low water a time or two. I suspect he laid the bonds aside in a box marked with a fictitious name in the vault. With the help of the Chief Cashier, Broome, who was devoted to William Blow and Penelope, she obtained the bonds, which her father then ordered her to take to London, sell, and place the funds in her own name at another bank in the City. He instructed her to act as trustee for the money, using it for the benefit of herself and her sisters as she thought fit. Thus, if the annuities did not suffice, there was a fund to make them up.'

'Did Miss Penelope tell her sisters of this, sir?'

'No. William Blow forbade her to do so unless utterly compelled. After the death of her father, his estate was made-up and distributed to various charities. It was only then that Penelope found out that she had committed a felony by not disclosing the sum in her name. It seems that gifts so shortly made before death are part of the estate and must suffer death duties. She remained silent about it all out of very fear and thus didn't reveal it.'

'So, she had the burden of all that money on her mind...'

'Yes. She gave much of her own share, she told me, towards another Salvationist charity. After her father's death, she took great interest in them, for he had told her of what they had done to him in the way of showing him his folly, and she felt she owed them a deep debt.'

'And what about the rest of the money, sir?'

'Katherine Blow married and she and her husband were very close and dear to each other. Penelope felt she could trust them and took them in her confidence. She gave them their share.'

'And Honoria?'

'Honoria was irresponsible part of the time...She felt...'

'You mean, sir?'

'Yes, Inspector...There was a strain of madness in the Blow family. I may as well tell you...I didn't want to bring it in on account of my dear dead love. You might have thought she did herself violence. That's what I thought at first when I heard she had died, God forgive me...I thought they had so tried her that she had become demented. You see, it was some years after we parted that she discovered her own grandfather died insane. After that she refused to marry me...Now you know, Inspector.'

'I'm truly sorry.'

'You also see why William Blow went unhinged when the weight of his sin became manifest to him. Honoria had an unfortunate love affair in her youth. She suffered a break-down...to call it by its mild name. Since then, she has twice again been in a nursing home out of the way. Penelope felt she had better hold Honoria's share on her behalf. I quite agreed. Furthermore, when Penelope told me Honoria was saying someone was poisoning her, I thought that it was just another of Honoria's tricks...'

'Tricks?'

'Yes. When she didn't get her own way, she often traded on her weakness. At one time, she pretended to commit suicide by throwing herself in the river. Fortunately, there was only sixteen inches of water in it, so the sensation had its farcical side. I'm sure she knew it wasn't deep...'

'Did she ever tell you about her nephews, Ralph and Harold?'

'Not very much. Ralph married Lenore Broome, the daughter of the former Chief Cashier. Harold never married. They are both like William Blow; hot tempered and overbearing.'

'No signs of the family failing, sir?'

'I think not. Their father was the best of the Blows. Theodore was a nice man. So was Rufus, Theodore's father and William's brother. You wouldn't have thought he and William came of the same father and mother.'

'Was Lenore Broome's father the one who helped Miss Penelope cash the bonds?'

'Yes.'

'Do you think, sir, he might have divulged the secret to his daughter?'

'I would think not. Mr Broome was the kindliest of men with the highest integrity. But maybe, she overheard or discovered something about it. One never knows.'

'To the best of your knowledge, sir, nobody knew of Miss Penelope's nest egg, then, except her sister Katherine and her husband, and her father and Mr Broome...and, of course, yourself.'

'That is true.'

It was still raining outside. Water dripped and ran down the glass of the French windows, the wood of which was decaying and needed a coat of paint. No wonder little was seen of the housekeeper. She'd have her work cut out looking after this great, rambling ruin of a place. Mr Claplady kicked the logs, which collapsed in a shower of sparks, and put on another couple.

'Have you any idea who might have wished Penelope harm, Inspector? I can't think who could have done such a thing. She was so kind and good...'

'I have no idea at all, sir. But what you've told me has been of great assistance. It gives us motive, at least.'

'What do you mean, Inspector?'

'Everyone thought Miss Penelope lived on an annuity which died with her. Now we know she had quite a little fortune... But wait...the annuity didn't die with her. It went to Miss Honoria. That would be her sister Katherine's share, Penelope's, and Honoria's, if as you say, sir, the annuity was tontine.'

'But, surely, her own sister! You don't suspect Miss Honoria?'

'If she was subject to fits of dementia...why not? But removing the screws was not a woman's job...not a job for a woman of Honoria's kind, at any rate. Did Penelope leave a will, do you know, sir?'

'Yes, Inspector. She asked my advice and let me see the draft. She had saved a little from her annuity and under cover of that, left what she had to the family. She had about eight thousand pounds of her own after she paid for the annexe at the Salvation Army. Then, in her own name, was the ten thousand which really belonged to Honoria. So, she left the larger amount to her sister, consoling herself that death duties would, at last, be paid on it, and the smaller sum equally between Ralph and Harold. A small, decent lawyer drew up the will for her in Nesbury and the family were unaware of it.'

'Can you give me his name, sir?'

'Padfield. I remember because that was my own mother's maiden name, God bless her. Padfield was instructed to bring forth the will in the event of Penelope's death.'

'What happened if Miss Honoria died first, sir?'

'All the money then went to Ralph and Harold when Penelope died.'

'So, had the arsenic acted quickly, Miss Honoria would have died first...'

'Yes. What an awful thing, Inspector. You surely don't think the family...'

'Who else would it be, sir? Nobody else is involved.'

'No, I see that...'

The grandfather clock in one corner slowly and laboriously chimed the quarters and then struck four. Littlejohn looked at the watch on his wrist.

'Clock's a bit off the mark, sir.'

'Yes. It's rather like me, Inspector. It's older by nearly a century than I am and we both forget the right time. It's about noon, I'd say, from a series of rough calculations on the basis of what it at present indicates.'

'That's right, sir. May I use your telephone, please?'

'You'll find it in the hall, there, just by the chest. It's an old-fashioned instrument, but moderately efficient.' Littlejohn excused himself, found the telephone and dialled 999. Almost at once, the full-flavoured, good-humoured voice of Harriwinckle rumbled in the receiver.

Littlejohn asked if he could manage a second guest, the vicar.

'Of course, sir. 'Ighly pleased to see the reverend. You managed to cheer 'im up a bit? Good! We'll be seein' you then, sir. Roast pork, stuffin', biled potaters and sprouts from me own garden. Suet puddin' to foller and can Mrs H make 'em! Well, you know of old, sir...'

'Thank you so much, Harriwinckle. And could you get a bottle of Martel from the landlord at the pub? Charge it to me. It does the vicar's cold a world of good... We'll be seeing you soon...'

'You really have been a great help, sir,' said Littlejohn to the vicar when he got back to the hearth. 'It's remarkable how well-posted Miss Penelope kept you...'

The vicar shook his head.

'I have never told another soul what I'm now going to say. Before we parted Penelope and I swore never to marry anyone else. In fact, except for the blessing of the Church on us, we were husband and wife, Inspector. We were each other's all in all, and we each remained faithful to the end. I shall be meeting her soon, I hope, in better circumstances...'

Littlejohn was glad there was Harriwinckle to take the old man out of himself a bit. He muffled up the vicar in a greatcoat, a motor rug and Penelope's scarf and, after pacifying Mrs Younghusband for taking her master away, tucked him in the police car and whirled him off for pork and stuffing. And could Mrs H cook 'em!

10
TRY IT ON THE CAT!

Cromwell was sitting in the kitchen of the bank house before the fire in a rocking chair. Posted solicitously round him were Mrs Frazer, Mrs Minshull and Jelley. The sergeant was balancing a cup of strong tea in one hand and breaking pieces of rich currant cake from a slab on a plate on his knee and eating them with relish.

'Good cake...'

'Yes,' said Mrs Frazer cryptically. She used only the best for the staff below-stairs, especially for Mr Jelley, who wasn't very strong. Dolly, the kitchen-maid, had been closed in the scullery and given a lot of brass to clean during the conference. You could hear her banging around to express her indignation at the affront.

Cromwell, on Littlejohn's instructions, had made sure that the family were out and then introduced himself at the back door as Littlejohn's assistant. He had been received into the bosom of the staff like a long-lost brother. He looked extremely respectable, a cross between an evangelist and a gentleman's gentleman, and this went down very well with them.

'You was sayin'?' said Mrs Minshull, wriggling in her chair with voluptuous pleasure at the tea, the cake and the company.

'Oh, yes, the citadel. We were there last night. Nice place they've got now, thanks to Mr Blow...*and* poor Miss Penelope...'

Mrs Frazer wiped away a tear.

'Whoever could 'ave done such a thing, sir?'

'That's what we've to find out. But first of all, Miss Honoria baffles *me*. This poisoning... I can't make out why whoever was doing it couldn't have given her a proper dose and finished the thing in one, instead of making such a long, drawn-out job of it. So long, in fact, that people have tumbled to it and stopped it.'

The three servants exchanged looks. Cromwell glanced from one to the other.

'You all look very mysterious. What's the matter?'

Jelley cleared his throat and delicately bit a small piece from his portion of cake, sipped his tea and sighed.

'We must confess we don't regard it as seriously as some people... We think it was another of Miss Honoria's tricks, Mr Cromwell.'

'What tricks, Mr Jelley?'

They looked at each other very respectfully, like a couple of friendly dogs in a first encounter in which each wishes to assure the other of its good intentions.

'Well, sir... Ever since she was quite young, Miss Honoria has wanted her own way and, if she couldn't have it, has created a fuss. She is nervously unstable, Mr Cromwell; what they call nowadays, neurotic...yes, sir, neurotic. In my days, Mr Cromwell, they were simply regarded as naughty and treated accordingly... Firmly, sir...just firmly.'

The two attendant women made noises of warm approval and nodded admiringly at the man who believed in a strong hand, although, to see him, he looked on his last legs.

'More tea, Mr Cromwell...?' And Mrs Frazer filled up his

cup and without his permission slid another large dollop of cake on his plate.

'Yes, Mr Cromwell, we are all three of the opinion that Miss Honoria took the poison herself.'

'What?!'

The remainder of the party confirmed this by unanimous acclamation.

'Yes, sir. We think she took it herself. Not enough to kill, or even seriously injure herself, but sufficient to make her sick and, if the doctor called, make her story seem true.'

'But why?'

'Well, we've talked it all over together, Mr Cromwell, and we're all of one mind; Miss Honoria had something to do with the decease of Miss Penelope. We think she was after her sister's money and planned her death.'

The two women were agog with excitement. It was evident there had been a severe staff conference between them and Jelley, they had pooled their views, and reached a measure of unanimity. Jelley was their spokesman, but as he told his tale, they punctuated it with cries, nods and groans of assent.

'But I thought the three daughters of Mr William Blow had an annuity each. In that case, the death of any of them wouldn't make any difference.'

'Oh, but it did, sir. You didn't know Mr Blow, sir. Oh, no. It wasn't as simple as that...'

'Oh, no,' clamoured his women.

'He left them what were called tontiny annuities or something such. Meanin' that the annuities or annuity went on and on till they all died. And when one died, the other two got her share between them. When two died, the relict got all the annuity...three times what she had when three were alive. Follow?'

Cromwell, feeling his way through Jelley's mathematics, nodded assent.

'But what good would that do Miss Honoria? She didn't need

much money from all accounts. She rarely went out or did anything with money.'

'Didn't she?'

The two women sniffed, and Mrs Frazer chuckled; 'Oh, Oh, Oh,' like an old witch.

'She did, Mr Cromwell. Mr Harold was the apple of her eye. He's always short of money. His practice at law is very poor. People don't like him and won't go to him. He's extravagant and only needs to go to his aunt to get everything she's got out of her. Between you and me, sir, I wouldn't be surprised if Harold had urged her on to do it...'

'Urged her on...' said Mrs Frazer with relish.

'Let's get this straight, Mr Jelley. You suggest that Mr Harold has been so pressing of late for money that Miss Honoria took her sister's life to get him more? Come, come, Mr Jelley, that's very grave, isn't it?'

Both women began to clamour in unison at this doubting of their official spokesman.

Jelley raised a feeble hand authoritatively for silence.

'She was a bit queer, you know, sir. There's a queer streak in the family, if I may say so. It came out in her. If I could tell you the things we know...'

'Oh...' chanted the women. It was like a scene from a novel of the Gothic school.

'Such as...?'

'Sleep walking, sir... Screaming in her sleep...going right off her head with temper and attacking people...hysterics...actually once shutting herself in her room and turning on the gas fire to do away with herself... If only I told you all the goings-on...'

The housekeeper and the cook moaned, and Mrs Frazer filled up Cromwell's cup again and gave him another slab of cake.

'Can I come in, now? I've done me brasses...'

Dolly completely destroyed the atmosphere by putting in an unruly red head and a face flushed with the speed of her efforts.

Mrs Frazer was angry.

'No. You can't 'ave done 'em in that time. Go and do 'em agen...'

'But, Mrs Frazer...'

'Do as you're told, miss, and don't be cheeky. And stop there till I say when. This is private, see?'

The head withdrew and the door slammed.

'Imperent madam,' muttered the cook.

Jelley resumed, stabbing the air with his bony forefinger for emphasis.

'I'll tell you straight, Mr Cromwell, what we think. Miss Penelope was always talking of a famous man at Scotland Yard who was a friend of a friend of hers. We knew who that was. Mr Claplady, sir. She had a special way of saying "friend" when she meant him. Well... We think Miss Honoria wanted Miss Penelope out of the way. She's cunning, sir, and must have planned the box to fall when Miss Penelope leaned on it to water the plants. But, without her sister out of the way for long enough, how could she unscrew the screws? I say, how could she unscrew them?'

'How could she unscrew them, in any case? It's more than a woman of her kind could do...'

'All in good time, sir...'

The women couldn't wait. Their voices rose in a fierce shout. Mrs Minshull, having a deep and powerful contralto when exerted, won.

'Who knew the way Miss Penelope watered the bulbs... putting her weight with one hand on the box while she used the water in the other? It was habit and the can from the bathroom that she used was 'eavy. There was only Miss Honoria, Mr Ralph, Mr 'Arold, Mrs Ralph, Dolly, Mr Jelley and me ever was there, at one time or another, when she did it...'

'That's as may be, Mrs Minshull… Allow me to go on,' said Jelley, firmly, taking the reins again. 'Miss Honoria wanted Miss Penelope out of the way for a good time. She also wanted an alibi and to be out of the house when the police called asking questions after the so-called accident. She was cunning, sir. So, she took a little of the arsenic, made herself ill, told Miss Penelope, put poison in her mind, suggested she went to Scotland Yard for your advice…and then unscrewed the box when her sister was away.'

'I heard her say to her sister, "I'm bein' poisoned, I'm sure. It would be such a scandal locally." I was changing the linen, Mr Cromwell, and heard that with my own ears,' whispered Mrs Minshull, respectfully interrupting again.

'But out of the way, what about going to Miss Penelope's room, unscrewing the screws and getting back again? I thought she was ill in bed.'

'Ill in bed!' muttered the housekeeper scornfully. 'She was up and down, up and down; she wasn't all that ill. If she wanted anythin' and we didn't answer the bell like lightning, she was up in a temper and got it herself and whined about nobody carin' what happened to her. That is so, isn't it, Mr Jelley?'

'That is quite correct, Mrs Minshull. Miss Honoria wasn't bedfast, although she would have liked us to think she was. She must have crept into her sister's room unseen and done it. We couldn't have heard her here. The walls are too thick and we're too far away.'

'But unscrewing those large screws… A feeble woman…'

'Ah… That's just it, sir. Please step this way.'

To the annoyance of the women, now immersed like mediums in a seance, Jelley led Cromwell upstairs. On the landing the butler paused.

'That is Miss Honoria's room and that was Miss Penelope's, Mr Cromwell…'

He paused and opened a door of what might have been a box

room, but which turned out to be a workroom, with bench, vice, lathe and a lot of tools neatly arranged in racks on the wall.

'This is Mr Harold's workroom, Mr Cromwell. His hobby is the making of model aeroplanes and railway rolling-stock...'

He said it with pompous contempt as though he himself had passed quite out of the juvenile stage and regarded Mr Harold as being mentally arrested.

'... In the attic is a complete set of railway lines, with engines, signals, stations, and such like. Mr Harold spends a lot of time there and derives much pleasure from it. He attends conferences of his fellow model railway and aeroplane gentlemen... Here he makes, as I said, rolling-stock and mechanical parts...'

Opening a drawer in the bench, Jelly took out a neat, compact contraption which Cromwell, who had one of his own and used it with great pleasure, recognised as a power-driven screwdriver. Jelley pushed a plug in the wall and switched on the gadget, which whirled merrily in his hand with easy precision.

'Miss Honoria knew of this, sir. She bought it for Mr Harold for his birthday and he taught her how it functioned. I think she used this on the screws, sir.'

They descended and joined the women, much to their satisfaction.

'I've shown Mr Cromwell the electric screwdriver, ladies, and told him how it was used...'

'Cunnin', wasn't she, Mr Cromwell?' hissed Mr Frazer.

'That's all right for a theory, I'm sure, and I thank you for telling me. But what about the poison? Where did it come from and how much did Miss Honoria know to take?'

'Ahhhhhh...'

'At one time, Mr William Blow went...well...to put it mildly...*queer*. He tried to take his own life by drinking a preparation then sold in the shops for fly catching. It was known as fly-water, Mr Cromwell. Well known to contain arsenic, and therefore dangerous. We used to use it here. I got the stuff from the chemist's, soaked blotting paper in a mixture of the fly-water and sugar. Then we placed them about the place and the flies came for the sugar and were poisoned by the arsenic… Most efficacious, it was…'

'*Very* effectuous,' butted in Mrs Frazer, 'very effectuous, and Mr Blow took a drink of it to make away with himself, but not enough. The doctor came in time…'

Jelley took up the tale.

'We never used it again, but the bottle Mr Blow used disappeared. They said he had concealed it. But we know what happened to it…'

'We do,' chorused the women.

'It was taken and hidden by Miss Honoria, thinking in her queer way, maybe, to prevent a scandal. Or, perhaps, to use for her own purposes in the future. You see, sir, what her father used and didn't properly poison him, she might use again…'

'I see. Just a bit thin, though, isn't it?'

Mr Jelley and his friends were affronted and looked it. 'At any rate, we found it… It is here…'

Jelley walked solemnly to the plate cupboard, unlocked it with a key from his waistcoat pocket and held out a pint bottle, half-full of clear fluid, to Cromwell.

HOPLEY'S FLY-WATER

An Infallible Method of Killing Flies.
These pests, which carry disease,
are instantly eradicated by the use of
this old established mixture.

POISON. NOT TO BE TAKEN OR USED
NEAR CHILDREN OR ANIMALS

Then followed a lot of directions for use in type Cromwell couldn't read without his glasses.

'It was hidden in an old trunk of Miss Honoria's, under a lot of dresses. Mrs Minshull found it.'

Cromwell could imagine these three people, embittered by the treatment received from the Blows and the death of their last friend in the family, turning the house upside down in their curiosity and vindictive researches.

'And she took a dose... But how much did she know to take...?'

Cromwell looked at the label. Children or...animals!

'Wait a minute. The cat!'

The three retainers were flabbergasted. They looked at Cromwell in awe and admiration.

'How did you know?'

'The man at the Salvation Army told us. Miss Penelope said the cat was ill just before Miss Honoria took bad.'

They all looked annoyed then. What did the Salvation Army want interfering in their business? It wasn't right!

'That was it. Simon, the cat...he's somewhere about now, was Miss Honoria's. She fed him. She gave him some rice pudding the day he was ill. He was terribly poorly and nearly died. But we gave him warm milk and brandy and he took sick and got it all up. He was soon himself again...'

'Did you see Miss Honoria actually feed him that day?'

'No. None of us did, but she always made a habit of it. He was hers and she was very jealous and particular about him.'

'But somebody might have doped the rice pudding she gave him.'

'But who but her had the poison? Answer me that.'

Mrs Minshull was getting hot on the trail again.

'It does look like it...'

Cromwell rose, almost too full of tea and cake to walk,

brushed the crumbs from his trousers, carefully placed his cup and plate on the table, and thanked them for their help.

'That's all right, sir. We want justice doing to Miss Penelope. She was good to us,' said Jelley. 'Call again, any time, and ask as many questions as you like.'

Having made sure there were no signs of the family, they all saw Cromwell to the door and parted with many expressions of approval and friendship. The sergeant crossed to his hotel, where he had arranged to meet Littlejohn over dinner. He was a bit dazed from a surfeit of information and victuals. If what the staff said was true, the case was solved. But was it? It sounded easy in theory, but proof was another matter. Suppose there were somebody behind the reputed half-wit, Miss Honoria, someone using her as a catspaw for his or her own ends. It would be easy. Penelope had arrived at Scotland Yard in Littlejohn's absence — and all the world knew he was absent, because the papers were full of the murder trial and Littlejohn's evidence in the case. She'd been sent knowing she couldn't get at him. If she hadn't mentioned Mr Claplady's name, maybe Littlejohn wouldn't have taken an interest, and they'd have got her out of the way long enough for the box to be fixed in her absence... Even then...

'Tea, sir?' said a waiter.

Cromwell, full to the brim with tea and cake, winced. Littlejohn found him sleeping it off in a chair in the lounge when he returned an hour later.

11

HE WOULDN'T STOP TALKING

Paston was decidedly uncomfortable. Superintendent Hempseed was still laid-up with his lumbago the Chief Constable was due to return in a day or two, the police had offended and been turned out by the Blows and were carrying on their investigations by back-stairs methods. It gave him the jitters. If Littlejohn didn't succeed in the case, Inspector Paston would be broken good and proper, and he already had, in the still hours of the night, visions of himself again pounding the beat or, worse still, sacked.

So when Littlejohn suggested taking a walk and interviewing Cuthbert Broome, ex-chief cashier of Blows' Bank and father of Lenore Blow, Paston grew hot under the collar.

'But he'll tell Lenore, sure as eggs...and then the fat'll be in the fire. She'll pass on the good news to her husband and he'll be over here like a shot...'

'We'll have to risk that. Things are beginning to get more concentrated and easier to understand. We've got a motive now and Broome's the only one who can tell us where the funds which old Blow salted away have been placed... If anyone complains, say I did it all. Say I interfered and you couldn't get rid of me. Say anything, but let's get ahead. We're not far from the winning-post if I'm any judge.'

'You think so?'

'I do. The motive is the Blow treasure controlled by Miss Penelope. Somebody's either had it or is after it. We've to find out where it is and how much there is left of it. The existence of the hidden hoard was supposed to be a secret known only to one or two trusted people. We've to find out who betrayed confidences and to whom. We also know that Honoria is subject to crazy fits and thanks to Cromwell's hobnobbing with the Blows' staff, we learn that they think Miss Honoria killed her sister. They think she administered the poison herself to herself to get Miss Penelope away to London and leave the field clear for operations on the box... That seems a bit fantastic to me... All the same, we've got to get on quickly. The right direction is Broome. I take it I have your concurrence, Paston?'

'Yes... I suppose that's the best. Carry on, sir...'

Littlejohn thanked him and Cromwell grunted approval. The sergeant was returning to London to interview Mrs Buckley, who kept the boarding house near Egton Square. Maybe she could throw some light on Miss Penelope's last journey and her last days.

Cuthbert Broome lived in the house he'd occupied for more than fifty years. It was an old Georgian place in a side street ten minutes from the main square. Time had taken the tide of residential life away into the country suburbs, but Orchard House, Haxton Street, remained. The orchard and gardens had been sold at profitable prices and were now covered by a chemist's shop, a fish and chip restaurant, and a tobacconist's, followed by a cheap tailor's, and a grocer's, who had been apparently trying to build a Tower of Babel of tins of whale meat, coarse fish and soup in his window. Orchard House towered above the modern tile and tin shop fronts like an indignant old dowager. Captain Broome hadn't moved out of town with the rest. He couldn't, in the first place, afford the expense and, besides, what was the use? His heart wouldn't stand up to exercises of a country nature, his old cronies were all dead, and he was such an old bore that new friends fled from him. He might just as well stay indoors... He'd been a Captain in the Volunteers as long ago as that — and retained the title. He was that sort.

Littlejohn rang the doorbell and was admitted by the housekeeper, a small, stout, masterful woman who looked like Queen Victoria, even down to the perpetual mourning which she had worn since the death of her husband, a former messenger at Blows' Bank, thirty years ago. Lenore paid for the housekeeper; her father couldn't afford it. He had been unlucky in retiring from the bank before it was taken over by a large, joint-stock undertaking with a proper and generous pension fund. In the old days, Captain Broome had guarded the cash of Blows' Bank through thick and thin, with his life. The partners had treated him like a domestic servant until Ralph grew old enough to notice the beauty of his daughter, Lenore. Then it had been a bit better. But a threatened run on the bank many years ago had given Broome a heart attack and necessitated retirement. The gratitude of his employers for a lifetime's faithful service as monetary watchdog had been expressed in the form of an annuity yielding two hundred and fifty pounds per annum. It would have been much less had the bankers not persuaded the insurance people that Broome was as good as dead already. He had cheated them.

Littlejohn was ushered in Mr Broome's private den by the housekeeper. The Captain, he had learned, was eighty or more, but the man who stood on the hearthrug awaiting him didn't look that age. He was tall and spare, with a stoop and a head of snow-white, carefully groomed hair. He wore tweeds and was smoking a curved pipe. He bore a white military moustache, long and carefully trimmed and curling upwards at the ends, his complexion was ruddy, more from blood pressure than the out of doors, and his linen was spotless. Only the mottled veins of his cheeks and his neat shrivelled hands revealed his age and physical condition. He was holding Littlejohn's card between finger and thumb. Behind him over the mantelpiece hung the head of an enormous deer. Captain Broome said he had shot it in the highlands, but nobody knew whether he was joking or not.

'Good afternoon, Captain Broome...'

They'd told Littlejohn he would be starting off on the right foot if he used the title.

'Afternoon, sir. To what do I owe this honour...if honour it is?'

He looked curious and uneasy.

'Sit down...'

The room was basically Victorian with the addition of odds and ends which an old campaigner might accumulate in his travels following the flag. Mrs Broome's father had been a Major, a regular, and was thought to be well-off during his lifetime. When he died, however, he left a lot of debts and a collection of junk gathered from the Sudan, South Africa, Egypt, Ashanti and India. On the wall hung the Major's photograph, in antique glengarry cap and heavy moustache, and all around were his treasures. Spears, ivory temples, Chinese vases, ebony chairs and chests, native leatherwork, Indian brassware, and a large buffet inlaid in gold, the present of the King of Ashanti who had been the Major's personal friend. Captain Broome retained them all around him in the hope that visitors would think he had garnered them in his own campaigns, although he'd never been out of the country himself. In cold weather he suffered from senile amnesia, and then declared confidently that they were actually presents from the grateful recipients of his military services.

'What can I do for you, sah?'

As time went on the Captain became more and more the old campaigner and less and less the ex-cashier.

'I'm here investigating the death of the late Miss Blow. You were a friend of the family, I hear, and particularly of the late William Blow and Miss Penelope.'

That did it! His daughter, who was very fond of him because he still symbolised her happy childhood and was all that was left of her former peace, had already told him about the re-opening of the case and her husband's reaction to it. Lenore had related it all with the bitter humour she employed when speaking of her husband. She had married him for her father's sake and rued the day ever since. Captain Broome was on his guard when Little-john's card had been brought in by Queen Victoria. But now... Well... A friend of the Blows, who in the old days had made his knees knock by their very presence and who, even in taking Lenore in the bosom of their family, had let it be known that he didn't share the privilege and needn't think he did... Well...

'Oh, yes. Great friend of 'em... Colleague of old William for best part of me life. Official of the bank when wasn' soidierin'. Want to know somethin' about 'em...? If you do, just say so... Whisky and soda? Not supposed to take it maself... Heart, cherknow. Two tots and three pipes are all the doctor lets me have. Eh?'

He looked so eager for a drink himself that Littlejohn gave him the excuse. Lenore paid for the whisky, too.

The Captain served the drinks and helped himself.

'Now, sir...'

'You were, I believe, Chief Cashier of Blows' Bank, sir, when the late William Blow went slightly off his head and had to be confined to his room...'

'Brumph... No, I was retired then, sah, but still in the confidence of the bank. People said he got a touch of religion. I say poppycock, sah...poppy cock... Been drinkin' too much. Alcoholism... The bottle, sah...'

'I see. In any case, he was too mentally unstable to make a new will when he became convinced he ought to do so...'

The Captain rose to his feet.

'Who's bin talkin' too fast? That was a strictly private affah, known only to a trusted few...a trusted few...'

'All the same, we have ways of finding these things out, sir. He was mentally incapable of making a new will and knew it. He wished to put right certain wrongs in such a document. So he made a present of a nest egg he'd laid aside for a rainy day to Miss Penelope, in trust for herself and her sisters...'

'One moment, sir. Let us be clear on one point. If you are attemptin' to involve me in such transactions, I acted strictly in my capacitah as a retired but still trusted servant of the bank. Let that be clear from the outset...'

'Of course. That is understood. You were in the confidence of Mr William Blow at the time. In fact, his most trusted man...'

'Yes. And bankin' was bankin' in my days, sir, let me tell you. Sovereigns... Gold... Not dirty bits of paper printed by the damn' government... Gold, sah. And Blows' was Blows', too. On the spot...not somewhere in an office in London with Nesbury just a name on a map. Blows' were Nesbury and Nesbury was Blows'. If Blows' didn't like you, sir, you went bust... Those were the days, sir...'

'Were they, sir?'

'Yes. Do you doubt it, sir?'

They were sirring one another like old boots and it looked like developing into an argument. Captain Broome had the reputation for bearing two grudges about which he grew very talkative and quarrelsome. Banking wasn't what it was, and modern mechanised warfare wasn't warfare at all — it was an industry.

'To get back to our point, sir... Mr William trusted you to the extent of asking you to cooperate in his scheme for putting right the wrong he'd done to his daughters in his will. He got you to take bonds valued at £30,000 from his private strong box in the bank's vault and sell them.'

Captain Broome turned a sickly purple colour and looked ready to have a stroke.

'Don't be annoyed, Captain Broome. The past is dead and done with. I'm not an Inland Revenue investigator. I'm on the case of Miss Penelope's death and that only...'

'I'm glad to hear it, Inspector, for I see you're aware of the full facts. Yes, sir, I did take the bonds and sell 'em at my old chief's request. I'd do it again, sir... I'm proud of my service with Blows' Bank, though I can't say I find the present institution inspirin'. Too inhuman... No warm blood in it... Men just numbers... Women about the place, too... Can't bear women messin' about in commerce and bankin', any more than I can bear 'em in the army. Why, in my day...'

'You sold the bonds, sir, and banked the money in a secret account?'

'I did, at the old chief's request. Nothin' to do with me that death duties weren't paid on the proceeds. You see that, don't you? I was merely actin' on instructions.'

'Of course.'

'Whatever I tell you, Inspector, is in the strictest confidence. I know you'll get it one way if I don't give it to you another. I'm an old man, sir, though you wouldn't think me eighty, would you? All I ask is your discretion, Inspector...and, most of all, that my little gel won't suffer... My gel's Mrs Ralph Blow, you know.'

'Yes, I know that, sir.'

The old man brooded and looked in the fire.

'Between you and me, Inspector...wish I'd died when I had the heart attack that finished me off in the bank. Wouldn't have been a burden then to my little gel. When Ralph Blow started courtin' her, I thought it was a godsend. Got her comfortably settled and she needn't work anymore for that blasted Liberal politician... She was his secretary, Inspector, and to an old Tory like meself, that was wormwood and gall, sir... Still, one has to live... And I was a bit dependent on her... Only got my pension,... Turned out she was in love with another chap. Turned him down for Blow and he went off and got killed in the war... Troubles me a lot, sir, my little gel's marriage... Misfired sadly... But why am I talkin' like this to you, a stranger...? Forgive an old man, sir, who hasn't anybody to talk with... Is that all?'

Captain Broome rose, a rather ridiculous figure among all his fake trophies and with his spurious campaigning style, but very human and pathetic when you scratched the surface and saw what was going on underneath the veneer.

'Is that all...?'

'Could you tell me the bank where you deposited the funds, Captain Broome?'

Broome put his tired hand to his forehead in confusion.

'Afraid I can't, sir, but I'll look it up at once. Memory's givin' out. Turned eighty... Wouldn't think it, would you? Eighty-two in May... What were you asking...?'

'The bank...'

'Oh, yes...the bank. I kept the papers just in case...well...you know, might have been accused of takin' a bit for myself, cher-know, Mr William being a bit beside himself and Miss Penelope not knowin' much of finance. Kept details and receipts as proof, if needed. But they were never needed. Penelope was a good gel... Trusted me and treated me like one of themselves. Often called to ask after me. Only one who did...'

The old gentleman turned to a heavy carved oak bureau, made of sandalwood and brought by his father-in-law from Suez. He opened the top and started to rummage among its neat contents with trembling, impatient fingers. Littlejohn looked around the stuffy room with its great fire and antique-shop air. There were campaigning pictures on the walls, photographs of

the late Major, and a few of Mr Broome himself in camp with
fellow officers, dressed in numerous uniforms, including sun-
helmets, forage caps, and even bearskin busbies. Over the fireplace, at eye level, hung two delicate miniatures on ivory. One
was of Lenore herself; the other of one who must have been her
mother. Dark, handsome, with a proud look and a haughty
nose, Littlejohn saw in a flash whence came Lenore's aristo-
cratic bearing and almost spectacular beauty. The Captain,
aware of the Inspector's silence, turned.

'Lookin' at my little gel's picture. I'm proud of her, sir. Might
have done better for her, but... Well, she's always been a
beauty... Like her mother, sir. Fine woman, her mother. Died
twenty years ago. Never married again... Couldn't find her
equal. Honourable Alice Greelam, she was... Met her payin' in
for her father at the bank. Love match. Not good enough for her
by half, but she was a good wife. Tried to keep up with her...
Failed... Damn...damn...can't find those papers... You have a
try, Inspector...'

The old man was in tears. Frustration at his inability to find
what he wanted, self-pity at his loneliness, and grief at the loss
of past happiness...

'You married?'

'Yes, sir.'

'Happy?'

'Extremely...'

'Look after her, then. My own fault I lost mine. Took her
boatin'. Rowin' boat on Windermere. Storm blew up. Boat
capsized. I couldn't swim... They hooked me out... If I'd learned
to swim instead of shootin' and showin' off in uniforms...
Well... What are you waitin' for...? Search the papers there.
You'll find what you want.'

Littlejohn was in a black mood. His work often led him into
stark tragedy, but it was the irony here that seemed to stab him
to the quick. Hastily he turned over the bundles of papers and

envelopes. They must have been accumulated over all the years old Broome could write. The stamps on some of the envelopes would have made a philatelist's mouth water.

Birth, marriage, and death certificates; legal documents; private letters; what looked like love-letters, as well, tied up with pink tape; a bundle of correspondence addressed to the Captain and his wife in a girlish hand, which might have been Lenore's news from school. They bore Swiss stamps and the Lausanne postmark. Finally, a small envelope marked 'William Blow — Contract Notes, etc, Sale of Bonds'. That was it. Little-john passed the packet to Captain Broome, who was pouring out two more whiskies.

'You'll join me, Inspector? It's one too many for me. But I need one... Somethin' about you makes a man talk... Never spoke about my affairs to a soul for years... Not since my son left us...'

'You have a son, then, sir?'

'Yes. In Australia. Sheep-farmin'. Doin' nicely. Won't come back here. Never see him again...'

'Why?'

'Ahem... Told you so much of my private affairs. May as well know the rest... I can trust you. My boy was in Blows' Bank. Junior cashier. Wrong in his cash. Turned out he'd been helpin' himself. I'd retired then. Ralph said if Lenore would marry him, he'd fix it...no prosecution, understand? Only a hundred pounds or so, but they threatened to call in the police. After all my years with them. Offered to put it right meself, but Ralph had it just as he wanted. Lenore...'

'I see. I'm sorry. Why didn't you go out to him if he's "doing well?"'

'I can't leave Lenore to the mercies of the Blows, sir. I'd have gone otherwise... Too late now... Besides, Lenore's still unhappy.'

The old man fumbled vaguely with the papers, screwing a

monocle in his eye, an instinctive piece of further affectation, and turning over the contents of the packet one by one...

'Take 'em...'

Littlejohn sorted out the stockbroker's contract note for the sale of the bonds and then beneath it turned up the advice of receipt of the funds, £30,433 5s 6d for credit of the account of Miss Penelope Blow. Doubleday, Ward & Co, Bankers, St. Paul's Churchyard. Littlejohn made a note of it.

'So the account is still likely to be there, Captain Broome?'

'Doubleday's was a private bank, since taken over by one of the big ones. You'll have to find out. But the money should still be there. What would Penelope do with it? She was a scared, timid little woman. No spirit, like my gel. You got all you need, now?'

'Yes, sir. Thank you very much. And thank you for your great confidence and kindness in this matter and others as well...'

'Nice to meet you, Inspector. What did you say it was all about? Penelope's death? But she had an accident... Why should Scotland Yard be here? There surely was no crime in that...'

'No, sir, not in an accident. But we think maybe it wasn't an accident but a well-planned murder.'

'Murder. Good gad, sir! But who...? It's that damned Honoria! Lenore told me about her. Always after Penelope's money to give to that wastrel Harold... Never was any good, Harold. Expelled from school for stealin' some exam. papers, I think it was. Sponged on the family. Got 'em to buy him a solicitor's practice to make believe he was workin' but sits there with his feet on the desk half the time. Lived on his aunt, Honoria, who thinks him a little tin god! Honoria's a bit weak in her wits. He's put her up to it. Lenore told me Honoria'd been takin' small doses of poison and blamin' Penelope so they'd say Penelope was losing her wits and put her away. Then Honoria would get control of her sister's affairs. You ought to look into Honoria, sir... To think I let my little gel into such a family. God forgive and help me...'

'Leave it to me, sir. I'll straighten it out. But I want to ask you a favour...a difficult one, I'm afraid...'

'Granted before asked, Inspector.'

'Please don't tell Miss Lenore, I mean, Mrs Blow, I've been here, or that you've told me anything. Ask your housekeeper to keep it quiet, too...'

'She won't say anythin'. Job to get her to answer a civil question let alone talk about my affairs. I'll see to it, Inspector. Though I generally tell Lenore... She comes here to me when she can't stand any more of that cad, Ralph...'

'Cad?'

'Yes, sir. Cad. Nothin' about other women or such like. But a bully and a cad, all the same. Hit my little gel once... Told him if he did it again, I'd get out my old service pistol and shoot him like a dog. Mean it, too. Hang the consequences... A mean little cad... Cruel, jealous, suspicious...all the vices of the bounder that he is... Wish I was younger... Horsewhip...'

'And Lenore puts up with it?'

'Yes. Don't know what she'll do now. Penelope was good to her. Tried to make up for Ralph's bein' a cad...'

The word seemed to please the old man. He repeated it over and over again, like somebody playing a well-loved gramophone record.

'I must tell you, sir, that we've tried to get in the Blow household to ask a question or two about Miss Penelope's death. Mr Ralph showed us the door. We can't make any headway in that direction. Could you persuade your daughter to call here and answer some questions without the family knowing? And, by the way, did you ever tell her about the secret funds in Miss Penelope's name?'

'Daresay. But I'd have to tell her then that you'd been here.

You asked me not to... And I did tell Lenore about Penelope's money. I told my gel everythin'.'

'Maybe she wouldn't find much wrong in keeping the matter of meeting me from her husband?'

'Certainly not, if I tell her not to speak of it to him.'

'Very well, sir. Tell her and ask her if she's willing to talk to me. If you care to ring me up at the police station, I'll call at your convenience.'

'Very good, Inspector. She'll be here this evening, no doubt. You can come then if she turns up. I'll be delighted to see you again. You've done me a lot of good. I feel younger by years, knowin' somebody's watchin' over my gel. You will keep an eye on her, won't you, Inspector?'

'I'll do my best, sir.'

And with that, they bade each other goodbye and parted, and Littlejohn went on his way wondering how deeply the old man's little gel was mixed up in the Blow tragedy. He hoped for the best.

SELECT APARTMENTS

C romwell turned in at Egton Mews and sought out Mrs Buckley's house. He regarded the fly-blown card, 'Select Apartments', with distaste, sniffed at the smaller one beneath it, 'Vacancies', and then knocked. Footsteps sounded on the oilcloth of the passage and Mrs Buckley opened the door. The hawk eyes and insolent expression travelled from Cromwell's head to his feet. She noted that he had no luggage and crossed her hands over her bosom.

'Yes?'

'Mrs Buckley?'

'Yes.'

'May I come in, please. Police.'

That was enough. Mrs Buckley looked up and down the mews and hastily admitted the sergeant before anyone else discovered who he was. She had only just put down the daily paper. Spies, Communists, Gangsters, Murderers... One had to be careful who one took in these days. Had she...?

Cromwell followed her down the dark passage, the doors of which were closed as though hiding men in flight or bent on secret things. All the lower rooms were let, and Mrs Buckley took Cromwell to her kitchen at the end of the lobby. There, behind a protective screen, he found a large table covered with a baize cloth, an ancient leather settee, its dilapidations hidden by an old travelling rug, an armchair and seven small chairs drawn up like victims of a firing squad against the wall waiting for the bed-and-breakfast lodgers next morning. Framed pictures from Christmas almanacs on the walls, a small cooking range with a fire burning, a gas stove holding a kettle on the boil and a plant stand crowned with a large aspidistra. This completed the inventory. The window was fastened and looked out on a sheet of whitewashed wall. The other side of the wall must have given on a garden, for all the time Cromwell was there someone was working a motor mower, the whine of which rose and fell as it approached and receded.

'Yes?'

The asperity had gone from Mrs Buckley's voice. She was trying to be pleasant, almost fawning. Her lips drew back in a travesty of a smile, revealing two regular rows of white false teeth.

'I've called to ask if you know anything of Miss Penelope Blow?'

Mrs Buckley was relieved. Her stays creaked from relaxation and her hands fell to her sides as the tension was released.

'Yes... I once worked for the Blows. Years ago... When I was young.'

Cromwell found it difficult to imagine Mrs Buckley as being young. She looked the sort who had endured the same for ever and ever, in darkened rooms, suspiciously watching her lodgers, prying into their affairs when they were out, almost hating them because she depended on them.

'...Miss Penelope and Miss Honoria stayed here when they came to town. They didn't like big hotels. They were shy ladies, always. I made them comfortable and was always glad to accommodate them in my 'umble home.'

The fire was scorching, the air stuffy and Mrs Buckley appalling. Cromwell wanted to get it over and be off. One almost expected the street door to bang, footsteps to sound along the passage, and Uriah Heep to fling open the door, kiss Mrs Buckley and say their 'ouie was very 'umble...

'Miss Penelope stayed here with you a few days before her death?'

'Yes. Poor Miss Penelope! To think...just to think of it! When I kissed her goodbye as she went, I was lookin' on her for the last time in life. We never know when it's goin' to be our turn, do we, sir? We never know when the 'and of the Lord will fall upon us and call us 'ome...'

'No. What made Miss Penelope come to London this time, Mrs Buckley?'

'Do sit you down, sir. I'll tell you all about it.'

Mrs Buckley swept one of the victims of the firing party from the wall, dusted the seat with her apron and extended it to Cromwell, who gingerly sat down on it. The back legs shook with age as they received his weight.

'As I was sayin'... Such a nice, Christian lady, Miss Penelope. One as could ill be spared, sir. And she always stayed with her old Buckley, as she used ter call me. She was a good friend. The Lord hath given, the Lord hath took away...'

Mrs Buckley worshipped with an obscure sect in Chelsea and was proud of her religious education.

'Why did she come to town at all?'

'Oh, yes. You was askin' that... Well, she confided in me a lot. Bein' an old servant and one of the fambly, as you might say... She came to see a gentleman at Scotland Yard.'

'Did she say what about?'

'No. That was the queer part of it. She didn't seem to know quite herself. Said the Reverend Claplady — 'e used to be a minister in Nesbury, sweet on her he used to be...well, she said the Reverend had told her to call and see some friend of his there. I forgot the name of the friend... Maybe, you can tell me...'

'She didn't say what about?'

'I just told you, No. She came here all a-flutter and looking that scared. I was properly sorry for her. Tried me best to make her comfortable. She went out every day she was here and came back in such a state. I gathered the man at Scotland Yard wasn't in. Now, if she was just makin' a friendly call, why get in such a stew? I couldn' make 'ead nor tail of it. Why come at all, if it was just friendly? I think she was goin' queer. I told Mr 'Arold that.'

'You saw Mr Harold then?'

'Yes. He came to take her 'ome. At once, he said, and made her pack and off with 'im right away.'

'How did he know where to find her?'

'I let the fambly know. I was gettin' anxious about her. She was actin' that queer, like.'

'Are you on the phone, then?'

'Yes. Not that I use it much. But Dr Fallows...not a real doctor, but they call 'im that...uses it a lot. 'E's a massure, goes round to the big houses hereabouts massaging patients for rheumatics and such like. 'E must 'ave a telephone for his appointments. I telephoned the fambly to say she was 'ere. They was very relieved, I can tell you, sir. Mr 'Arold come down and took her 'ome right away. Poor lamb.'

'Did she ring up to book her room?'

'It was Miss Honoria, I think, rang up. Said she was in bed ill, but they had a telephone at the bedside.'

'Miss Honoria, eh?'

'Yes. Funny.'

'Very.'

'Can you tell me the exact dates Miss Penelope was here?'

'I've got them in my book. I'll get it.'

Mrs Buckley hurried off upstairs where she apparently kept her private papers. Cromwell could hear her tramping across a room overhead. He rose and looked out of the window, through the long lace curtain which obscured it. A blank, whitewashed wall, a coal shed, some large plant-pots containing shrivelled brown plants, and beyond, the motor mower whizzing away. It must have been a large lawn...

Suddenly, Cromwell had the vague, unaccountable feeling that he was being watched and, at once, he knew where from. Overlooking the yard and at right angles to the one where he stood, was another window, the one of the next room along the passage. This window, too, was covered in curtain-net to obscure the room behind. He could see a white face peering through the lace in his direction, but the material intervening in his own and the other window made it quite impossible to distinguish the outline. The face vanished as he tried to make it out.

'The inquisitive lodger,' thought Cromwell and in imagination, he could see all the rooms of the house, containing lodgers with nothing to do but spy on Mrs Buckley, as she did on them, and on her visitors.

The woman was back. She wasn't quite comfortable, after all. Her smile was too overdone.

"'Ere we are. March 21st to 24th was the time poor Miss Penelope was here. Her last days on earth, wasn't they?'

Cromwell was very interested in those days. They were exactly the ones when Littlejohn was absent from the Yard. The newspapers had announced that by making prominent his attendance at the court at Lewes. Every day, there was something about him. Easy to guess he'd not be in London but tied down as a major witness in a murder trial. Then, when the papers announced the summing-up and it might be as good as certain that Littlejohn wouldn't be needed again, someone calls and takes Miss Penelope home.

'You rang up Mr Harold and told him she was here?'

'Yes.'

'But surely, hadn't Miss Honoria told him?'

'I don't know, sir. The funny thing about it is that Miss Honoria answered the phone when I rang. She must have told Mr 'Arold, who came right away.'

'Was he angry?'

'No, sir. Just firm. She didn't seem responsible or able to make up her mind.'

'Did she tell you anything that happened when she called at Scotland Yard?'

'No. Except that the gentleman wasn't in and she'd 'ave to call again. I said, why didn't you ask for somebody else, then? I said that. But she was that timid, sir. Oh, I couldn't do that. I don't know anybody else and I couldn't tell anybody else what I want to tell 'im. He's Mr Claplady's friend, you see, she sez. She was that way, poor lamb. Timid.'

Across the yard, the curtains were moving in the window again.

'By the way, Mrs Buckley, who's your lodger in the room next door? He or she, whoever they might be, seems very interested in what's going on here...'

Mrs Buckley started, and a look of horror crossed her face. Then, she pulled herself together.

''Ow dare he! How dare he! I'll jest tell 'im where he gets off. See if I don't. I'll...'

She was on her feet and flounced out before Cromwell could stop her. She hurried down the corridor to the door of the room and he could hear her slam it. No voices were raised. She must have almost been whispering. She was away quite a time and returned looking red and irritable.

'We won't be bothered agen, sir. I've told 'im to pack up and be off. We want none of 'is sort round 'ere. Spying. You got to be careful these days who you take in. You never know, do you?'

'Miss Blow was out when Harold arrived to take her back?'

'Yes. He waited about two hours. Mad 'e was, too. Said he'd better things to do than chase his aunt all over the country.'

'What did he say when he arrived?'

'Oh, he jest asked me where she was and what she'd been doin'. I told 'im, she'd been tryin' to see a friend at Scotland Yard.'

'What did he say then?'

'Seemed struck all of a 'eap, like. Said what did she want there? I said I knew about as much as 'e did, that was why I thought it best to let the fambly know. He thanked me and said she was a bit queer at times and I'd 'ave to overlook it and say nothin' about it. I got to tell you, sir, though, you bein' from the police. Is there somethin' funny about the death?'

'It was sudden and violent, as you no doubt know, Mrs Buckley. We wish to be quite sure that it was accidental.'

'But I thought… It said in the papers…'

'You don't want to believe all you read in the papers, Mrs Buckley.'

Mrs Buckley wished she didn't believe it all! All these spies and Communists and murderers got on her nerves. And now Miss Penelope!

The motor mower had stopped, and you could hear the gardener tinkering with it. He sounded to be hitting it with a hammer.

'Well, Mrs Buckley, I guess that's all. Thank you for what you've told me.'

'A pleasure, sir, I'm sure, to help the police. Though why you should think anybody would do violence to Miss Penelope…'

'Who said anyone would do violence…?'

Mrs Buckley started again, and her colour rose.

'Well, you did say you wasn't satisfied…'

'I didn't; all I said was…'

Cromwell picked up his hat as he talked, passed round the screen, the door behind which was open, and slowly made his way down the passage. He halted at the door of the room behind which the mysterious occupant was silent.

'...I only said, we had to be satisfied that there'd been no violence. A lot of difference, isn't there?'

'I guess there is...'

They stood for a minute without speaking. Not a sound in the house, which seemed to be watching every move none the less. Then, behind the door at Cromwell's back, the creak of a shoe.

Cromwell seized the knob and flung open the door.

Mrs Buckley gasped sharply.

'You can't...'

Standing inside the room, glaring with guilt, was Harold Blow! He recovered his poise at once, but beads of sweat sprang on his bulging forehead.

'What the hell do you mean by this? This is a private room.'

'Good morning, Mr Blow. Sorry I startled you, but I'm as interested in you as you are in me.'

'I'll make you sit up for this, you nosy cop! Calling here pestering Mrs Buckley. And by what right, may I ask? What are you after here?'

'You know as well as I do, sir; so why ask?'

'I know that the interference of Scotland Yard in a matter already investigated and closed by the Nesbury police is quite unwarranted and that someone will be made to sit up about it when it is reported to the proper quarter.'

'That remains to be seen, sir, and is a matter I can't argue about...'

Cromwell was beginning to marvel inwardly at his own eloquence and boldness. It wasn't often he was called upon to justify his duties, and he flattered himself he wasn't doing so bad. He'd have a tale to tell his missus when all this was over. He bade Mrs Buckley and Harold Blow good day and left without the greeting being returned. He wondered what they'd have to say to one another when his back was turned.

As Cromwell made his way along the mews to the kind of tunnel which gave access to the main street, he saw on his right a small wrought iron gate of beautiful design which gave on to the garden in which all the noisy mowing had been going on during his talk with Mrs Buckley.

'Might as well take a squint,' he said to himself, for the hidden gems of London were very dear to him, as a Londoner himself, and he never failed to seek them out when he could. He found the gate unlocked and walked in.

The scene truly gave the sergeant a surprise. He whistled with pleasure. On three sides were high walls like the one which shut out Mrs Buckley from this tiny paradise. The fourth side held a small house, with a forecourt of crazy paving and a lawn as flat and green as a piece of velvet. The front of the house had been treated with white cement, its steel casement windows were painted green, and a marvellous wrought iron screen closed a porch beyond which stood a solid oak door.

Sheltered by the surrounding tall buildings, from wind and weather, the lawn, in the middle of which stood another wrought iron masterpiece of a well-head, was sprouting with spring and the gardener was giving it its first cutting, gently and carefully with respect for the young shoots. He was an old man, who might, in better times, have been a coachman. His appearance, at any rate, spoke of horses and days when the mews outside harboured fine coaches and equally fine animals to draw them.

'Mornin', he said to Cromwell in a drawling voice which spoke of Western places far enough away from London. 'Takin' a peek around?'

'Yes,' said Cromwell, edging up to the man. 'This is a wonder. I never knew...'

'You never know... That's the pleasure of bein' about

London. You never knows what you'll be findin' next. Pretty, ain't it?'

They stood quiet for a while enjoying it. Cromwell offered his new friend a cigarette. The man looked a countryman still. Grizzled hair, sideboards and a chubby red face.

'You stayin' in these parts?' asked the man at length.

'No, just visiting. Made a call on Mrs Buckley. Business.'

'Oh, that one. Ain't got much use for 'er. Proper tartar, she is. Wouldn't like to be one of her lodgers. Sleepin' under that roof don't appeal to me.'

'Why? She doesn't seem a bad sort.'

'Hard as nails. They say she does a kind o' money lendin' with her rooms. If you can't pay one week, your rent goes up. Be that as it may, I don't like the look of her.'

'Bit hard-boiled, eh? Oily smile.'

'Yes. But neither smile nor oil to them as she gets agen. Some of the neighbours could tell you a thing or two. I don't know much about that, but I do see her actin' suspicious-like now and then. Maybe, she does a bit o' the old black market now and agen for customers as can pay extry for bacon and the like for their breakfasts. An' I did see her follerin'...shadowin', I believes they call it on the pictures, a poor old body who seemed to be stayin' with her a few weeks ago...'

Cromwell pricked up his ears. He hadn't seen Miss Blow, but from talk in Nesbury perhaps he could manage a passable description.

'What was her lodger like?'

'Oh, little oldish lady...'

'Dressed in black and a bit scared looking...?'

'That's right. How did you know?'

'The woman died later and I'm making some inquiries. That's why I was there at Mrs Buckley's. I'm from the police.'

'I knew that. No mistakin' you once one gets to know you.

Now, my lad's in the Devonshire Constabulary. Only a constable as yet, but one day he'll be more than that.'

'I hope so. Maybe, you can help me, then.'

'Oi, maybe. All I can say is I saw this little body comin' out of old Buckley's just as I was goin' into the Unicorn at the end there for a drink. Thirsty work, gardenin'. I went in and stood at the counter with my half-pint, lookin' over the screen in the window. No sooner had the little lady got goin' along the street, than out comes Mrs Buckley, dressed up, and follers her. I knew she was a-follerin' of her on account the way she behaved. Once, when the little un turned round, Buckley stops and pretended to be lookin' in an art shop. She's no interest in art, that 'un. She was follerin' 'er. Next day, the same. Soon as I got me half-pint, one passes and then the other. What old Buckley was up to I can't say, but it was no good I'll warrant.'

'I'll bet it wasn't...'

'And a few days later, I was knocking off my work and leavin' by that gate, when I sees a cab drawn up and the little un gettin' in it. With her was a tall, fierce-lookin' chap, and he was mad at her, too. Nearly threw her in the cab and off they druv. But it was the look on Buckley's face as I see most. Cruel and evil, that's what it was. Smilin' at the gent and noddin' at him as if she was approvin' what he done. Ar, a bad un is that there Mrs Buckley...'

Cromwell had heard enough, and they went on to talk of gardens and the West country, and he told his new friend that he married a girl from Truro, which sealed their friendship for good. Long after the case was closed, Cromwell visited the mews and spent an hour when he could with Samuel Hawkins. At that time, however, they both thought that a call at the Unicorn, to seal their friendship and view the exact spot whence Sam had witnessed the 'shadderin'' of Penelope Blow, was the right thing to do.

13

DOUBLEDAY, WARD & CO

Cromwell jumped from a bus at St Paul's Churchyard and looked around for the place he was seeking. There it was, between two more imposing blocks of offices, a humbler-looking, stone-fronted building, seeming anxious to efface itself, with tall windows screened by tasteful wrought iron grilles. 'Central Bank, Limited, Doubleday, Ward & Co Branch,' said a brass plate on the right of the main entrance. On the left side another old brass plate, almost worn away by polishing, said simply, Doubleday, Ward & Co, Bankers. Established 1763.

Cromwell entered. It was like going to church. The banking-hall was lofty and austere. The cashiers were all dressed in morning coats and they and the clerks moved silently about as though barefooted or rubber shod. Now and then, someone coughed sedately, and it echoed solemnly round the building. There were four tellers, all of them grey and past middle-age, and they dealt with customers calmly and quietly, with no haste or fluster. Clients, in their turn, approached the counter reverently; like making offerings on an altar. From somewhere far away came the dim noise of machinery. The large banking company which had digested the old firm had insisted on mechanised bookkeeping, but this was properly muffled in remote regions. Here, in the public place, all was as it had been a century ago. You entered the foreign department by the next door down the street and did your commercial banking in the branch over the way. Doubledays' Branch was for private business, and the last surviving Mr Doubleday saw to it that it remained so.

The clerk who answered Cromwell's ring at the inquiries counter, took his card, looked at it and turned pale. Scotland Yard! His eye ran from one to another of the four very respectable tellers. Which one...?

'May I see the Manager, please?'

'The Manager?'

The clerk looked surprised. The Manager here was rather small fry. He ran the office and looked after the profits. Mr Doubleday was the big noise. Mr Doubleday, the Director, the man who hobnobbed with the lords of the City and kept locked within his breast the secrets of great families, unknown to even the closest business associates of millionaires, ducal guinea-pig directors, and members of the wealthy and impoverished aristocracy. The clerk produced a slip of paper. Cromwell eyed it, took out a pen and filled it in.

Mr Cromwell of Scotland Yard
To see Miss Penelope Blow.

When the clerk saw the name of Blow, he hastily scribbled 'Director' in the spot left bare by Cromwell, pulled himself together and sedately vanished into the interior.

He was back in a few minutes.

'This way...'

The clerk lifted a flap in the inquiry counter, led Cromwell through a maze of mahogany and down a dark passage. He tapped on a heavy door at the end of a long turkey-red carpet.

'Come,' said a fruity voice. They went.

'Detective Sergeant Cromwell, sir,' said the clerk and vanished.

Cromwell took a second or two to recover his composure. It was the room which upset him. He didn't know such places existed in the City, outside the films, of course. Red carpet again, with thick pile, on the floor; a great open fireplace with logs burning in it; fine, large portraits of dead and gone Doubledays and Wards looking down from the dark panelled walls; St Paul's itself towering through the leaded panes of a fine, large window; and, sitting at a large period desk which must have cost a fortune, Mr Doubleday himself. He must have been around seventy, but the retainers of the office still called him young Mr Doubleday or young Mr Richard. He had a pink complexion, silky-white untidy hair, and a fine brow. His blue eyes sparkled with a sense of fun. There were papers on his desk, but he was reading Wisden when Cromwell entered. He spent a lot of time at Lords and the Oval in summer and was sharpening his appetite for the cricket season to come.

He put down his vade-mecum and took off his shell-framed spectacles.

'And what can we do for Scotland Yard, Sergeant? Sit down.'

Cromwell seated himself gingerly on a genuine Chippendale and put his bowler on the floor beside him.

'It's a little matter about one of your customers, Miss Penelope Blow...'

'Ah! The late Miss Blow, eh? And what about her?'

'She kept an account with you, I believe, sir.'

'She did. Been a customer here for many years. Came of a good old bankin' family. But that, of course, you know, Sergeant.'

'Yes, sir. What I've come to ask may be a bit awkward, sir. I know that banks must respect their customers' confidences...'

Mr Doubleday smiled gently.

'You do?'

'Yes, sir. I know that as a rule, they can't divulge information about accounts without the protection of the courts...'

'Ah! Quite a man of the law, Sergeant.'

Cromwell, somehow, didn't feel nonplussed by the comments. He felt there was no sting in them. In fact, just the old man having a bit of fun to himself.

'Well...sir. I've been mixed up in a few such cases before. I found the banks a bit sticky...'

'And you think I won't be?'

'Well, sir, I hope not. But let me tell you what happened so far.'

Cromwell thereupon told Mr Doubleday of the case on which they were engaged in Nesbury. He told him of Miss Blow's death and their suspicions of foul play and of William Blow's religious conversion, and of his tucking away funds with Doubledays' banking-house in his daughter Penelope's name by way of recompense for the unfair will he had made.

Mr Doubleday listened courteously, saying nothing, playing with a jade paper knife.

'We were quite at a loss to think of a motive, sir. Who would want to kill such a harmless little body? And then, we found out about the large account at your bank. Thirty thousand pounds, I believe...'

'How did you find that, Sergeant?'

'She'd confided it in an old friend, sir, a parson she'd known all her life...'

'I see...'

Mr Doubleday rose. He was rather small and portly. Unlike his staff, he dressed comfortably. Well-cut, easy grey suit, cream shirt with soft collar attached and a silk tie slightly awry. He opened a Sheraton cabinet at his elbow.

'Sherry? I usually take a glass at this time...'

Cromwell felt it would be very rude to decline even if he

were on duty. Such a nice gentleman, Mr Doubleday. Old school... He accepted. He'd never tasted sherry like it before. He wondered where it came from.

'You wish for some particulars of the account, Sergeant?'

'Well... If you'd be so good, sir.'

'What kind of particulars, may I ask?'

'We know, sir, that the account was opened about 1937 or 1938. We know, too, that during the War, Miss Blow withdrew about £5,000 to help the local Salvation Army build a sort of canteen...'

'And then...?'

Cromwell felt a bit put-out. Littlejohn had asked him to call at the bank and find out what they knew about Miss Blow's finances from their angle. An ordinary commercial bank manager would have said Yes or No without much ado. But Mr Doubleday didn't seem that sort. He had a paternal way with him. It reminded Cromwell of his boyhood when he tried to persuade a shilling out of his father for a football match or the films. A real inquisition into the whys and wherefores...

Mr Doubleday looked at Cromwell with sparkling eyes. He seemed to see right into his mind and to be enjoying the mental sorting-out that was going on.

'You want me to tell you if there's been any jiggery-pokery going on in the account, that it?'

'That's it, sir...' Cromwell was relieved.

'But we don't have jiggery-pokery in our accounts...'

Mr Doubleday laughed outright this time. If only the police-man, sitting there with his hat by his side and sipping his sherry like a hen drinking, knew what he knew about some of the accounts on their books and what went with them! Jiggery-pokery! By God...! Mr Doubleday laughed again. Then he pressed a button at his elbow. A young man rather like a tailor's dummy entered. He wore a black jacket, striped grey trousers, a white shirt and starched white collar and his hair was plastered with brilliantine.

'Yes, sir?'

'Get me Miss Penelope Blow's account, please, Cudmore...'

'Yes, sir.'

One minute Cudmore was there: the next he'd vanished with the rapidity of Aladdin's genie of the lamp. He was back almost at once.

'Right, thanks. Leave it there.'

Mr Doubleday opened the ledger at the right page. From where he was now sitting on the other side of the desk Cromwell could see a large red label marked 'Caution' in black type fixed on the top of the page. From where the banker sat 'Deceased' could be plainly seen written on the ticket.

'Ah, yes... We've already heard about this from her solicitor in Nesbury. Evidently, there's going to be no evasion of Death Duties this time. Not that there'll be much evasion here. The balance is under five hundred pounds...'

Cromwell sat up with a jerk.

'So, besides the Salvation Army money, over ten thousand has gone as well...'

'Your arithmetic's a bit at fault, Sergeant. Over fifteen thousand pounds.'

'I don't understand it. From what we heard there were thirty thousand pounds to begin with...'

'A little more, but that will do for our purpose... Yes?'

'Then, Miss Katherine and her husband had Miss Katherine's share of around ten thousand. Then, the Salvation Army five... Miss Honoria should have had ten... Miss Penelope regarded that as a sacred trust, I hear. Maybe she gave it to Miss Honoria...'

'I'm afraid not... With the exception of the two sums you mention, nothing was drawn until three years ago... Then the account went down by a series of withdrawals...'

'Well, well... I don't suppose you can give me any details, sir?'

Mr Doubleday smiled and then grew serious again.

'Within limits, I'm prepared to help you. Miss Blow is dead. Therefore, certain information will do neither her nor anyone else any harm. The sum of fifteen thousand pounds has been drawn over the past two and a half years from this account by cheques payable to "Self". In other words, Miss Blow drew the money in cash.'

'I don't understand it at all. She must have given her sister her share, ten thousand pounds, then...'

'Maybe. We must look further into this. She may have called here and taken the money. In that case, I haven't seen her. Must have been away from the office. We'll see...'

He rang the bell again. Cudmore came in like a shot.

'Please send in Mr Hobday...'

'Yes, sir.'

A man in a morning coat followed quickly on the heels of the private secretary.

'This is Mr Hobday, our Manager. Mr Cromwell, of Scotland Yard. He's inquiring about Miss Penelope Blow's account.'

'Ah, yes. What can we do about it? She's dead, I gather.'

'She is. We want to know, Mr Hobday, the circumstances under which these three items to "Self" were paid. Was cash withdrawn at our own counter...or what? Can you tell me?'

'Just give me a moment, Mr Doubleday. I'll look into it. The files, you know...'

Mr Hobday, tall, heavy, with the appearance of a successful KC, withdrew. He was soon back.

'Yes... A rather funny affair. Here's the start of it...'

He passed a file to his Director, the top sheet of which was a typewritten letter. Mr Doubleday read it hastily, turned over the rest of the papers and then, to Cromwell's surprise and delight, and the Manager's apparent consternation, passed the lot over to the Sergeant.

'Hm. Look at the top letter, Cromwell. Then, another one of the same kind earlier, and yet another earlier still. All the same you see...'

The latter was dated from the Old Bank House, Nesbury, early that year, and typewritten, with Penelope Blow's signature at the foot. The other two a year before and two years before. They were very similar.

To Central Bank, Ltd,
Doubleday, Ward Branch,
St Paul's Churchyard.

Dear Sirs,

I shall shortly be investing in some property, for the settlement of which the solicitors will require five-thousand pounds in cash. As I wish this matter to be confidential, I do not wish to make arrangements through our own bank. I shall, therefore, ask you to forward the amount in cash — banknotes by registered and insured mail — addressed to me at the above address.

On hearing that this is convenient, I will send you the necessary cheque on my account.

Yours truly,
Penelope Blow.

Cromwell handed back the file. He was nonplussed. So Penelope Blow had drawn the money herself! Was it blackmail...or more acts of charity? Or had she really invested the money?

'Would you do me a great favour, sir?'

'Name it, please.'

'May I borrow the three letters?'

The Manager gasped and looked hard at Mr Doubleday.

'Yes. Give Mr Hobday a receipt for them. Do you want the three cheques as well?'

Mr Hobday almost fainted. Then, he imperceptibly shrugged his shoulders. The old man was obviously losing his wits. The very idea...!

'Do you mind, Hobday, having the cheques turned up for the Sergeant?'

'Of course, sir, if you say so... Ahem... But, is it wise... Why, they might...?'

'Exactly, Mr Hobday. They might... In the first place, I cannot imagine Miss Blow sending a typewritten letter to us. She belonged to a past age, as I do, when it was considered the height of bad manners to write a private letter on a machine. I see it has passed through your mind that her signatures might have been forged on both letters and cheques. Someone ought to have thought of that before. Not now! If they *are* forged, let's know and be put out of our misery. Give the papers to Mr Cromwell and let Scotland Yard experts test 'em. If they're forged, we've made a thumping bad debt, Mr Hobday...'

The Manager made a hasty and bothered exit. The sooner the old boy retired the better. Absolutely nuts!

As they waited for Mr Hobday to have typed the receipts and covering letter for the documents, which Cromwell later signed, the banker talked cricket with Cromwell...

Then: 'What are you going to do with those now you've got 'em? I often wonder what you do at Scotland Yard. Commissioner's asked me over and over again to call and see, but, somehow, I never get the time.'

'Test the signatures, sir.'

'Have you got specimens?'

'No, sir. But we soon will have them, now...'

On his way out, Cromwell noticed a number of curious faces, including those of a few nice-looking young ladies, peering at him round corners and over the counter screen. He felt a great detective for once. Even the hitherto imperturbable tellers raised their heads from their money changing and eyed him with faint awe...

From the Yard, Cromwell rang his chief at Nesbury. 'Well done, Cromwell. Now we'll see what we can do.'

Littlejohn, just in from his visit to the Broome house, put on his hat again and made for the tradesmen's entrance of the bank house.

'You on to something?' asked Paston as he left the police station.

'Looks like it. Tell you when I get back. Things are boiling up and this is urgent.'

In the kitchen, the little maid was cleaning up again. She squealed when she saw the Inspector.

'Oh, sir. The fam'ly's *in*,' she said in terror.

'And what of it, madam?' said Mrs Minshull, popping her head round the door. 'You speak when you're spoken to, milady. Get on with them brasses... Good afternoon, Inspector. Was you wantin' someone?'

'Yes, Mrs Minshull. Mr Jelley free?'

'Of course, sir. We're havin' a cup o' tea together. Do join us.'

They were always having tea together! But this time Littlejohn told Jelley and his two women, who gave him most friendly greetings mixed with warnings that the family were *in*, that he couldn't stay. It was urgent.

'I want to know if you can find me samples of the writing of Miss Penelope and the rest of the family. Just routine, you know.'

'Surely not counterfeitin', sir...'

Jelley meant forgery, but the longer word sounded better to him and impressed his women more.

'Oh, no, no, no. A routine check.'

'It will be h'easy, sir. Now let me see... Yes. A letter of condolences from Miss Penelope when my sister was ill and I went to stay there. And Miss Honoria...well...shall we say one of her books, sir, with poetry written on the flyleaf, as she used to do. Did you want the gentlemen and Mrs Ralph's as well?'

'All of them, if you can...'

'I can manage Mr Ralph. He wrote to me sayin' after my sister died, that if I didn't come back by weekend, he'd fill my place... That should do fine...'

Jelley smacked his lips with relish at the thought of it.

'I could manage Mrs Ralph's, I think,' said Mrs Minshull. 'That stupid Dolly, went an' got herself a fresh job last year. Mrs Ralph sent a reference for her to her new employer, Mrs Witney, I think she was called. Then Dolly wanted to come back again. So, maids bein' hard to come by, we let her come back. She'd got her reference with 'er! How she got it from Mrs Witney, to whom it was wrote, I don't know, but she 'ad it. It said Dolly lacked intelligence and wanted a lot o' tellin'. Also, she was a bit insolent...all of which is true. But Dolly might have had all the virtues in the world set out in that there letter, the way she prized and clung to it. She'll 'ave it now. Probably got it out of the Witneys' wastepaper basket, or else got it flung at 'er 'ead when she left. I'll get it...'

She disappeared to interview or browbeat the unfortunate Dolly. Voices were raised in the kitchen, the words 'imperent', 'h'igneramus' and ''igh-and-mighty' were bandied about. Then sounds of wailing, snivelling and sobs followed. Dolly could be heard going aloft for her treasure and she soon appeared hugging it to her opulent bosom.

'Give it 'im,' snapped Mrs Minshull.

'I'll see you get it back, Dolly,' said Littlejohn. 'Meanwhile console yourself at the pictures...'

He handed Dolly half-a-crown. She looked at him, passed him the letter, took the coin, burst into tears and fled.

''Ussy,' said Mrs Minshull. 'You shouldn't 'a give it 'er, sir. Far

GEORGE BELLAIRS

too many pictures and shameful novels that girl gets. One day she'll get 'erself into trouble...'

She smacked her lips at the thought of the trouble Dolly had coming to her.

'That leaves Mr Harold.'

'Easy,' said Jelley. 'He's just left a letter for post in the hall. Writin' off for more railway engines...'

Jelley's women clicked their tongues and shook their heads.

''Ingines,' said Mrs Frazer with disgust. 'If 'e 'ad to drive 'em, slow goods, all over the country, day and night, fog and rain, like me uncle Arthur once did, 'e'd soon change 'is tune. Fell off in the end and was killed...'

Littlejohn didn't stop to inquire further into the awful end of Mrs Frazer's uncle Arthur. He was in a hurry for the specimens of writing. Jelley was not long in getting them.

'Bring 'em back soon as you can, sir,' said the emaciated butler. 'And as for Mr 'Arold's letter, could you see it was posted when you've tried the writin'. I suppose you'll be steamin' it open, or what other new scientifical devices you 'ave at The Yard...'

He rubbed his hands in glee. He'd certainly got it in for his employers. The women eyed him with admiration for knowing so much of what went on at police headquarters. And the familiar way he said, 'The Yard'. A man of the world was Mr Jelley!

'I'll look after them, Jelley, and thanks a lot.' Littlejohn hurried back to the police office and then told Paston what it was all about.

'Well, I'll be damned,' said the local Inspector. 'You do work fast. I guess the case'll be solved and the lot folded up when The Yard have gone over those things. Who do you think did it?'

But Littlejohn ventured no guess. He'd been disappointed so often before. And he was in for another. He parcelled up his exhibits and sent them down by next train to London. There

Scotland Yard worked on them all night. Cromwell arrived, after a good night's sleep at home, full of great expectations.

'Well?' he said to the expert whom he sought out eagerly.

'Well?' said the expert, who'd been up half the night, thanks to Cromwell.

'Okay?'

'Depends what you mean by okay, Serg...The cheques were forged, if Penelope's writing in the letter is a true specimen...'

'Of course it is... Littlejohn wouldn't...'

The expert went on peevishly...

'And, as far as we can tell, the signatures on the letters to the bank are false, too. Odds are against Miss Penelope doing them...'

'Good, good! That'll be great. I'll get off to Nesbury and tell Littlejohn the news. He'll be glad, I'll tell you...'

'Wait a minute, smartie. That's not all. The cheques and letters weren't forged by any of the people, male, or female, whose specimens you handed in. So you'll have to look again.'

'But they must be... It can't have been anybody else.'

'Who's doin' this job, you or me? I tell you they weren't done by any of that lot. And you can put that in your pipe and smoke it and tell it to Littlejohn and old uncle Tom Cobley and all, and I'm going home to bed now and be damned to you...'

'Oh, don't take it that way, Ashley. I was only a bit surprised. It means starting all over again, now.'

'Well don't cry about it. Where's my hat...?'

Cromwell hadn't the heart to fight for a bus. Instead, he took a taxi on the embankment, carefully hiding the cost of it in his expenses sheet under the cryptic head of *sundry trav exp*, and ruefully made his way to Paddington and his boss.

14

TWO WOMEN

Honoria Blow didn't want to see Littlejohn when he called a second time at Tankerville's Home. She was sitting up in her room and greeted him peevishly.

'Really, Inspector, I don't see why you need to keep calling on me! There's no more mystery about things. Penelope wasn't in her right mind and tried to poison me to get my share of the annuity. Then, when they found out, she killed herself...'

Just as simply as that! She must have been thinking it out and had satisfied herself about it all.

'How long had you been ill, Miss Blow?'

'On and off for months. She mustn't have known much about poisons or I'd have been dead by now.'

Honoria had had her hair done professionally and had rouged her cheeks. Littlejohn didn't flatter himself that it was on his behalf. It must have been for the fish-like Tankerville!

'Did you call in the doctor every time you felt unwell?'

'Of course. Dr Cross has been our family physician ever since he was a young man and is practically a member of the family. We have the utmost confidence in him...'

It was said with an earnest vehemence and a heightening

of colour which made Littlejohn sure that the rouge and hair 'do' were neither for Tankerville nor himself. They were for Cross!

'Are you expecting him today?'

'Of course... He calls every day. He should be here in half an hour. Why do you ask? It's nothing to do with the matter.'

'I was wanting to see Dr Cross myself. I wondered when would be the best time.'

She volunteered no information, but the excuse had pacified her.

'...Yes. Dr Cross's family have been in the town for untold years. His father before him was our family physician and his grandfather, too. He is a great man in the district...'

Honoria was on her favourite subject and looked like continuing in praise of Cross for the rest of the time if a stop weren't put to it.

'Do you mind telling me, Miss Blow, how Dr Cross treated you when these attacks came on? Did he know they were poison?'

Stupid question, but a feeler put out on the spur of the moment.

'Certainly not! That is a silly question, Inspector. Do you think he would have allowed Penelope to go on giving me arsenic if he'd known?'

'But *you* knew?'

'I found out by accident, as I've said before. If I hadn't, I'm sure I'd have been dead by now.'

'Did the doctor give you medicine for the attacks?'

'Really, Inspector, you seem to have called to ask me the most stupid questions. Of course he did.'

Littlejohn was sure she'd have dismissed him if she'd had anyone else to gossip to about Cross. As it was, he was a foil for her to talk to about this man of whom she appeared strangely fond.

'Do you know how the poison was administered, Miss Blow?'

'In my food, of course. Dr Cross...'

'How do you think your sister obtained it?'

'From the chemist, I reckon.'

'It's not quite so easily obtained as that. Have you ever heard of arsenical fly-water?'

It was a bombshell! Honoria Blow's jaw fell as though she'd lost control of her facial muscles. Beneath the rouge her colour drained away leaving the paint isolated and raddling her cheeks. She was obviously terrified... She rose and stretched out her hand to the bell which hung over her bed, but Littlejohn, who had been standing, reached over and took it between his fingers.

'Not yet, Miss Blow. I'm going in a minute and I'll ring when I'm ready. Please answer my question.'

'No... I never... I... What do you mean by such insinuations? I'm not well... I want the nurse...'

'Very well...'

Littlejohn pressed the bell and the sister appeared.

'Oh, sister. He's been upsetting me terribly... Please take him away... I feel so ill...'

The nurse showed no sign of resentment or alarm. She gave Littlejohn an understanding look.

'I'm going, sister. Thanks for allowing me the time...'

'He says, sister... He says I took the poison myself...'

Both Littlejohn and the nurse gazed at Honoria aghast. Littlejohn shook his head.

'No, I didn't, Miss Blow, but I'm glad you've told me. That clears your sister's name, at least. I guessed as much, but you've kindly confirmed it. No harm done, really, and now you can go home and feel safe. The family will be very relieved.'

Honoria Blow was weeping copiously and in a state of semi-collapse. Tears washed away the rouge on her cheeks and made runnels to her chin. She looked suddenly very, very old.

'Please calm yourself, Miss Blow. If you don't wish it, the family needn't know. Sister here won't say anything, I'm sure...'

'Of course not, if you say so, Inspector. But Miss Blow must dry her eyes now and be good. Dr Cross will be very annoyed with me for allowing her to be upset.'

It worked like magic! The thought of Cross arriving and finding her like this galvanised Honoria into frenzied activity. She got busy on her make-up.

'You're sure nobody will know, Inspector?'

'Quite sure. You'll leave this place and go home and not do it again.'

'I promise...'

'The fly-water was found hidden in your drawer, Miss Blow. It is safely disposed of. But it was very cruel of you to try it on the cat to find out what a safe dose would be...'

'I didn't intend to hurt him. Nobody took any notice of me at home... I thought...'

The sister looked bewildered. This was the limit! Taking mild doses of poison to attract family attention to her.

'I promise, Inspector. And thank you. I thought with Penelope being dead, I could safely say...'

'You ought to have thought of her memory and of her good reputation, though. It was unfair...'

'Has Dr Cross come yet, sister?'

That was foremost in Honoria's mind, and now that the poison interlude had been safely got through, she was back again on her main obsession.

'He'll be here in about ten minutes. Then, he'll probably let you go home.'

'I'll have to go to bed till I'm quite cured, though. He'll have to call every day till I'm right.'

'That will depend on the doctor, Miss Blow...'

Littlejohn and the sister went out together and she accompanied him down the corridor to the door.

'Well! That's the cat's whisker! Poisons herself to get everybody's attention... I've been nursing some time and met some queer patients, but Honoria's capped the lot.'

'Not everybody's attention, nurse. Just that of Dr Cross.'

'Ah! I thought so. I might have guessed, the way she behaves. She's crazy about him. He doesn't seem to have twigged, however. Rather wrapped up in himself. Plenty of lady admirers, I guess.'

'You don't say so, nurse!'

'Yes. He's a bit bald, has a beard and won't see fifty again, but some women find him attractive. He's the virile sort, you know, and very charming when he wants to be. It's not professional to talk like this, I know, but you're the police and I suppose you're discreet...'

'I am.'

Littlejohn smiled.

'On duty, he treats the likes of me with strict propriety. But get him when he lets his back hair down... At the hospital ball, for example. He's a great dancer, especially with the good-looking ones. I don't wonder he's no eyes for Miss Blow. He likes them younger.'

'Indeed! Quite a dog.'

'I'll say. I've danced once or twice with him. Now, I dodge him when I'm without a dance-partner or else get someone to take me and look after me.'

She laughed. Littlejohn wasn't surprised, if Cross was a ladies' man. The sister was a bonny, apple-cheeked, fresh-looking girl...

'Long before his wife died...about five years ago...they say there was talk about him on the quiet. You should have seen him at the Christmas dance with Mrs Ralph Blow... He's fallen for her, hook, line and sinker. Mr Blow looked mad. He's no dancer and the doctor was monopolising Lenore...'

Littlejohn raised his eyebrows.

'I see. A romantic man, our doctor.'

'Now and then... Poor Miss Honoria.'

'Yes. Poor Miss Honoria. I know it's rather unethical for you to discuss cases, but as we're in Miss Honoria's secret together, perhaps I might ask you something...'

'Go ahead, Inspector.'

'Has Dr Cross ever discussed Miss Honoria's case history with you, nurse?'

'No. But I've overheard him and Dr Tankerville talking. What did you want to know?'

'How long this business of stomach trouble has been going on?'

'That's easy. I heard Dr Cross tell Dr Tankerville that he'd stake his professional reputation that the stomach trouble only recently changed to arsenic poisoning. He said he'd treated Miss Honoria for it for a long time; that he regarded it as purely nervous or hypochondriac; and that, until lately, he'd sent his assistant because it wasn't at all serious. He got tired of being called in for nothing.'

'That explains it. As long as her pretended ailments ensured frequent visits from Dr Cross, Miss Blow was happy. Then, when he got tired and ignored them and stopped calling, she made sure he'd come by making herself really ill. So she resorted to arsenical fly-water after making sure she didn't take an overdose by trying it on the cat...'

'It would be laughable, if it weren't so tragic.'

'It would...'

They had been talking in the porch and now their interview was suddenly brought to a close by the arrival of Dr Cross, driving up in a smart two-seater coupé. The sister said goodbye and hurried indoors.

Funnily enough, now that Littlejohn had obtained more background about Cross, the doctor seemed and looked quite another man.

Instead of the stiff, formal, irritable, self-opinionated family doctor, Littlejohn saw the conceited lady-killer, the dancing-man, the passionate middle-aged widower whom intrigue had touched and who fancied dalliance and pawing with good-looking nurses, on the young side, at local infirmary hops.

Dr Cross raced his engine, shut it off and braked his car. Instead of the top hat he wore for the funeral when Littlejohn first met him, Cross now had on a jaunty black slouch hat, slightly overbroad in the brim, worn a little askew. He slid from the coupé gloved in clean cream chamois, still wearing his dark broadcloth, his linen spotless, a smart foulard tie round his soft collar. In his buttonhole he wore a small bunch of the first primroses of the season. Instead of his stiff, lumbering gait, there was spring in his step. He looked annoyed when he saw Littlejohn, as though clouds were beginning to appear in his blue skies.

'Good afternoon, doctor...'

'Afternoon...' and the doctor was gone, ever so slightly deflated.

As Littlejohn went through the main gate, a familiar figure entered pushing his stock-in-trade ahead of him. 'John WM Slype, Window Cleaner, fully insured, Est '21.' The little man looked Littlejohn full in the face and bade him a cheery good morning. He was totally different. His squint had gone, and he wore his rectifying spectacles. He seemed very pleased indeed about the whole matter.

'How-de-do, Inspector... Got me spectacles, you see. Eyes straight now, you'll observe. Good thing, too, in my job. Bit of a risk four stories up on a winder-ledge when you can't see straight...'

'I'm glad about that, Mr Slype...'

''Ere we are agen. Always 'ere. No sooner finished one round o' these winders than I start at the beginnin' agen. Contract, renewable quarterly... Nice car Dr Cross 'as got.'

'Yes. One of the new American export models by the look of it. Wonder how he's managed it.'

'Ways and means; ways and means...'

Mr Slype tapped his crooked nose on one side and closed one eye.

'...I remember the days when Dr Cross 'adn't two pennies to rub together. Used to bicycle on 'is rounds, like me. Funny if 'e'd bore a sign like me too, wouldn't it? Dr Cross, Physician etcetera, Fully Insured...'

Mr Slype burst into roars of choking laughter which reminded Littlejohn of infantile croup.

'...Oh, oh, oh, oh dear me. Life's good when you've a sense of 'umour, isn't it, sir?'

'It is, Mr Slype.'

Tears streamed down Slype's cheeks and he removed his glasses and mopped them away with a grubby rag used for putting the finishing touches on windows after he'd leathered them. His eyes immediately slid into squinting position again. When he replaced his spectacles, they slowly resumed their normal straightness.

'I never did like Dr Cross. 'Orrible snob, sir. Ill becomin' one as 'as known poverty, sir. Very low he once got in his early days. You see, sir, he tuck over his old father's practice, which 'ad got very run-down owing to the old man's drinkin 'abits. He tuck that way after 'is wife died. Expect 'e realised the futility of medical skill when it comes to a pinch and your dearest and best lies 'elpless and you can't do nothin' for 'em. The Lord tuck 'er and old Dr Cross tuck to drink.'

Mr Slype shook his head sadly and wrung out his wash-leather in a spasm of emotion.

'Young Dr Cross, the one we jest seen go in, was in 'is last year at the medical college. Walkin' the 'ospital, 'e was, when 'is father went bankrupt. The old man 'ad borrered money up to the 'ilt to get his son through. Overdraft at Blows' Bank, they said. It was whispered, sir, that old William Blow stopped his tap. I mean, foreclosed or somethin'. Any rate, the bums, I mean the bailiffs, went in... The old man was found on the floor of 'is dispensary, dead. He'd tuck a dose of his own pizon, sir. Young Dr Cross came tearin' 'ome too late. Somehow he managed to raise money to finish 'is studies and then built up the ole man's practice agen. And, 'ang me if 'e didn't become the Blows' doctor in course o' time. Wonder 'e didn't pizon the lot of them for what they done to 'im...'

Mr Slype suddenly woke from his reveries.

'Got to get on. Contract job. I'll 'ave matron after me. S'long, sir. Nice to 'ave 'ad another word with you.'

Paston was very annoyed when Littlejohn told him of Miss Honoria's faked poisoning.

'Well, that's the limit. And after all the trouble we took. All the same it's a relief. That part of the case is out of the way. But what about Miss Penelope? What was she sent to London for? Why send her off to Scotland Yard for you? Miss Honoria was putting herself in grave danger. She might have been sure you'd find out it was all a put-up job...'

'I wonder. Maybe now that Miss Honoria's got over her first shock she'll talk sensibly. I'll go back to the nursing home and ask her. May I take your car?'

'Sure. What are you thinking?'

'Tell you later...'

On the way, Littlejohn passed Cross returning to town in his natty little car. The primroses had vanished from his button-hole. The Inspector wondered where he'd left them.

Miss Honoria was in a good temper when the sister once again ushered Littlejohn into her room. She was holding a book tightly in her fingers. From the edge protruded the stems of the primroses she was pressing...

'Doctor didn't stay long and you're soon back, Inspector,'

said the sister. 'I'll just take you in and leave you. I've my rounds
to do. Ring you need me.'

'I won't be a minute. I'll see myself out...'

Miss Blow opened the book, smiling like a young girl.

'See what the doctor left for me...'

It was pathetic!

'I forgot to ask you something which interests me personally,
Miss Blow. Why did Miss Penelope come to London in search
of me? Surely, knowing the situation, you didn't send her on
such a wild goose chase frivolously.'

'No, Inspector. As you've been so kind about it all, I don't
mind telling you. At first, Penelope wouldn't believe me when I
said I was being poisoned. I told her because I wanted some
attention. I was being neglected, Inspector...'

She even created sensations to make poor bewildered Penelope run about after her!

'I told her... She said I must be mistaken. Nobody would do
that to me. Well, something happened which made her see it
was true. She overheard a certain person plotting to poison me.'

'I beg your pardon, Miss Blow. Is that quite right? Surely,
you said you were poisoning yourself...'

'Yes, but...'

'What exactly did she overhear? Tell me word for word.'

'She heard a certain person say as she passed the dining
room, "But we've got to get auntie out of the way..." Now, if that
didn't mean a certain person was going to poison me, what did?
Get auntie out of the way. That was me. Auntie. And out of the
way meant kill me.'

'Who was the certain person?'

'That's just it, Inspector. I wish I knew. I don't. Penelope was
like that. She wouldn't have trouble in the family or unjustly
accuse anybody. She just said, "a certain person" and wouldn't
say more till she'd proof. She rang up Mr Claplady and he

recommended she saw you as to what we ought to do. That's why she came.'

'Thank you, Miss Blow. That's all I want to know.'

'Is it safe for me to go home tomorrow? Dr Cross said I might go tomorrow afternoon. He said I could go to bed... He'll come to see me there. Isn't he wonderful?'

'He's a good doctor, I guess. Well, thank you again, Miss Blow. I must go now. Goodbye.'

'Goodbye, Inspector. Thank you. All has ended well, and we can all be happy together once more, although poor Penelope...'

Yes, thought Littlejohn, poor Penelope.

15

ORCHARD HOUSE AGAIN

It was after dinner when Littlejohn called again at Cuthbert Broome's Georgian house in Haxton Street. The housekeeper who looked like Queen Victoria let him in and led him to her master. The same warm, fuggy air, the same smell of stale tobacco, and the same odds and ends of travel round the Empire which gave the place the air of an auction room.

'Come in,' said the old man. 'Lenore's not turned up yet. Told her over the telephone you were comin' and she promised not to say anythin' till after she'd seen you. Can't understand what's keepin' her...'

The Captain was again standing on the rug, toasting his back before a large coal fire. He was dressed for dinner, being conservative in custom and anxious to preserve the traditions he'd assumed when he married into the local gentry. 'Always dress for dinner,' he told Lenore when she tried to make him change his habits. 'Sign that a fellah's goin' to pieces when he gets slovenly in his ways. Sure sign that the rot's settin' in...' He looked tired, but a fine figure for all that.

'Sit down, Inspector. Have a pipe of 'bacca...'

They filled their pipes and started to smoke. Littlejohn, after gingerly surveying a number of seats, including that presented by the King of Ashanti, at length settled in a cane armchair which creaked and groaned under his weight but safely held him The brassware and ivory shone under the shaded lights.

'I can only think Lenore's busy gottin' ready for her trip. Did I tell you, my little gel's shortly goin' out to Australia to see her brother? Marriage misfired sadly. Great trouble to me, sah. She's tried... By Gad, she's tried. But Ralph's turned out a cad. Well, she's determined to make the best of it. Said she'd go away for a bit. See her brother in the Antipodes... When she comes back, if bein' apart hasn't done 'em any good, well...it'll have to be a divorce. Goes against the grain with me, sah...very much against the grain. Marriages made in heaven...orthodox churchman...old-fashioned. Consider it adultery, sah, to marry with intention of divorcin' if it doesn't work out. Call it prostitution hidin' under the blessin' of the church. But I'm a back number, sah. All the same, my gel's done her best. Defy anybody to say she hasn't...'

Broome puffed his pipe and brushed his moustache with his forefinger. It was difficult to know which part of his behaviour was a pose and which genuine. He was like a character out of Kipling.

'You'll join me, Inspectah?'

The whisky bottle was out again, in spite of doctor's orders.

'Dr Messiter says I oughtn't to, but what's a fellah to do? On my own most of the day. Exercise forbidden... Short life but a gay one, eh?'

He filled two tumblers and passed one to Littlejohn. 'Your health, sah...'

'And yours, sir. You don't use Dr Cross, then?'

Captain Broome scowled as he swallowed his drink.

'No... Outsider... Not much good as a doctor, but worse personally. The Blow family have him. Tradition. Father to son, so to speak. They have short memories. I remembah, sir. Cross's father went bust...spending too much on the bottle. He owed Blows' Bank a packet, too, and...well...business is business. They sold him up. His son never forgave the family. Out for revenge, sah. I've told my little gel and the rest of 'em, but they think I'm just in my dotage. Well...Cross was responsible for the family shuttin' up old William Blow in his room, or I'm a Dutchman. Can't prove anythin', but never liked Cross. Bounder, sah...'

'A queer-looking chap, I must admit, sir.'

'Queer ways, too. Fond of the ladies. Made passes at my little gel, sah. Made a point of callin' on him myself. Told him to leave her alone. Married woman, too. Get my old campaignin' revolver out and shoot the bounder in cold blood if he dared harm my little gel...'

'Probably just gossip, sir.'

'Perhaps. That's what he said. Got offensive and said he'd throw me in the street if I made such accusations. Even mentioned blackmail in his temper. Best thing for my gel to go abroad for a bit. Let things blow over...'

'It was recently, then?'

'Last autumn. My housekeeper heard in town they'd been seen out in his car together. They both denied it. I asked my gel straight to her face if there was any truth in it. She said, no. Wouldn't tell her old father lies...'

'What was the rumour exactly, sir?'

'You interested in gossip, Inspectah? Why?'

'If I know the details of the rumour, I can deny them if I encounter anything in the course of my investigations.'

'Ah, yes. Nothin' much. They said he was takin' Lenore to his country cottage. He has a place somewhere not far from here. Weekend cottage. My housekeeper heard that somebody had seen 'em in Cross's car goin' in that direction...'

'Have they been friends, then?'

'No. Just professional, through Cross's attendance at the

house. And they're on the committee of the local Arts Club. Both of them do a bit of sketchin'... My gel did those two... Not bad, eh?'

He indicated two framed watercolours, country scenes with cattle, rather pale, but very competent.

'Very nice, sir.'

'Lenore's good at it, though I say it meself...'

'Cross paints, too, then?'

'Yes. Remember the days when he wanted to be an artist. Said to be good at black and white work, pencil and etching... and I must say what I've seen at local exhibitions of the Club, he's not at all bad. His father made him take medicine. Family tradition and practice all ready and waitin' for him...'

'I see...'

There was a sound of footsteps, crisp and purposeful; outside, a key was inserted in the front lock and after a minute, Lenore Blow opened the door of the room and stood there a moment. She was wearing her fur coat and skin hat again. Her cheeks glowed from her hasty walking. She was very beautiful, and her father eyed her with great pride.

'You're late, gel...'

They kissed each other warmly.

'Why are you troubling father, Inspector? He's old and tired. You won't do any good bothering him.'

She was into the fray without hesitation. Her fine eyes shone with annoyance.

'Mustn't get angry with my guest, Lenore. He's been very good to me...'

'Good! Pestering you with his questions. I may as well say, Inspector, my husband has heard again of your inquiries. Someone has told him you've been questioning the servants. He will report it to the Chief Constable as soon as he returns, and he's coming to the police station to ask you for an explanation tomorrow.'

'I will do my best to satisfy him, Mrs. Blow. Meanwhile, I haven't been worrying your father, I hope. He's been most helpful and hospitable...'

'There you are, you see, gel. He says I've been helpful. Want to help him find who caused poor Penelope's...'

'So that's it. Can't you let her rest, Inspector? It was proved an accident. What more can you hope for...?'

'I must say, Mrs Blow, I didn't call to discuss the ways and means of Miss Blow's end. We are almost sure she died by violence. We want to know by whose hand...'

Lenore threw aside her coat and sat down. She looked tired and impatient. A harassed expression drew two furrows across her forehead.

'But who would want? Who could have...?'

'All in good time, Mrs Blow. I hope to tell you that later. Meanwhile, I hear you are proposing to join your brother in Australia shortly. I must ask you not to go until this matter is settled...'

The two Broomes, father and daughter, both began to talk at once.

'Father! You told him that?'

'What do you mean, sah? Not leave till... You surely don't suspect my gel...? I won't tolerate it...'

'Why did you tell him, father? You know it's not settled, yet.'

'Thought you wouldn't mind. But as for not goin'...'

Littlejohn raised his hand.

'Please. There's no sense in getting so excited. I only want the case clearing up before any of the Blow family leave this town.'

'I shall go just when I wish...'

'Very well... We'll have to take steps...'

'How dare you, sah? Leave my house. Can't talk to my gel like that under her own roof. Lenore, show the Inspector out.'

The old man, quivering with rage, pointed a shaking finger

at the door like an outraged father in a melodrama. Littlejohn expected 'cad' and 'bounder' to follow him and threats of thrashin' and shootin' in cold blood. Instead, the old man marched to the whisky bottle, poured out a stiff peg in a tumbler and turned his back on Littlejohn.

'You'd better go...'

Lenore rose and held open the door. Littlejohn walked quietly out after bidding them goodnight, and the last he saw of them was Lenore trying to coax the old man away from his drink, which in his palsied rage he was spilling down his white shirt front.

Cromwell was waiting for him when he got back to the hotel. He was arguing with another military-looking gentleman in the lounge.

'I'm tellin' you yoga's quieter... No need to be disturbin' neighbours early every mornin' with your bumpin' and thumpin' on the floor. Gave up physical jerks in my youth and took yoga. Learned it when campaignin' in India. Fakir taught me... Lived over hundred and twenty and still goin' strong. At any rate, I'll be grateful if you'll stop that noise overhead every mornin'. Spoils my early cup of tea in bed and readin' *The Times*... Yoga, that's what you want...'

'Ah...' Cromwell clutched at Littlejohn and led him to the bar in great relief.

'That fellow has the room under mine. Says I'm annoying him with my early morning exercises. Fears the ceiling will fall on him as he reads his *Times* in bed. He says yoga...'

In Cromwell's eyes glowed the light of a new fad. He wondered whether yoga...

'I've had a bad time in London. The cheques were forged right enough, but not by anyone at the Blow house...'

Cromwell told his chief of the interview with the banker and of all that had transpired at Doubledays' bank.

Forged cheques... Money sent by post in cash... The letters

explaining that she was buying property, also forged according to the expert. But none of the Blow family had written either the cheques or the letters.

'Funny... I wonder...'

'You wonder what, sir?'

'I'm just running through the possibles. If it's not the family, who can it be? The servants? Too illiterate for a thing like this. What about Cross?'

'The doctor?'

'Yes. Do you remember Chesney Wilson...?'

'Yes. The counterfeiter?'

'Himself. Remember what his first conviction was for?'

'Passing forged cheques...'

'Exactly. He was an engraver by trade, but an expert forger because he could draw so well. He could copy a signature just like drawing a dog's head or a landscape... Both Dr Cross and Lenore Blow are good artists.'

'How do you know that?'

'I've just been to see her and her father at the old man's place and been kicked out for asking too many questions.'

'But how does Cross come in?'

'I don't know. But rumour has it he's keen on Lenore Blow. Gossip says they've spent some time at his cottage in the country.'

'Well, I'll be damned! Dr Cross, a lady-killer!! You don't say?'

'I do. I've had it on good authority that he fancies himself with the pretty ones.'

'How does that affect us?'

'In the first place, Lenore Blow is one of the few who know of Miss Penelope's nest egg. Her father, who helped sell the bonds and open the account with Doubledays', told her in confidence. Suppose she told Cross and between them they forged the letters and cheques... Yes... And now her ladyship proposes making a trip to Australia to see her prodigal brother. That all ties up. I wonder if Cross is going abroad, too...'

'We want a specimen of Cross's handwriting now, don't we? How can we manage it?'

'Let's go across and see Paston'

They finished their drinks and put on their hats and coats. Across the square, the blue light shone over the police station. The neon signs of a few shops and the glaring ore of a new cinema threw a blue and red glow over the vast cobbled space. The pubs were having a busy time, too. Inside some of them they were singing loudly... A figure at the door of the hotel greeted them.

'Good evening, gentlemen... Self-denial?'

It was a Salvationist with his collecting box for the Lent subscriptions. They searched in their pockets for small change.

'Pleasant night, sir. You both still in town on Miss Blow's affairs?'

It was one of the men they'd found on duty at the hostel.

'Yes...'

'Thank you both, gentlemen. We shall need every penny this year now that Miss Blow has passed on. We'd arranged to build another wing on the dormitories. We have to turn men away. It'll cost a thousand, so every penny counts. Miss Blow had promised to help... But now...'

'Miss Blow had promised more money?'

'Yes, sir. A woman never deserved the Land of Pure Delight more... An angel on earth... God's will be done, though... Good night, gentlemen...'

'Hear that, Cromwell? She was going to make another draw on the Doubleday account, or I'm a Dutchman. That means...'

'That means, sir, she'd have found the money wasn't there! There wasn't a thousand in the account! Somebody was going to be for it!'

To their surprise, Superintendent Hempseed was in the

police station. Muffled up to the ears, he was seated stiffly in his official chair talking earnestly with Paston.

'Doctor said I might get up a bit today. The pain's nearly gone, though I feel horrible on my feet. Weak, you know. Being in bed with all that heat takes one's strength. I got tired of sitting alone by the fire. The wife's gone to a whist-drive. I managed to get out and start the car, and here I am. Got to get back though. If I'm out when she gets home, there'll be merry hell, I can tell you.'

'Let's all take you home, sir, and we'll tell you all we know by your own fireside.'

'Good idea...'

Later, sitting by a glowing fire, drinking the Superintendent's whisky, Littlejohn and Cromwell told him and Paston the results of the inquiries they'd been making.

'But why should Cross...'

'I don't know, sir, yet. Do you know where his cottage is in the country?'

'Yes. Lapworth. He fishes and does a bit of painting there. Pretty spot.'

'We'd better inquire around if Lenore Blow's been seen there.'

'But the thing's preposterous. Lenore and Cross... Tommyrot!'

'Yes, tommyrot!' chirped Paston in warm confirmation.

'I know Cross is a bit of a philanderer. His father was the same. Family failing. But with a girl like Lenore. She's more taste than that and could do far better if she wanted to turn that way.'

'All the same, gentlemen, it's a link in the case that must be tested. We'll inquire in Lapworth tomorrow. Meanwhile, we want a specimen of Cross's writing as soon as we can. What do we do?'

'I'll get that as soon as we get back,' said Paston. 'Quake, the chemist, lives over his shop in the square. I'll knock him up and get a prescription. Quake owes me a good turn. He'll help us.'

'Right. We'll send it down by the midnight train to London and get Scotland Yard to vet it with the cheques and letters. We'll know by morning then. Ralph Blow's calling on you tomorrow. He's heard we're still on the case and he's coming for an explanation.'

'He is, is he? That means I'll have to come down, then,' said Hempseed.

'I'll look after him, sir,' said his Inspector loyally.

'No. I'm coming. We can't have you in trouble with this appointment as my successor not yet made. I've got to look after you.'

'Who's to look after what?'

It was the jolly Mrs Hempseed, the Superintendent's 'girl', returning from the whist-drive. She still wore her outdoor clothes, and in her arms, she held a large parcel.

'Hullo, girl. Had a good time? Our friends have called to see how I'm getting along.'

They all greeted her conspiratorially.

'Did you pick them up at the police station, Jack?'

'I...I...I...'

All four of them looked sheepish.

'I'm not a policeman's wife and daughter for nothing. You've been out in the car. There are wheel marks to the garage door. They weren't there when I left. You've been out...'

'I got bored, girl...'

'You're not fit to leave... As soon as my back's turned... Well, well... Some people won't be told. If you're in bed tomorrow, don't blame me...'

'No, I won't, girl...'

'You want some coffee, I expect... *And* some sandwiches... You know the doctor said to keep off the drink for a bit... I daren't turn my back...'

She embraced the lot of them in a comprehensive look of reproach. Then she smiled broadly at them.

'Like a lot of naughty boys, all of you. Look what I got.'

She opened her parcel and disclosed a large ornamental plant-pot, resplendent in gilt and many colours with two large tortured handles and a frieze of Greek girls dancing half-naked all round it in perpetual motion.

'What's that? You haven't won it, surely, girl?'

'No, I haven't won it and I'll ask you not to sound so scornful, John Allingham Hempseed. It was given to me. A present. It's the last night of the Women's Whist Club before we leave, and they clubbed together to give me this. It's very nice of them and I like it...'

She set her jaw in determined loyalty to her fellow card-players.

'Ow!' shouted her husband. 'It makes my lumbago twinge again...'

'It's not this, it's the cold night air.'

'Where are you going to put that in our new house? It's not decent!'

'I'll put it just where I please, mister. So there...'

She could hold out no longer and burst into roars of laughter. The men, greatly relieved, joined in.

'It's awful, isn't it? I nearly fainted...'

She left them and soon returned with hot coffee and food.

'Met some friends of yours on my way home. I passed the park wall and saw two people sitting on a seat talking with their heads together. So busy they didn't see me... Mrs Ralph Blow and her brother-in-law...that Harold... I can't stand him.'

The four men looked significantly at each other. They were all thinking the same thing. How much deeper and how many more men in Lenore's life!

After the little party broke up, Paston drove Littlejohn and Cromwell to Quake's Chemist's Shop in the square. There were lights and sounds of singing coming from the room above the shop. Paston looked alarmed as he rang the bell. Mr Quake answered. A little middle-aged man with a large bald head and round glasses. He peered in the gloom and tottered on his heels.

'Huuuuuullo, Inspector. Nobody ill at home, I hope...or nobody wanting poison or a prairie oyster or black draught... Mosht inconvenient if they do... My twenny-fifth weddin' ann'vershy... Silver weddin'... Twenny-five years of connubial bliss... Go' bless Mishis Quake, and me, an' all the li'l Quakes... Come in and drink our ver' good 'ealth...'

'I'm sorry, Mr Quake. Our best wishes, I'm sure. But we can't come in, much as we'd like...'

But Mr Quake was set in his purpose.

'Hannah...Hannah...' He bellowed up the stairs. 'Come down, 'Annah. P'leesh have called to add a blessin' to our annivershy... Conshtabulary greetin's to the 'appy pair...'

A huge form, twice the size of Mr Quake, appeared at the head of the stairs and slowly descended with elephantine steps and a lot of puffing.

'Do be quiet, Kenneth. You don't want to rouse the whole town. Ask the gentlemen up...'

'Can' come up. Bizzy on a case... Wanna wish you all the besht, my luv...'

Mrs Quake signified her great pleasure by shaking all over with mirth.

'You'll have to excuse my husband, gentlemen... This only happens once in a lifetime...'

'Here's to our *golden* weddin'...' roared Quake. Whereat a huge crowd of his children and grandchildren gathered at the stair-head to inquire what was going on.

Meanwhile, Paston had quietly told Mrs Quake what he wanted. She was as sober as a judge and a sensible woman. She said she would help, and she did. Quickly disappearing through a door into the shop, she switched on the lights, switched them off again, and returned with a slip of paper which she handed to Paston.

'That do? It's quite a long one. For Mrs Fitt's indigestion. Let me have it back, though. We've to claim for it from the National Health...'

'Wass goin' on?' yelled the happy chemist. 'What you wan' from shop? Ah...Rubbin' bottle for Mish'r Hempseed... Thassit...wot?'

He seemed satisfied.

'Less go up for a drink. Won' hear of no. Be insulted if you refuge. Jus' a li'l one for twenny-fifth wedding annivershy...'an...ish...not been a day too mush...' he broke into song.

'Come on, my ole Dush...'

His family were calling him, and he seemed to forget his visitors in the tumult. His huge Old Dutch led him unsteadily back to the bosom of his first and second generations and the police went on their way, Paston home and Littlejohn and Cromwell to the hotel, where they made a parcel of the prescription, the cheques and the letters to Doubledays' Bank, because the railway refused to accept them in letter form in an envelope. They put the evidence wrapped up in brown paper and string to abide by the regulations on the midnight train and telephoned the Yard to gather them up at Paddington.

16

PARCEL POST

Nesbury was a hive of activity when, early next morning, Littlejohn crossed from the hotel to the servants' entrance of the Blow household. Rain had fallen early but had now ceased and the air was fresh and bracing. The sea of cobblestones which made up the main square shone in the thin sunlight. Mr Quake, the chemist, was taking down his shutters, looking worse for wear from the innocent orgies of his silver wedding. A copious draught of his 'Special Pick-Me-Up, No 3' had not yet begun its work on him, and he pretended not to see Littlejohn as the Inspector passed his windows.

Drovers were already driving cattle into the pens which had been erected for the cattle-market. They chased and lashed the stunned beasts, beating them with canes on the head and buttocks to make them move. An auctioneer and a veterinary surgeon were at work, examining and valuing the animals for the auction. One roughly opened their mouths, examined their teeth and eyes, and the other followed, clipping away a circle of hair on their flanks and sticking labels over the tonsures. The victims bellowed and lowed with fear, sensing the approach of slaughter which was the fate of most of them. A travelling hot-gospeller who had pitched his caravan in the square was beginning the day with a hymn, assisted by a small knot of fellow workers.

> *All things bright and beautiful,*
> *All creatures great and small,*
> *All things wise and wonderful,*
> *The Lord God made them all.*

'I don't know that I'd like to share the responsibility of having made all that lot,' said a voice at Littlejohn's elbow. It was the little man in the coat with an astrakhan collar and spats and a Malacca cane whom Littlejohn had seen parading the square from time to time. His voice was an angry chirp and with his cane he indicated the brutal drovers, the humble, bewildered cattle, and a cat which had been run over by a motor-lorry and had died in agony. Then, he passed on without word to interrupt and argue with the evangelist.

'Don't take any notice of 'im,' said a large, fat, red-faced woman with a shopping basket on her arm and a small dog on a lead. ''E likes spoilin' people's pleasure. Crabtree-Mills, 'e's called. Proper ole atheistical. Ought to be put in the h'asylum...' The dog dragged her away to investigate a lamp post.

To add to the confusion, Nesbury Wanderers were playing Hawkside Albion that afternoon in a cup-tie. Charabancs were already disgorging visitors from Hawkside. They were yelling and shouting slogans already and punctuating their war-cries with rattles and bells. The men wore large club rosettes and scarves. One had a bowler hat, ornamented like a toffee-stick with the stripes of his favourites' jerseys. 'Up the 'Awks...' A Nesbury fan among the drovers shouted a counterblast. ''Hup the Tusslers...'

Jelley, the butler, greeted Littlejohn cordially. His two women were out buying in and Dolly, the little maid, was alone with him. He had been chiding her for dreaming about film stars and local amours instead of getting on with the potato peeling, and her eyes were red from weeping.

'Come in, sir, come in. Things are a bit upset, but you're welcome...' His voice quavered with the remnants of his rage against Dolly. 'And you get on with your work, my girl. Any more o' that and I'll ask you for your resignation...'

'Wow...ow... Yes, Mr Jelley... I'm a-doing of 'em...wow-ow...'

The girl's sobbing had changed to hiccups and she made choking cries as she turned the potatoes round and round under the knife, shedding thick skins as she worked.

Littlejohn felt he would always remember those servants' quarters. Bright, easily cleaned chromium taps in the butler's pantry, large brass ones in Dolly's scullery, a standing menace which called for ceaseless effort to keep them shining. The brown, grained woodwork, the gloomy walls, dark green below, light green above, with a hideous maroon line separating the two tints. The huge kitchen range about which, when it was cold, Dolly crawled and polished under the exacting double gaze of Mrs Frazer and Mrs Minshull. The two old-fashioned armchairs of the cook and housekeeper, the rocking chair of the butler, who was partial to heaving himself back and forth in lighter moments. From beneath the cushions of the three chairs peeped the corners of cheap daily papers and women's weeklies with long, melodramatic stories appearing complete or in serial form each week to be eagerly gobbled up by their subscribers. Mrs Frazer was in the habit of weeping copiously as she read of the cruel treatment of wronged servants, mill-girls and typists, and to give vent to the feelings which tears alone could not relieve, she was in the habit of prodding, poking, cuffing and pulling the hair of the unhappy Dolly. On one occasion, Mrs Frazer, more than usually enraged by her literary orgies, had threatened to choke Dolly to death.

'As I was sayin'...' quavered Jelley.

There was an eternal smell of cooking grease, kitchen soap, plate polish and vegetable water on the air. And there was the green baize door which divided the servants from their betters and beyond which the uneasy spirit of William Blow still prevailed...

'I was sayin'...these football matches. There'll be no work done today, you mark my words...'

Jelley wasn't doing much himself. *The Times* was on the table and a large, half-empty cup of tea. He was still in his slippers and his ankles reminded Littlejohn of a robin's legs.

'I called for a little more help, if you don't mind, Mr Jelley.'

The butler removed his green baize apron, washed his bony hands at the tap, put on his black coat, and looked ready for anything. From the scullery, the hiccups continued, fortified now and then by a spasmodic howl.

'Always ready to be of service, Mr Littlejohn, sir. And just stop that noise in there. It's not words Mrs Frazer'll give you when she gets in, my gel... It'll be a good box on the ears. Would you believe it, sir... She says she's savin' up to go to 'Ollywood... Akchewly writin' to film stars, she is... Oh, the disgrace of it! 'Ollywood, indeed!'

'Ow...ow...ow...'

'The question you were going to h'ask, sir?'

'Do you take in the post every day, Mr Jelley?'

'I do, sir.'

'Parcel and registered, as well?'

'Yes. I sign for the registered. It's allowed, you know, sir.'

'Yes, that's so. Now, I want you, Mr Jelley, to think very carefully...'

The butler assumed a profound expression with furrowed brow and set lips, like one being set a poser.

'...Do you remember, within the last six months, any large,

registered parcels arriving from London addressed to Miss Penelope?'

'Yes, sir, I do. I wondered what they held, because Miss Penelope wasn't in the 'abit of receiving much mail. Those were most unusual...'

'Give me an idea when they arrived, if you can, please, Mr Jelley.'

'Oh...weeelll... I'd say, sir, the first came, well, I'd say two or three...yes, nearer three...years ago. I remember it well. Then a year later, another arrived. The last came the day I left for my sister's, sir. Just before Miss Penelope went to London.'

'They came at the rate, roughly, of one a year?'

'Yes. They might have been presents, sir. I never saw one opened. Didn't even see the wastepaper afterwards, which was a bit unusual...'

'Why?'

Jelley coughed behind his hand.

'Just a little understandable 'uman curiosity, sir. You see, each member of the family 'as a wastepaper basket in their rooms. Dolly empties them, sir...when she doesn't forget...and brings them down here for the salvage bag. Well...you know 'ow it is, sir, with the ladies... Any envelopes, they look at 'em, trying to guess who they may be from. Just 'armless interest, if I might say so...'

'You join in the scrutiny, too, Jelley, I guess,' laughed Littlejohn.

'Yes, sir. They're h'all called to my attention, as you may say... Those wrappers never came. We remarked on it.'

'Registered and sealed, were they?'

'Yes, sir. A very good job, too.'

'Sort of job a bank might do?'

'You could not 'ave described it better, sir. Bein' in the profession, so to speak, all my life, I'd say it was the sort of packet a bank would make up with cash per post.'

'You took them from the postman, Mr Jelley?'

'Yes, sir.'

'Sure?'

'Why not, sir? Unless I'm out, sir, nobody else would answer the door and I'm not out so early in the morning, I can h'assure you.'

'You gave them to Miss Penelope?'

Jelley again entered into a state of profound meditation, contorting his thin, bloodless features in an outlandish effort of will.

'I don't remember, sir. I really don't. Now that's funny. If I'd given them to Miss Penelope, I would have remembered. She was always so pleased and grateful...profuse is the right expression, sir...so profuse...I'm sure I'd have remembered her pleasure and thanks. Yet, I can't...'

'Think hard. I know it's a long time ago. What about the last one?'

'I remember about that now, sir. I was packing a few things...greatly distressed I was too, because of my sister. She was my only sister and had 'ad an haemorrhage...a stroke to put it in popular terms, sir... I remember the bell ringing and as I descended the stairs, Mrs Ralph came out of the drawing room and stood there waiting to see who was at the door.'

'Did she seem in a hurry or eager?'

'I can't say, sir. My mind was on my own troubles and I thought only of them and answering the door. It was the post with a parcel for which I signed. I was taking it to Miss Penelope's room, sir. She'd had breakfast, of course. Always an early riser was Miss Penelope. I was taking it to her room, when Mrs Ralph stepped up to me. "I know you're troubled and in a 'urry," she said to me. "I'll see to this. Who's it for? Ah, Miss Penelope. I'll take it to her." I gave it up. Sort of line of least resistance, I guess, sir, because I had to pass Miss Penelope's room on the way back to my own.'

'And Mrs Ralph took it from you, went up as you did, and carried it to Miss Penelope's room?'

'No, sir. She went back in the drawing room. I guess she saw to it later.'

'Was it around breakfast time, you say?'

'Yes, sir.'

Jelley looked surprised at the catechism. It seemed very out of place. Bothering about parcels, indeed, when there was Miss Penelope's 'orrible end to be attended to!

'Why wasn't Mrs Ralph in the breakfast room, do you know, Jelley?'

Jelley sighed. This was getting ridiculous.

'I really don't know, sir. Mrs Minshull was waiting at table because I was due to leave early for my sister's. But I do know that Mr Ralph and Mr 'Arold were at table. Mrs Ralph was usually there, too, pouring out the coffee... She must have finished early...'

'The drawing room would be empty at that hour.'

'Most decidedly, sir.'

'And, now, Mr Jelley... Has this talk revived any memories of the other parcels?'

Jelley started...

'Why, yes, sir, it has. I forget what happened the first time...it was so long since, but a year ago, I remember it now. Miss Penelope was away from home...'

'Ah...'

'Beg pardon, sir.'

'Go on.'

'I remember thinking that. She didn't often go away, but that time she did. She went over, I recollect, to stay a day or two with Lady Clapp, a relative of hers. There was some sort of a village bazaar going on, and Miss Penelope being such a good needlewoman, her Ladyship asked her to come over and put the finishing touches to some fine needlework they were selling there. I remember it well, sir, because, if I may be allowed to say so, sir, it became a standing joke with the staff. Miss Penelope not being used to going away much, got very h'excited. For weeks before she went, she was bothering about what to take with her and how much. She was all of a twitter, sir, about goin' and then when she came 'ome, all of a twitter about havin' been. It got to be a family joke. "When I was h'at the Manor," she'd say a 'undred times a day, and then she'd tell what they did and what so-and-so 'ad said. It got quite a bore, sir. Until she got over it, people began to edge away whenever she started to say "when I was h'at the Manor…" She was a dear good lady, sir, and so little pleased and h'excited her.'

'What happened to the parcel that time?'

'I 'anded it to Mrs Ralph to re-address. She must 'ave seen it off herself. I never saw it again.'

'Did she seem to expect it?'

'I don't remember, sir. I do know she met me in the 'all that time, too, and took the package.'

'Did Miss Penelope ever know about the parcels arriving?'

'Meaning, sir?'

'After you'd handed them to Mrs Ralph, did you mention their arrival to Miss Penelope?'

'Oh, no, sir. I just left it at that.'

'Thank you very much, Jelley. That's been most useful.'

'Glad to be of 'elp, I'm sure, sir, though why…'

Steps and voices could be heard at the door. It was the two women returning from their walk round town.

'Well, imperence, and what 'ave you been crying at agen? Like turnin' on the tap, it is. Don't you think you'll soften my 'eart, madam. I've lived too long and seen too much for the tears of the likes of you to move me. H'idle, h'imperent 'ussy…'

'Ow…ow…ow…'

'Stop that noise… Well, look 'oo's 'ere. I didn't know you was in, sir. Excuse my h'anger at that girl. I never knew such a igorant, imperent 'ussy. I can scarce keep me 'ands off her. Pourin' the dirty potato water down the good sink, 'stead of down the outside drain... But, there, you don't want all my troubles, sir. What brings you 'ere...?'

Mrs Minshull joined the party and a strong smell of gin suffused the air.

'I'll just take me things off and then...'

Mrs Frazer transferred herself to her private quarters to remove a brown hat and mauve coat in extremely bad taste. Mrs Minshull remained behind to throw her own over an armchair and apologise for the state of her companion.

'She *had* to call at Mrs McAllister's to give 'er some sugar. Mrs Mc A asked if we'd like a cup o' tea... And as large as life her ladyship says something stronger would be more acceptable. And after one glass, she ups and asks for another. You'll 'ave to excuse her, Inspector. She just can't take it...'

Jelley raised his long thin hands and rolled his eyes to heaven, like an emaciated martyr calling down blessings on his inquisitors. Mrs Minshull was almost in as bad shape as Mrs Frazer.

The butler left the kitchen, presumably seeking out the offending cook for warning and reprimand. Littlejohn took his opportunity.

'Pity about Mr Jelley's sister. The only one, I gather.'

'Yes, very sad. 'E's not yet got over it...'

Alcoholic tears began to rise.

'Where did she live?'

'Todbury, I think. Quite a stretch from here. A poor, lorn thing she was, by all accounts. Now, he's not got a friend in the world beside us here...'

She sobbed and hiccupped at the same time.

'Excuse me.'

Mrs Minshull drew close to Littlejohn in confidential intimacy.

'By the way, sir, she's TOLD.'

'Told. What do you mean, Mrs Minshull?'

'She's told Mrs McAllister about you investigating Miss Penelope's death. That's what the gin's done... I warned her as she was talkin' too much, but she got quite cross...'

'Well?'

'McAllister's the bank messenger. She'll tell 'im when he goes home for his dinner, and this afternoon he'll tell Mr Ralph. Tells Mr Ralph everything.'

'Indeed. Well, it had to come out sooner or later. Might as well be sooner.'

Voices were raised in the passage and Jelley entered, flushed and trembling with anger, followed by Mrs Frazer with her hair rather in disorder.

'And 'oo are you to forbid me to take a drop in 'ealth of a fellow Scot-by-marriage, may I ask?'

'...Visitors present...lunch to prepare...highly degrading in a woman...disgusting, in fact...'

Jelley couldn't get his words out for rage.

'Wot did you say, Mister clever Jelley?'

Mrs Minshull rose in wrath.

'"Ow dare you, Jemima Frazer, with a police officer present...? Jest control yourself...'

Mrs Frazer compromised for the sake of peace and hurried off to bully Dolly, whose whispered protests could be heard from the scullery.

'An' leave 'er alone. Whenever you've 'ad a drop, you always turn on 'er. Let her be...'

Mrs Frazer returned, hands on hips, ready for a set-to.

'And who do you think you're checking, madam...? You h'imperent, h'igorant person, you.'

'The words is h'impident and h'ignorant, if you please, and don't be alwiz using 'em, for they apply very much to yourself...'

'Ladies, ladies, PLEASE...' quavered Jelley.

'I'm off; good morning,' said Littlejohn and found his way outside to the accompaniment of battle cries and shouts of feminine abuse.

'Hey, hey,' shouted a voice as he made for the door in the garden wall.

'Hey, hey...'

It was Betts, the handyman, emerging from his glasshouses and waving frantically as he tottered towards Littlejohn. He had a black eye given to him by his unruly son, who had last night returned home drunk and put the family out of doors.

'I want you...'

The old man was still chuckling and grinning, in spite of his disfigurement, and his almost toothless gums rotated with eager emotion.

'You said you'd come to me for another talk...'

'So I did, Betts. I'm sorry I've been so busy...'

'Come in greenhouse. Don't wanta be overheard...'

They crossed the empty vegetable beds and entered the largest of the glasshouses. It was warm and moist and smelled of strong twist tobacco. It was like a small garden under glass, soil in beds on the floor with cement paths between. The gardener seemed to have been bedding-out young tomato plants. In one bed, daffodils were in full bloom.

'Nice, ain't they? Flowers is better than 'umans once't you gets to know 'em.' Betts caressed the blooms and taking a huge clasp-knife from his pocket, picked the choicest daffodil, cut it, and slipped it through the buttonhole of Littlejohn's coat. He adjusted the bloom and patted the lapel back into position.

'From me, sir.'

'Thank you, Mr Betts. Have a smoke?'

The old man filled his clay pipe from the Inspector's pouch, lit it, and puffed contentedly for a minute or two. Littlejohn took up the baccy box from its shelf, opened it and laid bare a small piece of twist. He scooped out the contents of his own pouch and filled the box.

'Thankee, sir...'

Betts was not laughing this time. There was something on his mind.

'You wanted to talk to me?'

'Yes, sir. Two things. First a bit of advice, I wants. I kinda tuck to you, sir. Perhaps you'll give me your 'elp. Then, I've somethin' very important to tell 'ee about Miss Penelope...'

'First the advice then. What is it?'

Betts pointed to his black eye with his shortened forefinger.

'My son did this. I don't take that from nobody. Gave his mother one, too, which is worser. I'm goin' to take 'im up.'

'Was he drunk...?'

Littlejohn and the old man talked it out and eventually settled the business by Betts deciding to take his domestic troubles to the magistrates, assisted by Paston, for whom Littlejohn gave assurances.

'And now about Miss Penelope?'

'I oughter told this before and now you've advised me, I will. It was me as unscrewed the winder box...'

'You!'

'Yes, sir. I did it. I knows I should 'a come to police an' told 'em. That ud leave my ole woman and my gel without protection agen' our Joe. He'd murder 'em if I waren't there to take it instead. I couldn't tell perlice and get sent down an' leave 'em to 'im.'

'Not really, I understand. So you were the cause of the accident?'

'No, sir. Miss Penelope were *pushed* through the winder. I see it done.'

'Let's get this straight, Mr Betts. You unscrewed the window box. Why?'

'Them daffier would never a bloomed proper in that soil. 'Adn't been changed for fower year. Cruelty to flowers, sir. I told Miss Penelope, but she wouldn't 'ave them bulbs disturbed. So when she was away, I thinks I'll do 'em. I unscrews the box ready to carry down. Easier than takin' out all them bulbs in mid-air, carryin' down old soil, puttin' up new, and plantin' bulbs agen. So I was jest a-thinkin' I'd do it unknown to 'er. I'd got screws out, when up comes Mrs Ralph. Wants some daffodils from 'ere right away. Visitin' the sick, she sez. I gets 'em for 'er...about noon, it was. Then, out comes Mrs Frazer. Wants some lettuces and things for dinner. I gets 'em. With one thing an' another, dusk was a-fallin' afore I got time. So, thinkin' Miss Penelope wouldn't be back, I left the box without the screws. In any case, it were safe on that ledge, I thinks. A broad winder sill... I'd finish 'em first thing tomorn... Instead, Miss Penelope comes 'ome and starts a-waterin' of them bulbs. I was jest 'ere, as she puts on the light and I see 'er leanin' out with a jug, jest a shadder against the light, for by that it were dark, sir.'

'And you saw her topple out, Betts?'

'No, sir. She did not topple out. She were *pushed*. I see somebody suddenly come behind and stand behind 'er and it weren't a topple at all...it were a rush, as if Miss Penelope'd been pushed.'

'Who was it pushed her?'

'I didn't see, sir. As I said, they looked like two shedders.'

'Man or woman, would you say?'

'Couldn't even see that at this distance, sir.'

'I see...'

All the same, Littlejohn felt more satisfied. That made it a straight affair. No doubt now that it was out-and-out murder.

'The magistrates'll see to my missus and gel now, if I'm sent down, won't they?'

'You won't be sent down, Betts. I'll see to that.'

'You mean...'

'I mean, I'm glad you've helped me by telling me, Betts. I'll look after you.'

Betts said nothing, but started to weep, hard noisy sobs, with tears trickling from his black eye and slowly down his nose and beard.

'Wot a relief, sir. God bless yer...'

Littlejohn felt relieved somehow, as well.

17

THE FORGER

Whilst Littlejohn was in the throes of intestine warfare below-stairs at the bank house, news arrived at the police station from Scotland Yard. The experts were of the opinion that the writer of the prescription secured from the rejoicing pharmacist had forged the cheques on Miss Penelope Blow's account at Doubledays' Bank. That was Dr Cross.

Cromwell, instructed the previous night by Littlejohn, made his way early that morning to Lapworth, where Cross was said to have a country retreat. The idea was to find out if Lenore Blow had been in the habit of retreating there with him.

Lapworth lies about twelve miles north of Nesbury and is a great resort for fishermen and hikers. It is, as yet, unspoilt, but will not be so for long. The overspill from a large city is due, in the sweet by-and-by, to increase the population of 250 to 20,000 and, already, a host of jerry builders and developers are champing at the bit and spitting on their hands in eagerness for the Ministry to say 'GO'. Cromwell arrived on one of the infrequent buses and was dumped on the doorstep of the Miners' Arms well before opening time. There were no miners about;

the abortive lead-diggings were closed about the time they were erecting the statue of the redoubtable Blow in the main square at Nesbury.

The landlord of the Arms was standing at the door thinking how to make more money. He was always on the make and forever cudgelling his brains for further ingenious schemes, legal and illicit, to add to his ill-gotten gains. A little runt of a fellow, fat, coarse, illiterate and pop-eyed, he glanced at Cromwell with suspicion and disapproval. Then, his face lit up with an evil grin, showing a lot of irregular yellow teeth. He decided that the newcomer was something to do with the Town and Country Planning lot who were, by bringing droves of new customers, going to add to his balance at the bank.

'Mawnin',' said Slingsbee, for that was his name. 'Nahse mawnin'...'

'Yes,' said Cromwell. 'Looks like being a good Easter.'

'You betcha...'

The little tables in the garden at the side of the pub had all been green painted ready for next week's invasion of cyclists and hikers. On the hillside behind stood about a dozen little huts which Slingsbee rented for a week at a time to holidaymakers. They, too, had all had a vernal coat of paint. A gate nearby led to the river. *Fishing Tickets 1s a day. Apply Miners Arms* said a notice. And below it on a homemade sign: *Tresspaser's will be Prosected, by order T Slingsbee*. A path along the riverbank vanished among trees in the midst of which you could see clearings with a few more large huts.

Slingsbee held the rights over all the fun and games of Lapworth. Next week, sideshows would arrive, he would be selling ice cream and ginger beer as well as more potent drinks in the inn. All summer long, teas and refreshments would keep him and his on their toes seven days a week. And that was not all. Mr Slingsbee was up to his neck in the black market. If your credentials were in order, you could enjoy ham and eggs and juicy steaks with chips in an upper room at prices above the odds. You could, if vouched for, also take away home with you ham, eggs, butter, cream and nylons. Mr Slingsbee toured the countryside and neighbouring cities for fresh supplies every other day in an opulent car. The police had their eye on him, and he knew it, but Cromwell looked more like a planner than a snooper. All the same, Slingsbee was watching his P's and Q's.

'What brings you here?'

'I'm on a holiday in Nesbury. They said it was very nice out here and they're right.'

"Oo said?'

Mr Slingsbee was all ears for Cromwell's credentials.

'Dr Cross...'

'Ah, the doctor. Good sort. Bit standoffish, but a good sort. Customer o' mine... Keeps a little weekend place there through them trees. Gets 'is grub 'ere...'

'Does he come much? He seemed to know the place well.'

'Used to be 'ere every weekend. But now with the National Insurance, I guess 'e's bizzy... Only been once since Christmas.'

'Is he a fisherman, then?'

'No... Does a bit o' sketchin' round the place.'

Mr Slingsbee gave Cromwell a yellow leer. There was something behind the look.

'What are you laughing at, landlord?'

'Me thoughts... You know the doc well?'

'So, so. Met him a time or two and he said he was fond of this place,' lied Cromwell in a good cause. 'Fond o' the ladies, too, I guess.'

Slingsbee grinned lasciviously and spat a long jet across the cobblestones. Higher up the road a church clock struck ten-thirty.

'Openin' time.'

Mr Slingsbee removed his untidy body from the doorway to

denote that business was ready to begin. They went indoors. The lobby was long and dark, and the taproom plainly furnished. Cromwell draped himself on a leather upholstered bench which ran round three sides of the room.

'What'll it be?'

'Pint of bitter. Join me?'

Mr Slingsbee honoured his guest by drawing the drinks himself.

''Ere's 'ow...'

'Your good health, landlord...'

A blowsy barmaid thrust her head round the door.

'Where you bin? I'm havin' to attend to the bar meself.'

Slingsbee, standing by the bar, gave the girl a twisted grin and reached out a stumpy hand and fondled her, eyed her opulent bosom hungrily, and then gave her a push.

'Go an' get your 'air done, Ethel. That's not the way to appear before gents...'

He cackled and preened himself.

Nasty bit of work, thought Cromwell.

'Go on with you,' said the artificial blonde and flounced out.

'Bit of all right, wot?'

Cromwell's nose was in his beer pot, however.

'Dr Cross 'as an eye for the ladies, believe me...'

It was evidently the landlord's favourite subject.

'So I believe...'

'You've heard of it? Surprised at 'im. But we're all yewman, aren't we? Enjye yerself while yer can's my motter. Don't blame Cross. Won't say that little bungerlow of 'is hasn't been a love-nest now and then...'

Slingsbee had helped himself to a glass of whisky this time and his tongue was loosing nicely.

'Girls from the town?' asked Cromwell, feeling his way.

'Gels, did you say? Naw. The doctor likes 'em grown-up, like me. Machewer an' bonny, like Ethel. Not bits o' kids. Now, the last 'e brought, a few weeks since...well... If I was to tell you. Thought I 'adn't seen 'em. Took the path on the other side o' the stream and crossed by the tree trunk as lies across higher up. But there's not much round 'ere as Slingsbee don't see. I saw 'em. Reel lovely bit o' work, the doc 'ad with 'im. Tuck 'er to the bungalow, but they was soon back. She must 'ave rumbled 'im and turned 'im down. They wasn't there above 'alf an hour...'

Cromwell was getting sick of Mr Slingsbee's *Decameron* and rose to his feet.

'Off already?'

'Thought I'd take a stroll by the river a bit...'

'Comin' back for a meal?'

'What time's the bus back?'

'One thirty. Care to order lunch now? We'll get you off for the bus...'

'Righto. I'll be back then. Which is the doctor's shack? I'd better just pass it. He'll be asking if I saw it.'

'Oh, aye. Second along the path. Stands all alone by itself. Locked up and he keeps the only key. Not much to see inside, though. Peep through the winders...'

'Right,' said the sergeant and smiled wryly to himself.

It was sunny outside. Hens were picking among the cobblestones and on the manure heap in the small farmyard which stood by the pub. You could hear pigs yelling in styes, too. Mr Slingsbee's ham and eggs in the making!

A pleasant morning for a country walk. The willows on the bank of the stream were yellow with catkins and here and there clumps of daffodils were blooming in the fields. At regular intervals Mr Slingsbee's homemade and illiterate notices took your eye. 'Willful Damige', 'Camper's are Forbiden to Light Fires', 'Sight for 4 Caravans', 'Tip no Rubbish, by order, T Slingsbee', and more trespassers who would be prosecuted by Slingsbee's orders. After a brief walk, Cromwell came upon what must have been Cross's hut. It was a well-kept place, with a single large room and a small kitchen. Through the window, Cromwell could make out a plain chair, an easy one, a wooden table and a camp bed without mattress or clothes. He looked all round and then, taking a large clasp-knife from his pocket, coaxed from it an implement like a hook and tackled the mortice lock of the door with it. He was soon inside.

The place smelled a bit damp and airless, for all the windows were fastened. A large stove, with a pipe piercing the roof, stood by the inner wall. A pile of logs in a box beside it. Cromwell opened a plain wood cupboard hanging on the partition. It had three shelves. From the undersides of two hung white cups and two jugs. There were tins of tea and coffee, cans of milk and beans and a few other odds and ends of condiments and cutlery. Nothing much else.

Cromwell turned to the stove, opened it and examined the ashes. Just wood-ash; nothing more. The kitchen was equally unproductive of anything interesting. Cromwell returned to the main room ready to leave. Over the camp bed was a hanging bookshelf. The sergeant crossed and examined its contents. Two or three thrillers, a guidebook and map of the locality, a pamphlet on the local church by the vicar and, wedged between two crime stories, a leaflet with a gaudy back. South Africa. A shipping office handbook of routes and sailings, dated late the previous year and bearing the stamp of a Nesbury firm, 'Shelley's Tours, Nesbury.' Cromwell put it in his pocket and turned to the door. Peeping Tom Slingsbee was approaching along the riverbank, looking here and there cautiously, evidently on Cromwell's trail. The sergeant watched him until he was momentarily hidden by the bushes which sheltered the hut and then quickly slipped out, skilfully fastened the lock again with his hook, and when Slingsbee came to light, was eagerly peering in through the front window.

"Ello... Found it?'

'Yes. Not bad...'

'You ever wantin' a 'ut, let me know. Be able to mannige it for you...'

'Thanks... Can I get a taxi hereabouts? I don't think I'll stay for lunch. I got my feet damp by the river and I'll get cold if I don't change my socks...'

Mr Slingsbee eyed Cromwell up and down and mentally dubbed him a sissy. Why, with keeping an eye on things in the season, his own feet were never dry. All the same...

'I got a car. Cost you a couple of quid from 'ere, though.'

Cromwell's mind flew to his expenses sheet.

'Right.'

Half an hour later, the landlord of the Miners' Arms dropped his passenger in the square at Nesbury. On the way, egged on by Cromwell, he had disclosed the name of the doctor's last brief guest at the hut. A woman in a fur coat... Bank chap's wife, he thought. Seen her about the town and goin' in Blows' Bank. A real, nice, tasty dish o' tea, if you asked Mr Slingsbee. Wouldn't mind gettin' to know her himself...

'Fifty bob, did I say?'

'Two pounds...'

'Makin' a loss with a car like this... All the same, if I said two quid, two quid it is... S'long... Don' forget... If you want a bungalow yourself, lemme know. Bring your girlfriend along... I'm discreet... S'long agen...'

Cromwell exhaled hard to get the air of Mr Slingsbee and his flash car out of his system and turned in at a small shop in the square. There were posters of English and Swiss resorts in the window. *Shelley's Tours... Lugano this Year. Select Party...£30, inclusive.* They were tea-merchants as well. At the counter a platinum blonde was booking theatre seats for a little man. She finished the job and turned to Cromwell.

'May ay help you?'

Outside, the football fans were thronging the pavements and hunting for somewhere to have their lunches. They whirled their rattles and rang their bells. 'Hup the 'Awks...' The cattle-market was over, and men were dismantling the stalls and wheeling them away.

'Have you any information about South Africa...?'

'Yace. This leaflut will help... Any particulah infawmeyshun?'

'No, thanks. I'll study this and maybe come again for help if I need it.'

'Deelayted...'

'I hear Dr Cross is talking of a trip...'

The girl tittered.

'Yes. We told him all we could. Fares, currencay, the prace of tickets, and then he decayded to fly out...'

She patted her permanent wave gingerly.

'When is he going?'

'He said he'd let us know... Thet was some tame ago. He's not bin since...'

'Maybe I'll find myself with a companion...'

The girl giggled and was interrupted by a lady who wanted to buy a chromium cake-stand. Cromwell made his exit.

At the police station, he found Littlejohn, Paston and Hempseed, the latter looking much better and very flushed from argument. They were in the Chief Constable's room and the Chief Constable was with them. He'd just got back from London and Cromwell was too late to be in at the thunderstorm which had broken over Nesbury with his arrival. Ralph Blow had telephoned a complaint to him and he had returned, hotfoot and in a foaming temper.

Colonel Cardew was a tall, clean-looking, military man with a liverish temperament and a tendency to vent on his constabulary underlings the repressions caused by petticoat government at home. Fortunately, Hempseed had limped in a minute or two before the Chief Constable had hurled himself from his car and torpedoed his way in. Cardew was fond of Hempseed. Besides, the fellah was going on pension in a week or two. Just got over a bad bout of illness and, in the past, the Chief had owed the Superintendent a lot. After all, it would hardly be cricket to hit the fellah when he was down. It spiked Colonel Cardew's guns. He contented himself with asking: 'What the hell? Who the blazes?' and, turning to Littlejohn, 'Who the hell are you, sir?' and what in thunder Scotland Yard wanted messin' about...?

Hempseed took the initiative, and all the blame, was forgiven, and Cardew, taking a seat, asked for a full account. Then he rang up Ralph Blow and told him he'd better be at the police station as soon as he could get there and not to be long.

The storm had passed when Cromwell entered and he was introduced to the Chief, who said: 'What, another of 'em?', shook his hand and ordered him to sit down.

'You're only just in time, Cromwell,' said Littlejohn. 'Sorry, there's another rush job for you. Go on the half-past twelve train to London, call and see Mrs Buckley again and ask her exactly whom she was working for when she shadowed Miss Penelope, where she saw Miss Penelope go, and whom she reported to. Also, ask her what Harold Blow was doing there the day you called. Got that?'

'Yes, sir.'

Littlejohn passed a letter to Cromwell.

'That's interesting...'

It was on the official paper of Doubledays' Bank and had been sent by the Manager. It was addressed to the Nesbury police.

Gentlemen,

With reference to the call of an official from Scotland Yard to interview us recently on your behalf, I am instructed to inform you that Miss P Blow wrote to us a fortnight ago for her statement of account. This was duly forwarded. Mr Doubleday, who was unaware of this fact when he interviewed your representative, asks me to say he thinks this point may be of importance to you. Miss Blow had not previously had such a statement of account since the withdrawal of the donation of £5,000 to the Salvation Army in 1942. This, presumably on the assumption that there would be no change in the balance.

I am also informed by one of our cashiers, that a week ago, Miss Blow called here and asked for Mr Doubleday. I regret this, too, was not mentioned at the interview with your representative, as neither Mr Doubleday nor myself was aware until yesterday that she had called. The cashier, who has been absent through illness, reports that on being told that Mr Doubleday was absent, Miss Blow said she would not care to see anyone else, as he alone dealt with her affairs.

I hope this report will prove of use to you.

Yours faithfully,
Bannister J Hobday,
Manager.

'So, she knew all the time...'

'Yes. And maybe her call at Scotland Yard didn't entirely concern arsenic, Cromwell. What a pity both Doubleday and I were away at the time. Probably she'd still have been alive.'

'By Gad! Somebody's goin' to be made to sit up for this, sir,' said the Chief Constable, and he thumped the table.

Cromwell found Mrs Buckley in, drinking tea at the table with the American leather cloth, sitting on one of the platoon of chairs. There was a smell of greasy cooking on the air. A dishevelled daily help was busy making the beds and carrying slops from the rooms of the absent guests. Mrs Buckley was afraid this time. She asked Cromwell to sit down in a hesitant voice, rubbed her hands nervously up and down her large white apron and said she wasn't very well.

'I've only called for a minute, just to clear up a thing or two, Mrs Buckley,' said Cromwell in his blandest manner.

'I 'ope it's nothin' serious. I couldn't bear it. I'm that bad this mornin'...'

'Whilst Miss Blow was with you just before her death, you were instructed to keep an eye on her by someone. You followed her on her daily visits and reported back to somebody. Where did you see her go?'

Mrs Buckley's eyes grew wide with horror and her tightly corseted bosom rose and fell and made her stays creak with the strain. She opened a drawer, withdrew a bottle of smelling salts, sniffed gingerly at them and seemed to receive a measure of inspiration from the fumes.

'It was this way... Miss Penelope was a poor, innocent thing. Never able to look after 'erself proper. When she came 'ere, all worried and worked up, I tuck pity on the poor dear. She was...'

'Just cut out all the sob-stuff,' said Cromwell harshly. 'Miss Penelope was murdered after you supplied certain information. I want to know all about it.'

'Murdered! Oh dear... That on top of the way I feel this mornin'... Do you know, I've just received notice to quit. 'Is Lordship's agent won't renew me lease. Whatever am I to do? I've all my lodgers to think of...'

'I'm not concerned with that. Please answer the questions.'

'Well... As I was sayin'... I thought Miss Penelope wasn't fit to look after 'erself and the sooner they got her home the better. So, I telephoned the house at Nesbury right away.'

'Who answered you?'

'A woman's voice...'

'Whose? Now come along. This is murder...'

'Oh, dear...'

She sniffed hard again at her bottle and recoiled.

'I think it was Mrs Ralph, though I'm not sure. I told 'er. She said she'd see about it and went off and soon Mr 'Arold came on. He said I wasn't to let her out of my sight. Out of my sight! And me with all me lodgers to do for. I told 'im so. He said he'd make it worth me while. So I got Mrs Tetlow in while I looked after poor Miss Penelope.'

'Whilst you shadowed her... Go on...'

'The first day, she went straight up to the City. Called at a bank in St Paul's Churchyard. I forget the name, but I've got it down somewhere. I'll find it...'

'Never mind. Then what?'

'She never went there again. But she kept callin' at Scotland Yard. I telephoned Mr 'Arold every time I saw her go anywhere. In my 'umble opinion she wasn't 'erself. Goin' mad. It's in the fambly. What did she want in a City bank when they've a bank of their own, and what did she want at Scotland Yard? There's police in Nesbury if she must 'ave the police... That's all I know.'

'And Mr Harold came and took her away?'

'Yes.'

'Did he ask her here where she'd been?'

'Yes. Forced it out of 'er, like. She said she'd been seein' a mutual friend at Scotland Yard.'

'I see. That'll be all, thank you. Good morning, Mrs Buckley.'

'Good mornin', sir... I 'ope I 'aven't...'

'I don't know. I may call again. Otherwise, you'll read all about it in the papers...'

Cromwell peeped in the walled garden, but his friend was missing, so he hurried off for the next train back to Nesbury. Littlejohn was busy interviewing Jelley again. The old butler looked ready to pass out.

'We've spoken to the police at Todbury, where you were staying whilst Miss Blow was being murdered...'

'I had nothing to do with it, sir,' shrieked the palsied butler.

'I'm not saying you had, Jelley. Sit down and don't take on so. But the police tell me they know your sister very well. She's very much alive, and the time you were there seemed to be spent on a holiday, and that they saw you about the town with the one you were supposed to be burying...'

'I can't... I didn't... Oh, Mr Littlejohn, I didn't intend to lie to you. But what could I do? I'd told the family she was ill and then dead. What would they have thought...?'

'I don't care what they thought, Jelley. I want to know why you told such a cock-and-bull story... The truth, please.'

'I'd been through enough, sir, with the family. I knew something was wrong and I wasn't being in that house again if there was trouble. That's why I made up the tale. I had to get away... You do believe me, sir...you must.'

'What was the trouble, Jelley?'

'Miss Honoria was saying she was poisoned, and Miss Penelope had run away, sir. I overheard Mr Ralph and Mr Harold having a terrible quarrel. Mr Harold said she was as mad as the rest of them and that he was going to see Dr Cross and have her shut up in the old room that Mr William was put in. Mr Ralph got in a terrible rage, sir. Said he knew all that 'ad been going on and that he wasn't havin' any more public scandals. He said it had to be kept in the family proper this time. And that Miss Penelope was no more mad than he was. It was other people who were mad...'

'Was that all?'

'It was quite enough for me, sir. I'd had to do with things when the same sort of quarrels were going on about Mr William. I wasn't havin' any more of it. I told the tale about my sister and I went. I couldn't give notice. I can't afford to be out of a job and nobody else would take me on. Only reason the Blows keep me now is that I know too much.'

'What do you know?'

'Only what I told you, sir. About the matter of Mr William and 'is trying to poison himself and all that. And them knowing I'd overheard what they said about Miss Penelope.'

'I see...'

Paston entered smiling grimly to himself.

'Mr Ralph Blow has called and he's in with the Chief. They want you, sir.'

Jelley began to tremble like a leaf and turned the colour of putty.

'All right, all right, Mr Jelley,' said Paston. 'We'll see you off by the back entrance. Come on...'

Littlejohn rose and braced himself to meet Ralph Blow, and this time matters were different.

18

'NOBODY TELLS ME ANYTHING'

Under the steely blue eye of the Chief Constable, Ralph Blow was less formidable than he might have been. He was used to bullying and browbeating his inferiors, but rather at a loss in the face of stern authority. It was an experience he wasn't often called upon to endure.

'This is Inspector Littlejohn of Scotland Yard, Blow,' said Cardew brusquely. 'He's here investigating the death of your Aunt Penelope...'

'We've met...'

'Good afternoon, sir.'

'I may as well tell you, Cardew, I showed the Inspector the door and propose to do so again if he meddles in affairs which have been settled legally and don't concern him...'

'Don't be a damn fool, Blow!'

Mr Ralph, although freely perspiring, was wearing a large overcoat and gloves. He unbuttoned the former, removed the latter and clawed at his collar. The pulse at his temple grew inflated and you could see it steadily throbbing as his temper rose. Having relieved himself of his various sources of heat, the banker with angry hands gripped the desk and thrust his face as close to Cardew's own as he could without raising himself from the ground.

'I won't take that from you or anyone else, Cardew...'

'Sit down and listen.'

'I prefer to stand, thank you.'

'Very well, then. The case is re-opened, the Coroner is being notified that I'm not satisfied with the findin's of his court. Your aunt was murdered, and I'll trouble you, Blow, to cooperate with us in findin' out who killed her. That plain?'

Ralph Blow sat down this time. His eyes popped, revealing bloodshot whites and thin films across them as though he might be starting with cataracts.

'I never heard such nonsense! I'll make somebody pay for this. I'm a JP, don't forget, and I'll use the full weight of my power to make somebody suffer...'

'Who will suffer, might I ask?'

'The whole damn lot of you. Meddling police...interfering scoundrels... I'll have the law in at this...'

'That will do, Blow. Let me talk and then you can go on with your threats. Till I, or rather Littlejohn, has said his say, be quiet!'

'Let's hear what it's all about, then, and it had better be good...'

Littlejohn drew a chair to the desk.

'It's quite true your aunt was murdered, Mr Blow. We have witnesses to prove she was pushed from the window of her room. The window box rather drew a red herring across the trail. It wasn't the cause of her death. Someone from behind did that.'

'But the inquest made it clear...'

'The inquest was held before the full facts came to light. On the evidence then available, it looked like an accident. It was not an accident and we can prove it.'

'Give me the proof then...'

'Later, sir. For the present, you'll have to accept my state-ment. Last time I tried to interview you and inspect the scene of the crime, you showed me the front door. I was forced to continue my inquiries at the back door...'

'I heard of that. Damn scandal. Police sneaking round getting information from the servants. I've given the lot notice. Don't want informers in my house.'

'If you won't volunteer help yourself, sir, we have to get it the best way we can. The servants weren't to blame. I did the questioning...'

'GOAL!!!'

A titanic yell rose and floated over Nesbury like a thunder cloud of sound. On their ground behind the Blow house, the Nesbury team had scored a goal. Workmen, passers-by and hangers-on in the square halted in their tracks for a brief moment like petrified beings, looked at each other with approval, congratulated one another with broad smiles and then went on where they'd left off. To Ralph Blow it was as though nothing had happened. He heeded it as little as did the monstrous statue of his ancestor which the pigeons were copi-ously decorating outside.

'I wasn't going to stand for police all over the place. Besides, nobody told me it was murder. Nobody tells me anything.'

If he hadn't been so angry at the indignity of this inquisition, Ralph might have burst into tears of self-pity!

'You didn't wait to ask or even let me say my piece. You showed us the door and made threats. I want to know now, sir, if you're disposed to cooperate.'

'He'd better! If he doesn't, I'll damn well see his name's removed from the panel of Justices,' breathed Cardew hoarsely.

'No need for you to interfere, Cardew. Of course, if the law's been broken, it's my duty to cooperate, though I don't like the way things have been done. Object to bringing in the servants, that's all. Might have done the thing straight and above board.'

He was a stupid man whose mind seemed to run on mental tramlines. Cardew looked ready to burst.

'Look here, Blow...'

'Do you mind, sir...?'

Littlejohn was getting fed up with the sparring and snarling of the local bigwigs. Blow was beginning to show every sign of deflation and the Inspector was anxious to take advantage of it.

'Will you answer my questions now, sir?'

'Of course. Never said I wouldn't. It's Cardew who...'

'You were in the house when your aunt met her death?'

'Yes. My brother and I were in the hall seeing off the doctors who'd been consulting about my aunt. She wasn't an aunt at all; only a cousin, but being so much older than we were, we called her that since we were children.'

'There were just the four of you there?'

'Yes. We heard the scream and the thud. Then we broke up to see what was happening. That's as well as I can remember and it's all I know about it.'

'Where were the other members of the family, sir?'

'My Aunt Honoria was in her room...and so, of course, was Aunt Penelope. My wife had gone upstairs to help Aunt Honoria get some things together. Aunt Honoria was going at once to Tankerville's nursing home...'

'Are you sure your wife and your Aunt Honoria were together when Miss Penelope fell?'

'Look here... Are you...?'

'Answer the questions, Blow...'

'No need for you to come butting in, Cardew. I'm not forced to answer all this... Don't know if I will. Want to see my lawyer.'

Littlejohn brushed the objection gently aside.

'You'll have to answer sooner or later, sir. The inquest will be re-opened and there you'll be asked the questions on oath. Better here than in public.'

'I... I... Oh, very well. What do you want to know?'

'I asked if your wife and Miss Honoria were together when Miss Penelope met her death.'

'I don't know. They were upstairs. The whole place is carpeted. I didn't hear them moving about.'

'I see. The servants? Where were they?'

'Jelley was away burying his sister; Frazer and the maid were in the servants' quarters. I saw 'em as we ran through to the back to see what was going on.'

'Thank you.'

'That all? Because, if it is, I'll be going. Business appointment.'

'Not quite, sir. I'll try to be brief. Mr William Blow's will... Did you know its contents?'

'Of course. What's that got to do with it?'

It was obvious that the old man's last efforts were still a sore point with Ralph in spite of passing time.

'...He left the lot to a pack of silly charities.'

'With the exception of a tontine annuity to your aunts.'

'Yes; with that exception. Though what that's got to do with it, I can't for the life of me think. This is just silly...'

Cardew half rose and then subsided with a snort.

'To what extent did your aunts benefit under the annuity, sir?'

'At first, a thousand apiece. Then, when Aunt Katherine died, her share was divided. Fifteen hundred apiece.'

'And now, Miss Honoria enjoys three thousand a year which dies with her.'

'Yes; but... Are you suggesting that Aunt Honoria...?'

'I'm suggesting nothing, sir. Were you aware of any other moneys possessed by your uncle at the time of his death?'

'What do you mean?'

'What I say.'

'Of course not!'

He looked as if he meant it, too.

'You didn't know, for example, that he had deposited a considerable sum in your Aunt Penelope's name at a London bank before he died?'

'What *is* this? Just ridiculous. Why, if he had, we'd all have known.'

'That's just where you're wrong, sir. He told nobody but Miss Penelope and she had full control of the funds. He repented his harshness before he died.'

'This is ridiculous!'

'You may think so, sir. But Doubledays' Bank in London will confirm that it's true.'

'Why wasn't I told?'

'You were only his nephew. It was his daughters he was concerned about after he repented.'

'After *what*?'

'He repented what he'd done in leaving so much away from them. He was under restraint at the time and any will he might have made could have been contested. He was a bit queer and didn't quite see things right apparently, but he was sane enough to realise some bonds he'd laid aside for a rainy day and place the proceeds to the account I've mentioned. Your father-in-law assisted him and, with the exception of Miss Penelope, was the only other person in the secret. It had to be kept dark because estate duties hadn't been paid on the amount.'

'But why...? Why, I was the next head of the family... Why didn't he tell me?'

They could all have given a true answer, but they didn't.

'I don't know. Your father-in-law later told your wife about it.'

'Ah! Of course, *she* didn't tell me. Anybody but me. Nobody tells me anything. I actually heard about your investigations with the servants from the bank messenger!'

'Well?' asked Cardew.

'I don't like it. Why wasn't I told?'

'Damn it, man. Don't ask us. We weren't in the secret.'

'How much was there?'

'Thirty thousand pounds...'

Ralph Blow pawed the air and slumped in a state of semi-collapse. His body seemed to grow inflated and hung over the sides of the chair like a flabby balloon.

'My God! The old swine!! And all these years...Aunt Penelope...and she never said a word to me. I never liked her. Stupid old fool... Half out of her wits and trying to handle all that money... Well... No wonder somebody murdered her...'

He realised what he had said and with lowered head glanced round to see how the rest had taken it.

'Is it still there? Because, if it is... Her will... She left all she had...all she had...'

He choked and tore at his collar.

'Her will's in course of being proved, but I've seen it. It was a new one. She left all she had...'

Blow started to laugh. There was no mirth in it. It sounded like the boiling of thick fluids in his lungs. His neck grew inflated like a rubber tyre and hung over his collar, livid and floppy. His eyes protruded from their sockets more than ever, and flecks of foam oozed from the corners of his mouth.

'Blow!!! Dammit, man, there's nothin' to laugh at, if you're supposed to be laughin'. The poor old girl was murdered in cold blood...'

Blow threw back his head and with staring eyes and spasmodic coughing from his hideous mirth, spat out the words "Salvation Army..."

'She left all she'd got to the Salvation Army! First, Uncle William... Now Aunt Penelope... The whole damn lot to charity... It's true, we're all mad... All, all mad... Balmy Blows, that's what somebody once called us... But, by God, I'll fight it this time if it costs me every penny I have. I won't be humiliated a second time. I'll... I'll...'

'The money's all gone.'

'Say that again... Gone?'

'Yes. It's been withdrawn.'

'You mean to say old Penelope's blued it all in? No... No... It's a lie... What would she be doing with all that?'

'No. Someone else drew it out with forged cheques.'

That did it! Blow rose to his feet, his banking intelligence outraged, his mind completely befogged by the rapid march of events.

'Oh, come, come, come. You're joking. All that money. A bank wouldn't do that. You're mistaken. It's there all the time.'

He was like someone waking from a pleasant dream who tries to fall asleep again and return to illusion.

'No. We've got the cheques and experts confirm it.'

'You said only Lenore and her father knew besides my aunt. If they've...'

He didn't finish, but stretched out his podgy, well-kept hands, with a large signet on the left little finger, and made strangling gestures in front of him.

'No. It's neither of them.'

'But who else knew? Did they tell anybody else? I insist on knowing. After all, the money was as good as mine. I'll make them disgorge it. Damn me, if I don't.'

'Where did your aunt keep her private papers, Mr Blow?'

'In her box in the bank vault. We took them out after her death. She's actually made that snivelling little Padfield her lawyer and made two wills, one after another. The first left what she had to the family. The other, made the day before she left for London, left it all to the Salvation Army. I might as well tell you the whole damn fool tale. She'd made Padfield her sole executor. Not a cent for the family. Honoria, she said, would benefit enough under the annuity and her only other friend, a parson chap... Clapcoot or somebody...'

'Claplady...'

'That's it. How did you know? Been snooping round at Padfields? Left Claplady her love, because he'd enough money of his own. And her signet ring with the family crest that was her father's, she left that to the parson, too, in memory... In memory! It'll be many a day before I forget the way she and her loony of a father made a fool of me! But this money... You say it's all gone?'

'The bulk of it...'

'How much is left?'

'I can't say. It's immaterial for the moment. We want to know who withdrew it and what was done with it.'

'Well, don't look at me that way. I never knew it existed. Nobody ever tells me anything...'

'You've told us that before, Blow.'

'Well, I'm telling you again, Cardew, and don't keeping picking on me. Instead of showing sympathy with me in this mess, all you can do is pick on me. It's not good enough...'

Blow sat down limply and looked as if he hadn't a friend in the world.

'It's Lenore... I knew it... She's always hated me. Why, I don't know. I've always...'

'Your wife didn't forge the cheques, sir.'

'How do you know?'

'They've been examined by our experts.'

'Who did, then?'

Blow was beside himself. For some reason best known to himself, he took a pair of spectacles from his pocket and put them on. Then he took a cigar from his case, offered nobody else one, lit it and suddenly awoke to what he'd done. He looked at the cigar and then at the company.

'Who did it?'

Littlejohn was afraid to tell him. It would probably finish Blow altogether.

'Our investigations aren't complete yet, sir. I hope to be able to say very soon, though.'

'When? You're taking a hell of a time...'

'Tonight. I believe Miss Honoria is coming home this evening...'

'Yes. For dinner. Why?'

'I want you to invite us to your place after dinner. I have some questions I'd like to ask you all when you're together, now that you've offered to help us.'

'How many of you?'

'I suggest the Chief Constable, the Superintendent, and myself, with my colleague, Cromwell, to assist me personally.'

'All right. Do as you wish. Come over. Expect to arrest somebody, because none of our family would do such a thing. You'll find you're chasing a mare's nest. However, if you must, you must. Come at eight.'

'One other thing. I suppose Dr Cross will be accompanying your aunt from the nursing home. I'll be grateful if you'll arrange for him to be there, too.'

'What the devil's Cross got to do with it?'

'He was in the house when Miss Penelope met her death '

'Well? So was Tankerville. Want him, too?'

'No. Cross will do.'

'Very well. Seems a lot of rubbish to me. Still... Hope to recover the money?'

'I can't say, sir.'

'Mysterious, aren't you?'

'Just another question, sir, if you please.'

'Well? Thought you'd have had enough. What is it?'

'You say Padfield was sole executor. He took Miss Penelope's box from the bank to get out her will. Did you see the contents yourself?'

'Yes. He said he wanted a member of the family to be there. We went through it and made a list of what was there.'

'What was in it, sir?'

'The will and a lot of junk. Better ask Padfield.'

Quickly Cardew telephoned and asked the lawyer, who luckily happened to be in his chambers across the square, to come over to the police station. Almost at once, they saw Padfield crossing to meet them. He carried in his hand the list of contents of his dead client's box, which he had hastily snatched up.

There was nothing at all snivelling, as Ralph termed it, about Padfield. He was tall, lean and clean, with a kindly, clever face and, although he looked in his mid-forties, a head of thick, completely white hair. The type Miss Penelope would choose and trust.

'Yes?' he said after introductions.

'You're Miss Penelope Blow's executor, I hear, sir.'

'Yes. I brought the list of contents of her deed box. That's what you wanted, isn't it?'

'Thanks...'

Littlejohn put on his spectacles and read the details. A pathetic assortment of odds and ends. Keepsakes, jewellery, the will itself, a sad little bundle of early letters from the Rev Ethelred Claplady, scheduled as *seventeen items of private corre-spondence (unread) addressed to Miss P Blow, signed Ethelred,* a chequebook of obsolete cheques...

'The cheques, Mr Padfield. Obsolete, you say. Why?'

'They must have been kept as curiosities... Banking family, you know, Inspector. The bank has long been defunct...'

'Absorbed is the word, sir. Absorbed by a larger institution which carried on its business. Remember the name?'

'Double...something...'

'Doubleday, Ward...St Paul's Churchyard?'

'That's it. How did you know?'

'No statements of account at Doubledays'?'

'No. Nothing else.'

'I see. Mr Blow... Would anyone else have access to the box before Miss Penelope died?'

'No. At least, I don't think so. She kept the key in her purse, I know. I've seen her... She'd go in the bank and have it out of the vault and then...'

'Who would give it to her?'

'Let me see... The securities clerk. She'd have to see him. He keeps the key of the deposit vault... Gaukroger, that's the man.'

'Could you get him over, sir?'

More telephoning soon saw the stocky, middle-aged figure of a pleasant man putting on his bowler at the door of Blows' Bank and crossing the square to the police station with steady, mincing steps.

'Good afternoon, gentlemen... Oh, good afternoon, Mr Ralph. I didn't see you, sir... You wanted...er...?'

'Yes, please, Mr Gaukroger. Just a question...'

'Certainly...'

'Miss Penelope Blow kept a box in custody at the bank, I gather.'

'Yes, that's right. Mr Padfield opened it after her death.'

'It's before her death we're concerned with, sir. Did she always call personally and ask for it when she wanted to put anything in or remove anything...?'

Mr Gaukroger blushed and licked his lips.

'Now, sir, I want the full story, please. Did anyone else ever go into it?'

'Oh, no, Inspector.'

'Well, Gaukroger,' exploded Blow. 'What are you standing there looking so awkward about? Tell Littlejohn all you know.'

'No need for that, Blow. The fellah's doin' his best. You keep out of it.'

Gaukroger threw a grateful, fearful glance at the Chief Constable. Something to tell the boys when he got back. Mr

Ralph told to shut up! What a lark!! His eyes glinted with repressed fun.

'Well, sir. It's rather awkward. It was against the rules, but seeing that Mrs Ralph Blow...'

'Mrs Ralph Blow!! Keep my wife out of this, you! I won't...'

'That's enough of that, Blow. Go on, Gaukroger... I'll see you don't suffer... Shareholder of the bank as well as Blow... I'll see you all right...'

'Thank you, sir.'

'It's just that on one or two occasions I let Mrs Ralph have the box at Miss Penelope's request.'

'In writing, sir?'

'Well...no... I know it was irregular, but...well...it was a bit awkward. Being Mrs Ralph and Miss Penelope Blow... Mrs Ralph just said Miss Penelope had asked her to get the box for her and take it into the house. She wouldn't have it away above a minute or so. Which was right. She just wanted a piece of jewellery, Mrs Ralph said. Which seemed right. It was only out less than a quarter of an hour. After all, it was for the family... I couldn't... I hope there's nothing wrong, Inspector...'

'Of course not, Mr Gaukroger. I'm very grateful for your help. That's all, thanks...'

'Thank you too, sir. Good afternoon, gentlemen.'

'...And not a word of this at the bank... Understand?' yelled Blow after his clerk. Mr Gaukroger, a lonely figure in the empty square, returned to the office, closed for public business, but still hard at work. He was accompanied on his way by a dismal all-pervading groan which followed a burst of diluted cheering. The Hawks had scored an equalising goal against Nesbury!

'Sorry, Mr Padfield, but we'll have to see that chequebook. Could you get it? I know I'm a terrible nuisance...'

'Not at all, Inspector. Very glad to help...'

Padfield took a handkerchief from his pocket and trumpeted jovially in it.

'I'll have to go to the bank... It's still in the box... Luckily the key's in my pocket. I won't be long...'

He hurried out; they saw him cross to the bank and ring the doorbell. Someone let him in.

Blow was a wreck. Fury, indignity, surprise, disappointment, hope, they'd heaped them all on him. And now... Lenore was mixed up in it. What had she been doing with the box?

'My wife wouldn't do such a thing. Nor would my aunt. They both knew it was against the rules. I've always told them they've not to break the regulations and take advantage of the family position... How can you keep discipline when the family...? It's a lot of nonsense... Gaukroger's mistaken... I'll see him when I get back...'

'You'll damn well do nothing of the kind, Blow. I won't have him bullied. He's helped us. If I hear you've victimised him, I'll ask a question at the next general meetin' of the bank...'

Blow quailed. It was more than could be borne. A question at the general meeting... He burst into a sweat of horror!

Padfield was back with the chequebook. It was a very old one of Doubledays' Bank. Littlejohn examined the counterfoils. They bore exact details written by Miss Penelope of her withdrawals... Her sister... The cheque to self for the Salvation Army annexe... The Inspector checked the numbers... There were three gaps in the sequence. Three cheques had been carefully removed, counterfoils and all...

'Thanks, Mr Padfield... May I keep this? I'll see you get a receipt.'

'Certainly...'

Blow sat crumpled in his chair. His cigar had gone out and he sucked at it unaware that he held it in his mouth. Slowly, he removed it.

'Will somebody tell me what all this is about? Nobody ever tells me a proper tale. Nobody tells me anything...'

'We'll see you at eight tonight, then, sir. We'll try to tell you everything then,' said Littlejohn, and he handed the banker his hat and gloves. 'And meanwhile, please don't mention this interview to a soul, sir.'

'You hear, Blow? Not a word to a soul,' was Cardew's parting shot again.

19

THE RETURN OF HONORIA BLOW

As Littlejohn made his last call on the servants of the bank house, the home side scored their winning goal in the cup-tie. 'Scrapper' Bloor, the home centre forward, headed the ball from a corner kick and it struck the enemy's crossbar and bounded back into play. Scrapper headed it again; this time right into the net. Or so the *Nesbury City and Soke News* said later in a special edition. The succession of roars, culminating in a shout of triumph, sounded like those of the Giant in Jack and the Beanstalk. FEEEEE ... FIIIII ... FOOOOOO ... FUUU-UUUMMMM.

Jelley greeted Littlejohn on the back step, disgusted at the noises and pleased to see the Inspector again.

'Silly h'asses,' he shouted, waving a thin, bony hand in the direction of the football ground.

'Think so?' said Littlejohn, grinning. 'I bet if I took you there, you'd be shouting your head off along with the rest.'

They were almost too busy to talk in the kitchen. Miss Honoria was returning and there was to be a family gathering. Although nothing had been said about a welcome feast, Mrs Frazer felt it was up to her. Certainly, the servants had deserved a good feed and there would be plenty left over. Mrs Frazer had seen to that. She was busy at the oven, and Dolly was peeling potatoes and enjoying a quiet snivel again. She flourished on misery.

Littlejohn had called for a brief word with Mrs Minshull and tackled her at once.

'We've been forbid by Mr Ralph to 'ave anything to do with the police when they call 'ere,' she said. 'Of course, somebody told all about what's been goin' on. No names mentioned. But, 'oo's Mr Ralph to tell us what to say and what not to. We've our rights, 'aven't we? And the good Lord gave us tongues to speak the truth with, didn't 'E? You was sayin', sir...?'

'Where exactly were you, Mrs Minshull, when Miss Penelope fell to her death?'

Mrs Minshull smacked her lips.

'In my room. Insulted by the doctor, I was. I was that put-out. Accused me of h'evedroppin'. Me! As 'as been with the fambly untold years... I left the room... Went to me own room and I stayed there till Dr Clever Cross 'ad gone down.'

'Mrs Ralph was seeing to Miss Honoria ready for the nursing home, then?'

'Yes. They called me... But I must say I was a bit before I come out. I was that cut up at what Cross said. Shed a few tears, to be quite candid, I did. Come over a bit queer, too. So I had to undo me stays. It took me a bit fixin' myself up after they called.'

'Meanwhile, Miss Penelope...?'

'Yes.'

'Mrs Ralph and Miss Honoria were in the room together then?'

'So I should 'ave imagined. I heard Mrs Ralph go in Miss 'Onoria's room and shut the door heavy-like with tantrum at Mr Ralph tellin' her to do things.'

'Did either of them come out just before Miss Penelope...?'

Mrs Minshull didn't wait to hear the rest.

'That they did. Somebody passed my door on the way to the box room... I think it would be the box room. Probably it was Mrs Ralph goin' there for Miss Honoria's blouse-case, to pack up 'er things for 'er.'

'You didn't see though?'

'No. But it would be Mrs Ralph.'

'Why?'

'Well, I heard her steps along the carpet. If it had been Miss Honoria, I wouldn't have heard. You see, she hadn't had time to dress by then and would 'ave had to come along in her bare feet or house slippers, not her shoes. In that case she'd 'ave made no noise, would she?'

'A good point. Now can you remember if Miss Penelope fell whilst Mrs Ralph was passing your door, or after she'd got back.'

'I really couldn't say, sir. I was that put-out myself.'

'That's all then, thanks...'

'She might not 'ave been going to the box room. The bathroom's that way, too.'

'Thanks very much...'

Ralph Blow had fixed eight o'clock as the time for the arrival of the police. They met some time before and crossed the square together. Colonel Cardew, Hempseed, Littlejohn and Cromwell.

'Miss Honoria arrived by car with Dr Cross over an hour and a half ago,' Paston told them. He wasn't going to the party with them. Cardew said there were quite enough.

All their arrangements were made. Cardew had been over beforehand to have a word with Ralph Blow. They would see that Honoria retired to bed immediately after dinner; the interview might upset her too much and she had better not be present. On the way out, the Chief Constable had also had a quiet few words with Jelley. There would be three of them to carry on the police interview with the family, who would not know that Cromwell was also in the house. He was to sit in the lounge across the hall, with the door open and the room in darkness. As soon as the party arrived, Jelley had promised to smuggle the Sergeant to his place without revealing his presence to the Blows.

'I don't understand what all the fuss is about, Littlejohn,' Cardew had said. 'We're goin' to ask them a few questions about their movements at the time Penelope died, and test the reactions of all of 'em to the revelation about the money at Doubledays'. Why all the other stuff?'

'We know where everyone but Miss Honoria and Mrs Ralph was when Miss Penelope fell, sir. One of the two of them pushed Miss Penelope through the window. I hope to find out before we leave. I'll therefore ask you to swear out warrants against both of them; then I can use whichever I need...'

'But...but... Warrants? Are we so far advanced? I thought... Look here, Littlejohn, if we make a mistake now, there'll be hell to pay. Blows aren't just ordinary folk. They count round these parts. We'll have to be damn careful.'

'I'll take responsibility, sir.'

'Very well. But I don't like it...'

It was dark when they rang the front doorbell at the bank house. Jelley let them in and slipped Cromwell quietly to his watching place. Then he announced the rest. Outside in the square the drunken supporters of the defeated football team were noisily piling in charabancs and returning disconsolately home. The local supporters of the victors had crowded the pubs and you could hear their songs of triumph all over the town.

The family were all there. Coffee was over and they had gathered round the fire, which burned high in an old-fashioned broad grate. The room was heavy. Heavy furniture, heavy curtains, heavy carpet, and a heavy portrait of a dead and gone Blow glaring stubbornly down on them from over the mantel. The furnishings were dark, like the carpet and the hangings. Ralph and Harold were in deep armchairs by the fire; Lenore was sitting on a tapestry sewing chair by the corner of the hearth. It was Cross's half-day and his assistant was taking surgery. He was sprawling on the couch, a cigarette in his fingers, looking as if he owned the place. Honoria was on her feet with Minshull in attendance. The doorbell had been the pre-arranged signal for seeing her off to bed. She greeted the newcomers as Jelley brought them in.

'Good evening... I believe this is another police investigation...and I'm not to be present in my state of health. They're *making* me go to bed. Dr Cross says I'm not fit to stay up yet... Don't you, Jack?'

She looked coyly across at the doctor, who nodded assent. He seemed bored with it all. Honoria had evidently got herself up to please him. Her hair had been specially dressed again, and there were overdone patches of rouge on her cheeks. Her complexion, pale and pink, resembled enamel.

'Come along, Miss Honoria, dear...'

Mrs Minshull made a diminutive curtsey to the company and led away her charge.

Ralph Blow rose and further greetings were exchanged. He offered them seats, but although port and whisky stood handy, he didn't ask them to drink. They were all keyed-up except Cross and seemed to want to get it over.

'Well? I suppose it's a case of checking alibis... You'd better get on with your questions then, Cardew.'

'Not quite that, Blow. Littlejohn here has something to say and I want you all to hear it. No use wastin' time. Get on with it, Littlejohn.'

This was a bit different from what they'd all been expecting. They had evidently been ready with accounts of their movements, but a change in tactics had taken them off their guard. They sat up in their chairs and even Cross straightened himself and stared hard at the Inspector.

Littlejohn looked at the circle of anxious eyes around him.

'First, I would like to say that it has been established that

Miss Penelope was pushed violently through the window of her room. The investigation, therefore, becomes a murder case.'

It was obvious that Ralph had primed them all. They looked startled but there was none of the astonishment of a bombshell.

'From the first, all of you have been antagonistic and refused to cooperate with us. We have therefore been put to a lot of trouble, I might say a measure of indignity, in finding out matters from other sources...'

They had looked ready, all of them, to express their thoughts about inquiries in the servants' quarters, but the stern tone of Littlejohn's voice stopped all that. Only Harold protested.

'I've not been uncooperative. I've never been asked a thing.'

'Your brother forbade us the house. We were not prepared to chase you all over the place, sir, if we couldn't meet you here.'

Harold subsided and puffed hard at his cigar. His large head shone under the light of the standard lamps and his brown eyes bulged with resentment. Littlejohn caught Lenore and Cross exchanging sarcastic looks. Lenore seemed quite unmoved by the matter.

Littlejohn glanced at the ponderous oil painting over the fireplace. Obviously, William Blow, dressed in his robes as Mayor of Nesbury. A heavy, pugnacious, pink-faced man, with a cold, blue fishy eye, a bulbous almost vulgar nose, loose lips and an unpleasant bulldog chin. The artist hadn't spared him, but everyone seemed satisfied.

'It begins with the last years of Mr William Blow...'

'Look here! I don't want a lot of family history. Let's get down to facts... Don't want a whole night of this...'

Ralph was getting mad. He wasn't used to second place in any event, and this damned Scotland Yarder looked like holding the floor all the evening if he wasn't squashed.

'Please let me speak. This is very relevant. It's most important. Do I go on, sir, or shall we adjourn it till the re-opened Coroner's Inquest in public...?'

'Very well… Only get to the point.'

'In his last days, Mr William Blow had a change of mind. He had hated his family and hated his wife. Instead of giving him sons to carry on the business and family, she bore daughters. She also eloped with an employee of the bank. His original and only will gave his fortune to charities and left the family high and dry, with the exception of a tontine annuity, providing each of his three daughters with a thousand pounds a year. This sum increased proportionally as the daughters died. Miss Honoria is now due for three thousand pounds a year.'

'We know all that. What *is* this…?'

Littlejohn went calmly on.

'But something happened to change Mr Blow's outlook. He was originally not only going to leave his money away from the family. He was going to rub it in. There were to be charities labelled with his name all over the town to taunt them. The William Blow Retreat, the Blow Cats' and Dogs' Home, the Blow Citadel at the Salvation Army…'

'Look here…'

'In the course of planning what he thought would be a very ostentatious building, he called in the Salvation Army representatives and, strange to say, those good people changed his outlook. He became religious. He repented his wrong-doing…'

Cross laughed harshly.

'Probably I contributed a little to that, too. I gave him only a few months to live. He'd an aneurism…'

All eyes turned on the doctor. Littlejohn's voice was like a lash.

'That probably gave you the greatest satisfaction, doctor.'

'What do you mean?'

'You hated him. You hated all the Blows…'

The family looked amazed and you could feel them draw together, as they had always done in adversity. They were a compact lot, if nothing else.

'...You hated the Blows because they had ruined your father and put an end to your own ambitions. You were forced to take up local practice when all the time you had wanted to be an artist...'

Cross rose to his feet in fury. His short, dandified beard bristled.

'That's enough of that. My private affairs don't concern you.'

'You shouldn't have interfered then... I was saying that William Blow changed his mind. But he was, by this, so altered, that his family thought him mad. He suffered acute depression and tried to take his own life. He was locked up in a specially reinforced room upstairs. Thus, not being of sound mind, as the lawyers say, he couldn't alter his will.'

It was almost laughable. He had now reached the stage of knowing more than the Blows were supposed to know themselves. They obviously resented it.

'But Mr William had a way out. He had laid aside bonds to the value of thirty-thousand pounds for a rainy day and these he sold, with the help of Mrs Ralph Blow's father, ex-chief cashier of the bank and a very good friend. The proceeds were placed to credit of Miss Penelope Blow at Doubledays' Bank in London.'

They all pretended to be astonished, but hardly succeeded, except Ralph. Although the police had informed him of the nest egg, he behaved as though they hadn't. He was on his feet, ranting and raving about not knowing a thing about it. Did anybody else know? And why hadn't he been told? Nobody told him anything.

'Don't be so stupid; how could anybody tell you...?'

His wife rebuked him testily.

'Why?'

The dangerous veins in Ralph's temples began to drum again.

'Miss Penelope was Mr William's favourite. Miss Honoria was, I gather, unreliable and Miss Katherine had happily married. He could rely on Miss Penelope to do exactly as he wished. She, then, controlled this large sum. She paid out her sister Katherine almost at once, knowing she could depend on her and her husband to keep the secret. It was a serious matter, you see, because death duties had not been paid on the secret hoard. Miss Penelope then paid from her share a sum for extensions to her father's citadel. After that, the money remained for years... Until someone else found out it was there.'

You could have heard a pin drop. Cross fumbled in his case for another cigarette. Lenore tried to appear calm, but, from where he was sitting, Littlejohn could see small beads of perspiration on her upper lip. Harold looked like a chidden child, his eyes on the carpet. Only Ralph, the man whom nobody told anything, was obviously still incredulous. Ralph, the family big shot, laughed at behind his back, pompous ass who tried to protect the family honour and had ended up by being made a fool and who knew what else...?

'These people found it was there. They hatched a cunning scheme. They steadily withdrew the money from Doubledays' by forging cheques, and, lest the bank became suspicious, they wrote forged letters, in Miss Penelope's so-called hand, explaining why such sums were being withdrawn. They even took the precaution of having the money sent here.'

'Here! But this is nonsense. Nobody could...'

'They did, Mr Ralph. The parcels, all addressed to Miss Penelope, were intercepted...'

'But who could have...? Ah! Jelley! I thought so. He's been behaving funny for a while. Jelley...'

It was laughable. Ralph wouldn't give in. Impossible that one of the Blows...

'Sorry. I haven't got all night to listen to this. It doesn't concern me. I've patients to visit before I turn in. So if you don't mind...'

'We do mind, doctor. And it does concern you. You forged the cheques and letters...'

Pandemonium broke out. Ralph, Cross, Cardew and Hempseed all shouting at once and Hempseed separating Ralph from Cross. Ralph had seized the doctor by the lapels and was shaking him, trying to wring a denial from him.

'Sit down, all of you. Unless we can do this damn business quietly, I'll arrest the lot of you and finish the job at the police station,' yelled Cardew.

Hempseed glanced across at Littlejohn and raised his eyes to heaven. He had clapped his hand in the small of his back where his lumbago, shaken awake by the tumult, had gently reminded him of its presence.

'Go on, Littlejohn...'

'Yes. Go on and tell me the lot now. I'll make somebody suffer if this is true. If Cross has done what you say, I'll have him clapped in gaol...'

Ralph was beside himself and fortified himself with a stiff whisky which reminded Harold that he needed the same.

'Dr Cross forged the cheques and the money came here. Mrs Blow received it...'

There was a terrible hush. Ralph Blow was speechless with incredulity. The rest of them, knowing it to be true, could find nothing to say.

'Say it isn't true, Lenore... Say it isn't true, and I'll make this lot pay for their words. It's false, isn't it?'

'You may as well know... I can't disprove it and I suppose the police have proof. It's true...'

Lenore remained sitting and looked quite unrepentant. Her husband seemed to shake himself like a dog out of water. All his pleading and humility vanished. He rose swiftly, crossed to where the doctor was standing and struck him a heavy blow across the face with the back of his hand.

'You swine! You did this...'

They had to separate them. Cardew went and sat, scowling, by the doctor and Hempseed led Ralph back to his chair.

Cross wiped his mouth from which a thin trickle of blood was oozing.

'You can hardly blame me, Blow. It was your wife's idea. She got to know from her father and persuaded me... We're in love with each other and she wants her freedom. Then we can go away...'

Ralph Blow collapsed. It was more than he could bear. Dignity, family, wife and honour, all apparently gone...

Harold Blow sat with his great head in his hand.

'I tried to stop it all... I learned about it too late...' He said it, as if to himself, over and over again.

'I think you're making rather a mistake, doctor...'

Littlejohn's calm, brisk voice broke in.

'...Mrs Blow doesn't love you. She simply used you. She found out that you were a good forger; maybe you'd boasted about it at the Arts Club. The pair of you had meetings at your country cottage, but she only met you there for quietness in which to write the cheques and letters...'

'It's a damned lie! She told me... I know... Tell them, Lenore...'

'Yes, Mrs Blow. Tell him you had arranged to go to South Africa together with the money you got. Tell him, too, that *your* arrangements are for Australia, not South Africa...'

'Is this true, Lenore?'

Lenore Blow was on her feet like a tigress, her eyes flaming, her breast heaving.

'Be quiet, the lot of you. Like a pack of hounds snarling over a bone. I never loved any of you... I married Ralph for father's sake, but I never forgave the Blows for breaking my brother. When father told me of Penelope's money, I made up my mind to get it. It wouldn't pay for half of what they did to my family. With it, I was going to take dad to Australia and set up my brother properly. Since the Blows turned him out, he's lived miserably from hand to mouth. That's why I've put up with this awful house, this awful family, for so long. My husband...pomp and circumstance. I must be and behave like the wife of a Blow... How I hate it all! And his two half-mad aunts always at me, seeing I was conducting myself properly. No money, cooped up like a prisoner, dependent even for my clothes on a man I despised... Yes, despised, Ralph!... Harold was the only decent one of you. He found out what was going on and tried to put things right... And now you can arrest me... Do what you like with me... I've blotted the escutcheon of the Blows, and I'm glad...'

Cross, who had been standing like a statue, dumbstruck by the revelation, burst into a torrent of abuse.

'You little cheat! You common little tart...'

Harold Blow rose, almost ran to where he stood, and struck the doctor a savage blow, this time on the chin with his fist. Cross reeled back and returned to the fray.

Police, the Blows, Cross...all shouting and struggling. And then the front doorbell rang violently. There was a lull in the storm, and they all grew silent and started to straighten their clothes and ties. Strange how a reminder of the world outside brought them to order.

Jelley entered, raised his eyebrows at the pandemonium and calmly announced the visitor.

'The vicar, sir, to see Miss Honoria...'

In the doorway, his professional smile suddenly frozen to a look of horror, stood the Rev Maximilian Fidler, Canon of Nesbury, and Vicar of St Michael and All Angels!

20

THE MADNESS OF THE BLOWS

Canon Fidler knew when he was emphatically *de trop* and beat a hasty retreat, but his timely arrival caused a healthy fall in the temperature of the crazy family scene which had developed in the Blows' dining room. They looked like the survivors of a wreck at sea after the embarrassed vicar had bolted. Ralph's eyes were glassy and his face livid, like the victim of an epileptic fit; Harold, on the other hand, looked ready to faint or be sick; his fit of violence had left him prostrated! Dr Cross would have gone with the vicar had Littlejohn not detained him. Now he was pacing the room, demanding explanations, lawyers, apologies, anything to occupy his mind. Lenore, who, on account of the powder, paint and lipstick on her face, could not show the colour of her emotions, had sunk on the couch, limp, her head between her hands, with their scarlet fingernails.

'I'll make you pay for this!'

They all jumped. It was Ralph bursting again into eruption. He waved his fist in the direction of Cross, who snorted.

'I'll see you get gaol for this theft...and forgery... You dirty crook!'

GEORGE BELLAIRS

'Don't forget your wife's in it. If I go to gaol, she does. It was her doing from the start. She's an accessory...'

Littlejohn intervened.

'You can settle your personal differences later. Our main concern now is, who killed Miss Penelope?'

They'd forgotten that! There was dead silence.

'That wasn't the only thing happening in this house...the forging of cheques... There were other things...' Littlejohn went on. 'For example, Miss Penelope decided to make another donation to the Salvation Army and sent to Double-days' Bank for a statement of account. It was the first she'd had since the thefts. She was staggered by what she saw. Practically the whole of her balance had gone without her knowing it. At the same time, to add to her worries, Miss Honoria insisted that she was being poisoned... Her illness tallied with that induced by arsenic, according to some book or other she'd read. Strangely enough, when medical experts examined her after her removal to a nursing home, they confirmed her fears...'

'We all know that...'

Ralph was recovering his irritability.

'But you don't know who gave her the poison... She took it herself...'

They all spoke at once.

'Nonsense... Ridiculous... Rubbish...' and Lenore burst into shouts of hysterical laughter. Her feelings were getting the better of her and she looked wicked.

'It is true, because Miss Honoria has confessed. She took mild doses of fly-water, used in an attempt on his life by her father, and hidden away ever since the event. She tried it on the cat and almost killed him, to begin with...'

'But why kill herself?' Ralph waved his arms. He seemed to be the only one capable of shouting.

'She had no intention of killing herself. All she wanted was

248

medical attention! Dr Cross had been neglecting her and that was her way of getting him in attendance again...'

Cross strode across and thrust his face close to Littlejohn's.

'Liar! Liar!! Why keep involving me? I'll make...'

Ralph now thought fit to intervene again.

'Get out... Get out, you swine...'

He pointed a melodramatic forefinger at the door for Cross.

'I'm afraid that won't do, Mr Blow. I want the doctor here. He's got to hear all I have to say before we decide what to do with him...'

Cardew intervened violently. He seized Cross by the lapels and thrust him on the couch beside Lenore, who drew herself as far away from him as possible.

'Dr Cross had been behaving gallantly to Miss Honoria, I fancy. She resented his neglect. However, her sister's illness gave Miss Penelope a chance to inquire quietly from her friend, Mr Claplady, who would be the best to turn to for advice. Mr Claplady suggested me. But Miss Penelope not only wished to ask me about the poisoning of her sister. She wanted my help about the vanished bank balance.'

'So, that's what you were after all the time...'

Harold Blow found tongue at last.

'No. Miss Penelope never saw me. She called at Doubledays' Bank to get help from old Mr Doubleday... He was away, too. If either of us had been there, she might still have been alive. She had to come home without us... You knew that, Mr Harold. Mrs Buckley followed Miss Penelope on someone's orders and reported back on the telephone...'

'They weren't my orders, I swear that,' said Harold, obviously getting out of his depth. 'It wasn't till the day I went and brought her home that I knew what she was doing. She wasn't safe wandering about in London on her own. Aunt Honoria told me where she'd gone. I tried to get out of auntie why she was in London. She said something about paying a friendly call. I never got to the bottom of it. I even went back to Mrs Buckley and questioned her, only your man turned up and seemed to think I was the murderer...'

'I know all that, sir. Did you ever say to anyone: "We've got to get rid of auntie"?'

'Who told you that...? Walls have ears in this place. I told Lenore that I thought Aunt Honoria was going the way her father went. She acted so queerly... I said we'd have to get her away... I meant a home...'

Ralph Blow was on his feet again, blustering.

'But where's all this talk getting us? I guess Aunt Honoria could take poison to her heart's content without the police messing all over the place. And Cross...with his forgery and his affair with my wife...'

'Keep me and your wife out of this, you old fool,' yelled Cross. 'Do as you like about me... I'm fed up with it all... But what I get, I'll see your precious Lenore gets, too... It's the murder of Miss Penelope I want to know about. You can't pin that on me. I was in the hall with you and Harold and Tankerville when it happened...'

'That's right,' said Littlejohn. 'The men of the party are each other's alibis. The servants were all down below, except Mrs Minshull, whom you had insulted, Dr Cross, and who was in her room weeping and fastening up her stays, as she says, when Miss Penelope fell. There was a witness, too, to the fact that she was pushed from the window...'

'Who?'

'Never mind. That can wait. We know that Mrs Ralph Blow and Miss Honoria were in the latter's bedroom. Mrs Ralph was heard to leave the room and pass along the landing...'

Cross and Ralph Blow were both on their feet together.

'Look here...'

'Wait. Hear me out. Mrs Ralph was responsible for the forgeries. She knew of them and knows where the money is now...'

'Where is it...? You'll tell me, if I have to damn well choke it out of you...'

'That will do, Mr Blow. You can deal with your wife later...if she's still here...'

'What the hell do you mean?'

'I mean, she knew Miss Penelope had found out about the theft. She knew also, from Harold, and Mrs Buckley, who phoned and told her, that she'd been to the bank and Scotland Yard. She knew that if Miss Penelope lived, she'd get to the bottom of it all... So... She heard Miss Penelope calling to Minshull about the window box and the daffodils, she excused herself and left Miss Honoria on some pretext, crept into Miss Penelope's room and...'

There was pandemonium again. Cross seized a large poker from the grate and brandished it.

'If...'

Cardew seized the poker and with a quick chop on the side of Cross's neck with the edge of his palm, felled the doctor. Poor Cross was having a rough passage... This time he remained sitting on the floor, feeling his jaw with expert fingers.

'Mrs Blow...'

Hempseed looked flabbergasted.

Littlejohn stood over Lenore Blow.

'Lenore Blow, I hold a warrant for your arrest...'

This time the commotion was from another direction. The door into the hall flew open and there stood Cromwell, struggling and dishevelled, trying to hold a shrieking figure, dressed in a nightgown and dressing gown... It was Honoria Blow!

The two brothers, Hempseed and Cardew hurried towards the newcomers and together they held the now fighting woman and took her to the couch. Lenore Blow rose slowly, put her arms round Honoria and tried to soothe her.

'What's the meaning of all this? We've had quite enough... My aunt now! Can't you get out and leave us in peace?'

'There'll be no peace here anymore. You should have thought about peace long ago, Ralph. You tried to step into Uncle William's shoes, and look where you've landed us all. Aunt Penelope dead; Lenore — you've lost her; Cross, broken and disgraced; and now Aunt Honoria gone off her head...'

Harold intoned it like a dull chant.

'You keep out of this, you meddling young fool...'

Cromwell straightened his tie and smoothed his hair. He looked ashamed of being the centre of attraction.

'I sat in the dark in the sitting room. It was chilly...no fire. No sooner was the door of this room closed than Miss Honoria was down, listening at the keyhole. I did a bit of sweating when the parson called. She bobbed in the room beside me. We were only a few feet apart. She was chattering and chuckling to herself. When the parson left, she went back to the keyhole... She kept chuckling and whispering to herself... Quite pleased about something. Then, she must have heard you reading the warrant to Mrs Ralph. She went wild... Started to dance about... Uncanny in that dim light. I could see her from where I was in the dark room. She was whispering... "Good," she said. "Good. Now I'm rid of Lenore. I'll have Jack," — whoever *he* might be — "I'll have Jack all to myself. She'll hang for what I did..." Then, she saw me... I'd crept out to hear what she said... She flung herself on me like a wild cat...'

'Murderess! Thief!' Honoria had started again. 'She took Jack from me. Always after him. I saw her... He didn't want me because I'd not enough money... Oh, yes... I know he wanted money. I often gave it to him... Now I'll have Penelope's share, too... I'll have three thousand a year, Jack... And she'll hang...'

Ralph strode over to his aunt.

'Did you push Aunt Penelope out of the window, aunt...? Now tell me...I want the truth... *Did you push her out of the window?*'

'Don't bully me, Ralph, *please*. I can't stand any more. I'm ill, Ralph...I...'

'Did you?'

'It was only a little push, Ralph... She was as light as a feather...I didn't mean to... She fell before I touched her... She had my money... It was mine... I hated her because of the money... I sent Lenore for my suitcase... Then, crept out... In my bare feet, Ralph... She was so busy with the daffodils... I'm rich now... Jack, don't let them...'

Ralph Blow staggered back pawing the air.

'We'd better take her to her room,' said Lenore gently.

'No... Not that,' shouted Ralph Blow. 'Uncle's old room. The one with the bars...'

And then fell sprawling on the carpet.

HONORIA BLOW IS NOW in a home, hopelessly mad, and Ralph had died from a stroke. Lenore Blow had carefully deposited the stolen funds in an account in her own name and turned it over to her husband's family, from whom, in turn, a mixed body of executors took and distributed it, much of it to charity again. There was no prosecution, so she and her father left for Australia to join her brother.

The bank house is now the machine-posting department of the bank and the messenger lives on the upper floor. The family is broken, and Harold has gone away. Cross alone remains of the queer parties to the tragedy of the bank house. He carries on his practice, which is very diluted, for, like his father before him, he has turned to drink.

The servants are scattered. Minshull lives with her sister and they wish she would go, for she talks of nothing but the Blows and their strange ways. Mrs Frazer is somewhere in London, and Dolly, who snivelled so much because someone had stolen her virtue, was lucky enough to marry her seducer and bear her infant like an honest woman. Jelley, turned out with the rest, became a nominee of police charities. He now lives in William Blow's Retreat, in a small house of his own, next door to Simon Jacques, who finds him a good neighbour. Jelley is more cheerful, for he has been converted by his jolly friend, and he sings evangelical hymns in a quavering tenor as he does his housework.

Later that year...in the autumn to be exact...Littlejohn visited Bexhill to see Hempseed, who, leaving Paston as his successor, has settled down with his cheery wife, a dog, twenty hens and half an acre of ground by the sea. There, his lumbago has left him, and he cultivates his cabbage patch and a rose garden for his wife in peace.

ABOUT THE AUTHOR

George Bellairs is the pseudonym under which Harold Blundell (1902–1982) wrote police procedural thrillers in rural British settings. He was born in Lancashire, England, and worked as a bank manager in Manchester. After retiring, Bellairs moved to the Isle of Man, where several of his novels are set, to be with friends and family.

In 1941 Bellairs wrote his first mystery, *Littlejohn on Leave*, during spare moments at his air raid warden's post. The title introduced Thomas Littlejohn, the detective who appears in fifty-seven of his novels. Bellairs was also a regular contributor to the *Manchester Guardian* and worked as a freelance writer for newspapers both local and national.

THE INSPECTOR LITTLEJOHN MYSTERIES

FROM OPEN ROAD MEDIA

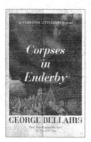

OPEN ROAD

INTEGRATED MEDIA

INTEGRATED MEDIA

Find a full list of our authors and
titles at www.openroadmedia.com

FOLLOW US
@OpenRoadMedia